To Claudia,

A History

of

Forever

A NOVEL BY

Beth MacDonald

Beth MacDonald

North
Ink
Books

This book is a work of fiction. While some of the places and people referenced are real, the events recalled and words spoken are not. *A History of Forever* is a novel, written to entertain. It was not written as an historically accurate account and should not be construed as such.

ISBN 978-1-7374760-0-9 (E-book)

ISBN 978-1-7374760-1-6 (Trade Paperback)

ISBN 978-1-7374760-2-3 (Hardcover Book)

Cover Artwork: Jennie Yu

Cover Design and Author Photo: Romy Klessen

North Ink Books

www.NorthInkBooks.com

Printed in the United States of America

A History

—of—

Forever

Cheesy + easy
compelling

Lydia de Treville, *The Visitor*, ca.1783-1790
(attribution Dr. Sarah Bolling, 1982)

— — — — —

Attn Tommy Gill:

Here's the letter and manuscript I found on that ratty wingback chair Sarah keeps in her office at the store.

Read it and let me know what you think.

Bob Roberts, Sheriff
Beaufort County

— — — — —

Fauxlonial Furnishings

Mid-Twentieth-Century
Early American Reproduction Furniture & Abstract Art
820 Bay Street, Beaufort, South Carolina 29902

December 7, 2016

To the law firm of Gill and Sumner:

If you're holding this letter, I am no longer with you. Sorry if that sounds overly dramatic, but I'm sure that it's true.

Please, sell the stock and fixtures from my store Fauxlonial Furnishings, the contents of my home, and my vehicles. After paying my outstanding debts, including your bill, see that all funds raised from the sales, along with all money remaining in my bank account, are given to the Sargent Leggett Memorial Scholarship Endowment at the University of South Dakota. Information to facilitate the sale of personal property and transfer funds to the University is on file at your office.

If any items do not sell, donate them to the Habitat for Humanity ReStore on Parris Island Gateway.

The attached manuscript should answer many questions. I've held lifelong secrets concerning the three years between 1972 and 1975. It's time to tell the truth. There is no one left to be hurt by it—not even me.

Sarah Bolling 12-7-16

Sarah Bolling

A SELECT MEMOIR
by
SARAH ELIZABETH BOLLING

PART ONE
November 7, 1972

—1—

I crossed the campus thinking the front of my head was going to freeze and fall off from the bone-aching South Dakota cold. I even pictured it—blindly kicking the shards of my frozen face down the snowy sidewalk to Nelson Hall. My nose started to run and not wanting to break stride I wiped it with the back of my mitten. The class I was heading to was held in the balcony of the old building's auditorium because classroom space was maxed-out. Draft deferments and the sheer number of us boomers had filled the campus to its breaking point, or, perhaps, past it.

I climbed the back stairs and took my place among the other stragglers. The *squeak*, **slam**—*squeak*, **slam** of the wooden seats falling into place grated on me while I fumbled with my fogged-up glasses. As we all shed our outer layers, the usual odor of damp wool and last night's bad habits drifted out mixing with the must of the worn auditorium. This morning it made me gag.

Professor Leggett took his precarious position in front of the balcony railing and began his ten o'clock lecture. After two months of classes in this location he seemed perfectly comfortable with the chasm at his back. That would never be me. I was thankful I had a safe, solid seat far away from the balcony's edge. Normally, Dr. Leggett's American colonial history class was one of my favorites, but today was different. I couldn't get myself to focus on his words. I kept thinking back to what Brian had said earlier that morning, "You just aren't enough, Sarah. You aren't who I want."

Damn, I was pissed. Who was he to call the shots? I knew this Election Day was going to be a bad one for him, but I'd had a few bad days in a row lately and I'd really wanted to talk with him. Topping off my unpleasant thoughts, I felt the now familiar sting of pending tears making my nose run again. I searched my scuffed patchwork purse for a Kleenex. No luck. I pulled the dirty mitten from my coat pocket and covertly used it for the same purpose I had earlier. God

I was a mess—I needed to pull myself together and figure out how to get on with my life.

As Dr. Leggett droned on, all I could think about was that I needed to leave. I knew I couldn't stay around here. But go where? In her letters Annie kept inviting me to come visit her. I figured she meant during the summer, but maybe I could talk Mom and Dad into letting me spend the interim term with her in Boston. And then stay? Probably? I'd miss my next semester at the U, but, really, what choice did I have? Spring on the East Coast might be a lovely option— well, that was one way to sell it to my parents and professors.

I flipped through my history text, at least appearing studious. A few days earlier I'd seen an intriguing illustration of a colonial painting of two children. Their faces bore some semblance of realism, but their bodies were as flat and ridged as paper dolls. Maybe I could research that kind of art while I was in Boston. There had to be some story behind it, some reason it looked like that. An independent study entitled "Aspects of Colonial Realism in Portraits of Children" by Sarah Bolling. Ok, maybe that title needed a little work. I just knew it sounded better than the truer "Fuck you, Brian—I'm Leaving."

Class ended. I re-bundled, grabbed my books, and gingerly took the aisle stairs toward the edge of the balcony to see if I could make an appointment with Dr. Leggett. If I was going to make this independent study thing work, I would need an advisor. Being the history department's expert on colonial America made Leggett the logical choice. That he was a good professor and nice to look at didn't hurt, either, although my primary motivator was expediency.

Walking down the stairs, my purse strap slipped to my elbow—a common occurrence. Weighed down with my ever present paperback dictionary and the stuff I needed to get me through my long days on campus, the bag was far too heavy for my small frame. As I swung the thick strap back over my shoulder, Dr. Leggett turned. My purse, with the power of a medieval mace, slammed into his arm sending the papers he'd been holding sailing over the balcony railing.

"HO-LYYY SHIT!" my involuntary expletive rang through the old hall as the professor and I watched all his handwritten class notes flutter like large white confetti onto the students walking into the auditorium below us.

I tore down the stairs to the main floor with Dr. Leggett at my heels. Hooting with laughter, students entering the auditorium for the alternating main-floor class were catching the wayward pages as they floated through the hazy air. Only a few of the papers had landed on the floor. Most had been saved from the ravages of the tracked-in snow melting on the gritty linoleum. I thanked god that the damp and dirty pages were still legible and that Dr. Leggett was smiling. A professor's notes are his tools, and I had just managed to scatter Leggett's—probably his only copy—from stem to stern in the orchestra level of Nelson Hall. I don't know that I would've been as cheery had our roles been reversed.

Part of the lecture papers were passed to me, part to Dr. Leggett. I had to face him at some point to hand over my stack—up until then I'd been avoiding eye contact. While originally I'd wanted to make an appointment with him, at this point all I wanted to do was hand over the papers and run for the nearest exit. But, when I finally looked up while holding the flopping pages out for him to take from my hand, Dr. Leggett was still smiling. I looked in his eyes and he started to laugh. His expression made me feel like he was seeing me for the first time and, yet, at the same time, it shined with a sense of recognition—like he knew me well. Confused and embarrassed, the tears that I had been holding back all morning slipped down the nosepieces of my octagonal wireframes and dripped onto my scarf.

That was the day he went from being "Dr. Leggett" to "Jon" in my mind. As we walked back to the stairs so that he could go collect the rest of his things from the balcony, he handed me his handkerchief and asked me not to cry. His eyes were warm and he seemed concerned that I was upset, a far cry from the way Brian had treated me earlier in the day. Jon said that we had managed to save everything, or, at least enough for him to put his lecture back together. I reached under my heavy glasses and clumsily wiped my tears.

I pointed to the balcony railing. "I really hadn't planned to attack you...sorry. I wanted to see if we could talk later in the week about some ideas I have for an interim project?"

He softly chuckled at my attack comment. "Ahh, certainly, we can talk. Would you be able to come by my office in the Humanities Building at, say, 3:00 this Thursday?"

I told him that would be perfect and I promised to bring back his handkerchief, clean and pressed, just the way he'd presented it to me.

—2—

I didn't live on campus like a normal college student—I had chosen to save money and live at home. It was sixty-five miles from Sioux Falls to Vermillion, a drive that I shared with an ever changing assortment of married grad and law students. Our first two winters the commute had been easy. This winter had been a challenge and it wasn't even December yet. My little group of carpoolers rarely missed a day on the road, but the morning after I'd knocked Jon Leggett's notes over the balcony, we opted out. The wind was blowing and although it wasn't snowing, the snow that had fallen days earlier was whipping through the streets icing them over and making it impossible to see outside the city proper. No class, no matter how edifying, was worth skidding out of control and freezing to death in an interstate ditch.

I holed up in my boxy bedroom. After making the appointment with Jon yesterday, I'd skipped lunch and gone to the library to see if I could find reference materials to begin my search for colonial artists. The library didn't have much, but I felt I'd found enough to fake my way through an independent study proposal. The fact that I couldn't find what I wanted should have been enough to convince any academician that I needed to travel to find source materials.

Now, as the apple tree branches outside my window slapped the frosted glass, I began working on my proposal. Not owning a desk, I'd gotten into the habit of piling pillows against my headboard to do my homework in bed. The furnace was working overtime, and, because of it, every time I pulled on the green acrylic blanket covering my knee socks, static electricity crackled and snapped.

Four hours later I had a rumpled bed and the outline of a proposal for an independent study class to fill my 1973 interim requirement. It would involve me keeping a daily journal and writing a thirty-page research paper. It would also require me to go to Boston, Massachusetts, and get as far away from home and Brian as possible, although no one on the official permission committee of parents and professors would ever hear Brian's name. I was already sorry that I had.

Brian and I met while working on the presidential campaign that summer. One of South Dakota's senators, George McGovern, was the Democratic candidate in '72. I'd started volunteering at the Sioux Falls campaign office in late July, soon after he'd won the nomination. Brian was a paid political organizer brought in by the national Democratic party to run the office. He was a smart, good-looking, twenty-five-year-old. A college graduate with a job; I'd personally been friends with only a few of those—well, other than my big sister Annie.

Every day, by late afternoon, scores of young people were hanging around the campaign office. However, because of my work schedule at a little mom-and-pop gas station where I ran the cash register and restocked the penny candy, I generally went to the office in the morning before most of the volunteers my age had climbed out of bed. Brian and I got to know one another during those quiet mornings. Neither of us was looking for anything long term, but we were both single and attracted to one another.

One evening in late August, after pizza and 3.2 beer with the office gang, Brian and I went to his apartment and made out. We were to the point where we both breathlessly wanted more, but I stopped him to ask if he had a condom. I'd been off the pill for a month for a prescribed annual break. Pregnancy was not something I was willing to risk. Brian didn't have one, so we cooled things pretty quickly.

The next time we were together at his place was in September. I had started back on birth control and

Brian had gone condom shopping. As a joke for my benefit, he had placed a bowlful of the colorful square packets beside his bed. I let him know that even though I was back on the pill, it would still be a good idea for him to use protection. He asked me to pick a color, then he slid the condom on while under the sheets.

I had a rare early shift at the gas station the next morning. About an hour after opening the register I started cramping, so I asked Rob, the owner and mechanic, to cover for me while I ran to the restroom. I felt like my period was coming, but that made no sense since I'd been on the pill a few weeks already. Sitting on the toilet I wiped myself fully expecting to see blood; instead, when I looked at the toilet tissue, it was bright blue. Honestly, I gasped; I had no idea what was happening, but it was horrifying. My first thought was that I had just expelled some sort of large blue parasitic worm. It took me awhile to realize that I was looking at Brian's condom from the night before.

For some reason that I still do not understand, I was embarrassed. Then I just got mad. Brian had to have known that the condom came off and he chose not to tell me. I thought, "What kind of asshole does that?" But, then I remembered how embarrassed I had been just a few moments before, and I had no reason to be—if there was an injured party in this scenario, it was me. Yes, he should have told me, but he was probably embarrassed, too. And, after the fact, there wasn't much either one of us could do about it. It was an accident. I assumed I wasn't pregnant since I was back on the pill and decided to be kind and not confront Brian.

Brian and I dated through mid-October. But the strain of a campaign that was looking more and more like a train wreck was beginning to tear him apart. He had to keep up a good front at the campaign office, but on the few nights when we could see each other he vacillated between taciturn and grouchy. I was busy, too, having started my Junior year at USD in September. What had started as a summer fling was fading as autumn blew in.

I had never assumed Brian loved me, or that we would stay together forever, but I thought I deserved more than his rude, quick dismissal the morning of the election.

After finishing my proposal, I decided to take a long bath while I was the only one at home. In a house where we shared one bathroom, it was a rare treat. I turned on the space heater, a rattly unit that had seen better days, and filled the tub with scalding water. I knew a tepid bath would be better for my dry itchy skin, but anyone who can take a lukewarm bath on a windy seven-degree day has far more discipline than I. After the soak I wrapped myself in my red and black flannel robe and flipped my hair over the bathroom sink for its weekly wash. The sink wasn't small, but my hair filled it to overflowing. I had gobs of hair—it was thick and hung to the small of my back. Most of the time I hated my hair, but my mother had convinced me that cutting it would be a bad idea.

I was born with a rare genetic condition that made my hair stand on end. In photos taken of me when I was a toddler, my head looked like a dandelion just gone to seed. Mom told me that people would stop her on the street and embarrass her by asking if she had given me a bad home perm. Eventually, she found that the only way to stop the stares was to cover my unusual blonde fluff with scarves until it grew long enough to braid. Mom insisted that I never cut it for fear it would rear its ugly head again. Her pun, not mine.

As I got older my hair turned kinky—not curly, not wavy, and especially not straight. I parted it in the center like all the other girls my age, but that's the last comparison I can make. While their hair flowed softly over their shoulders and could be tucked behind their ears, mine stuck out like a Christmas tree and would have required ears the size of catalpa leaves to hold it back. To tame it, I wore it in a single thick braid that hung down the middle of my back.

I finished washing the tangled mass, wrapped it in a bath towel to deal with later and started on my laundry. The unexpected day off gave me a chance to wash my mittens before the weekend. I also rinsed and ironed Jon's handkerchief, then pressed it into a perfectly folded small square so that it looked the same as when he'd handed it to me. The crisp cotton fabric was monogrammed with a beautifully embroidered cursive "L." I thought it a little odd that a man as young as Jon used handkerchiefs, but he dressed conservatively, so maybe handkerchiefs were just part of the package.

My mother was the first to hear of my January plan to study in Boston. She had never met (or even heard about) Brian, so had no idea that there was more to my trip than a scholastic adventure. I explained that if Annie could house me, I would use my savings to help her pay for groceries and rent. I told my mom that I needed her and Dad to cover my flights, but that I would pay them back during the upcoming summer when I could work more hours at the gas station. But I also explained that everything was still contingent upon the history department's approval of my project.

I didn't think that Mom would have any problems with me leaving for a month or more. When I didn't make waves, my parents treated me like a potted cactus—with benign neglect—I was sure I wouldn't be missed. But I was concerned that she might think that they couldn't afford the plane ticket with Christmas on the horizon. I was counting on her love for Annie; she knew that her older (read *favorite*) daughter was lonely and she would enjoy my company. Even though we were eight years apart, Annie and I had always been close.

Mom said she thought they could handle the cost of the ticket as long as it was a loan and she promised to talk to my father as soon as he got home from work. It went without saying she meant if he was lit-up enough to be jovial but not so much that he was combative. It was a fine line. Mom said if Dad agreed, we could call Annie long distance later that evening. She half jokingly said if she smoothed things over with my dad and we got Annie's hopes up, I'd better do a good job convincing my professors. I assured her that was my intention.

—3—

Thursday morning dawned cold but clear. The evening before, my father, drunk but still in a good mood following Nixon's election, had said I could join my sister in Boston "with all the other misguided liberals." While I wasn't a fan of his sarcasm, I was thrilled that he'd agreed to front my ticket. When we called Annie, except for the initial panic of getting a long distance call on a Wednesday night, she seemed overjoyed I might be coming for a visit. I told her I'd do everything in my power to see her in Boston shortly after Christmas.

As I waited in the chilly entry of my parents' house for my ride, I thought about what I would say to Dr. Jon Leggett to convince him that my project was worthy of his approval. For a more seasoned professor it would be no great risk, but I assumed because he was relatively new to the department he would be judged harshly if I crashed and burned. I had to show him that I was a serious, dedicated student with a penchant for old art. Piece of cake.

I climbed the stairs to the auditorium balcony in a much better mood than I'd been in on Tuesday. Today Jon kept my attention. He really was an excellent instructor. His lectures were straightforward and easy to follow, making notetaking a breeze. In many of my other classes I'd spend hours trying to make sense of what I'd scrawled in my notebooks. Not so after a Dr. Jon Leggett class. He was organized, but not simplistic. He made us (at least, me) want to think. He gave us a reason to read the text and delve into outside reading. I started feeing guilty about my preoccupation during Tuesday's class, but thought he might forgive me if he knew the circumstances (although, as far as I was concerned, he never would).

After class ended I walked toward the front of the balcony to ask Jon if we were still on track to see one another that afternoon. Yesterday's weather had forced the cancelations of many appointments and I wanted to make sure I hadn't had my time slot taken by some more important faculty matter. Jon exaggerated clutching his lecture notes to his chest as I walked toward him. I restrained myself from sticking my tongue out and just smiled. He looked at me again with a familiarity that made my pulse race. He assured me our meeting was still on his calendar and he was anxious to hear what I had to tell him. I doubted he was half as anxious as I was.

Three o'clock finally came. Jon's office was at the very end of a long hall next to the open broom closet, and, I soon learned, roughly the same size.

Seniority has its privileges; Jon's privilege was that he wasn't sharing a space with mops and buckets. I was amazed with all that he had fit into such a small space. Along with the old wooden desk and chair that the University had provided, he had created space for an extensive library, a shabby but clean plaid wingback chair, and an antique-looking side table topped with a shaded reading lamp. As I knocked on the open door, he was already pulling the plaid chair up to his desk so that I had a place to sit.

With the late afternoon sun shining through the office window, I laid out my plan. I told him about my research project; I showed him my proposed time table; I even explained that my older sister lived in Boston and that my parents, with whom I was currently living, approved of my adventure. Oh, and that I had the money to both pay for the class credit and fund my travels, although, from things he said, I don't think the financial information played any part in his final decision. Money, or rather, the lack of it, was always at the top of my mind, so I sometimes forgot other people didn't have the same concerns. Jon told me I'd made a good case for my proposal and carefully placed it in the top left-hand drawer of his desk.

As the little room gradually darkened, we talked about other things including the results of the election, which had disappointed us both. We agreed that McGovern started losing the election with his bad choice of Thomas Eagleton as a running mate and his indecisiveness when it came to dropping him from the ticket hurt even more. We talked about the war, which we both opposed. Jon said college deferments had let him avoid military service and being born in 1943 had made him just old enough to escape the draft lottery in 1969.

Talking with Jon was surprisingly easy. It was comfortable, just like the plaid chair he had offered me when I entered the office. I felt a connection that seemed more than academic, and from the way Jon continued to look at me, I guessed he did, too.

It was completely dark as I ran across campus to catch my ride back home. It wasn't until I reached the car with all my carpool mates waiting that I remembered I still had Jon's handkerchief in my purse. At first I was angry with myself for having broken my promise to return it to him that day, but then I realized it gave me a chance to visit with him again. I was smitten.

Damn, I had awful timing.

—4—

Jon called me at home on Saturday to tell me he had given my independent study project plan to the department head, Dr. Sargent, for his approval. He let me know that he had included a report of his own on his impressions of me as a student, his firm belief that the project would be of value to me, and that I would prove a credit to the University's history department. I silently hoped he hadn't overplayed his hand—I still remembered my optional title for the paper.

Before he hung up, Jon told me he was surprised to find out that I lived in Sioux Falls. He said when I'd told him I lived with my parents, he'd assumed I was a Vermillion townie. "When I was making the phone call to you, I noticed we have the same prefix. It turns out we make the same daily commute."

"Don't tell me you drove to Vermillion on Wednesday when it was so icy!" When he told me he had, I'm afraid I lectured him on the perils of early winter ice and blinding snow. I wasn't sure I should have scolded my professor knowing he had lived in South Dakota for a few years already, but I figured as a native Northerner I was more knowledgeable on the subject than he was. He thanked me for my concern, although when he said he had "learned his lesson," his tone was as patronizing as mine had been didactically maternal. He did admit, however, that the roads had been horrible.

Jon told me Dr. Sargent had been so distressed by the thought of him driving back to Sioux Falls, he'd convinced him to spend Wednesday night at his house in Vermillion. I asked Jon if any of Sarge's Platoon had come over that evening. For years, Dr. Sargent had attracted a group of history majors, nicknamed the Platoon, that met at his big house close to campus. Being a part of Sarge's Platoon was a huge deal for most serious history students. I would've loved to have been part of the group, but could never join them since I didn't live nearby. Jon said Wednesday wasn't a regular Platoon evening, so no. He and Dr. Sargent had spent a quiet evening doing professorial things like drinking and talking late into the night. I said, "I thought that's what the Platoon did." He laughed and said I was right, other than the Platoon wasn't known for being quiet.

I smiled as I hung up the receiver on the living room phone. I wasn't completely sure, but I thought maybe, just maybe, I might have been flirting with my history professor. I skipped back to my bedroom—I hadn't skipped since I was seven.

By Monday afternoon, Jon had Dr. Sargent's approval for my interim study project and the November weather was far more temperate. On a personal level, in less than a week, it appeared that I had been dumped by one guy, was starting *something* with another, and had made plans to live away from home for the first time (for a reason I was barely admitting to myself). My life was changing so fast that I was both exhilarated and scared silly.

On Tuesday, after Jon's class, I met him at the balcony railing with his handkerchief. As I handed it to him, I thanked him, and promised I wouldn't need it again. I told him I was embarrassed by my behavior— that I hadn't cried in public since the fourth grade. I explained that Tuesday had been a particularly crappy day. "Knocking your notes over the balcony ledge was like putting onion icing on a turd cake of a morning." Jon guffawed at my Midwestern eloquence and asked if I would like to walk to the commons for an early lunch. I was surprised he could think about food after my comment, but thrilled he had asked me to join him.

The breeze was from the south and warm. Most of the students had shed their heavy coats. Jon was wearing his tan corduroy sports coat, the professorial one with leather patches at the elbows. Coat open, his houndstooth tie flew up over his shoulder, while his moppish light brown hair blew back revealing a slightly receding hairline. At six feet, Jon was nearly a foot taller than me. As I looked up at him, the pre-noon sunshine accentuated the laugh lines at the corners of his golden-brown eyes. He wasn't classically handsome, but I wondered why I had never noticed his perfect aquiline nose and the gentle curve of his lower lip where it met his neatly trimmed beard.

The Tuesday special was always pork chow mein, my favorite. When I found out that in the three and a half years that Jon had been eating on campus he had never tried it, I cajoled him into ordering a scoop. He said he trusted my assessment, but he still threw a ham sandwich on his tray "just in case." We were joined by other students from Jon's classes. Although I would have preferred lunch to be just the two of us, I knew that there was safety from gossip if we ate with the group. I hoped no one noticed how we looked at one another. Professors had been dating students since the beginning of professors and students, but I was in one of Jon's classes—that made things more suspect for him. And, while I didn't normally worry about my reputation (a rather antiquated notion to my mind, though not my mother's), I didn't want to be thought of as "*the chick who got her grades by sleeping with her professors.*"

Jon agreed that the chow mein was worth the seventy-five cents that the commons grill charged and teased me when I couldn't clean my plate after bullying him to try it. My appetite was getting iffier by the day. Today the vegetables had gone down well, but the pork remained piled on my plate. I told Jon I thought I might be coming down with something. He softly chuckled and said that he was afraid he might be coming down with *something*, too. The look in his eyes let me know precisely what he meant. Had I ever thought the chemistry I was feeling was one-sided, that look and comment erased any doubt.

Jon and I didn't have lunch together after that Tuesday. Of course, we saw each other in class and at one very official meeting in his office on Thursday where we worked on the plan for my independent study. He was pleasant during the meeting, but seemed more formal than I had expected after Tuesday's flirtation. In one sense, I was thankful. Even though I had conceived of the project as a way to leave town, I was genuinely interested in my subject and I wanted the class credits. I needed his professional assistance with my project.

However, I would be lying if I said I wasn't disappointed. After Brian's dismissive behavior, Jon's attention had been reassuring and fun. And, I liked him. I really liked him.

When I got up to leave Thursday's meeting, Jon stood up and reached over his desk to shake my hand. As I grasped his palm, he pressed a folded piece of paper into mine. He was smiling, but then, Jon smiled most of the time, so I wasn't sure what to expect. I slipped the paper in my pocket to read after I'd left the Humanities building. I was shaking as I opened the note, and for a change, it wasn't from the November cold.

Jon gave me his address and asked if I would like to come to dinner at his place on Friday the twenty-fourth; he said he wanted to cook for me, but assumed I would already have plans for Thanksgiving dinner. I don't know what I had expected to read in the note, but the invitation to dinner surprised me. I guess, from his behavior earlier, I'd thought he might suggest we cool things down instead of ramp things up. I wasn't innocent enough to think that dinner alone with a guy at his house was all about eating. There were so many reasons I should have said no to Jon's invitation, but when I pictured him in my mind, not a single reason was more compelling than his smiling golden eyes and the way they made me feel.

Later that day, when I called his office from a wall phone in the commons to tell him I would be delighted to join him for dinner, the department secretary told me that Dr. Leggett had already left for the day. I was more nervous speaking to the secretary than I would have been talking to Jon. I apprehensively asked if she would leave a message on his desk—I told her my name and that my message was "yes." She asked me if that was all, and I said "yes." To this day I picture that she left him a note saying "Sarah Bolling, yes, yes."

On Tuesday, our last class together before Thanksgiving break, Jon gave me a smile and nod from the balcony railing that let me know he had gotten my phone message.

—5—

School let out for the Thanksgiving break, not a big event for me since I saw my parents and hometown every day, but I was looking forward to the break for the extra writing time it allowed me and the chance for some uninterrupted sleep. Ever since my early teens I'd needed a few nights a year when I'd go to bed in the afternoon and sleep until ten the next day. I was in desperate need of about two of those days in a row. Of course, not too far from my top of mind was Friday's dinner date; I actively tried to not think about it so that I could get other things done and calm the ping-pong balls in my stomach.

Thanksgiving Day was cold, but the ice and snow were gone after last week's warm spell. Travel was easy, so all of my cousins arrived safely at Aunt Thelma's for dry turkey and her (in)famous pineapple coconut sweet potatoes. I couldn't eat much, but my younger boy cousins took care of my share and no one noticed. Mom brought pies, as usual: pumpkin, apple, and pecan. I'd whipped real cream, but Mom and I may have been the only people who could tell that it wasn't Dream Whip. I think there's a point on Thanksgiving Day when people just keep forking food into their mouths without even tasting what they swallow.

The great thing about living just a few blocks from where you eat your Thanksgiving dinner is that you can go home and avoid eating the same meal for a second time in one day. Aunt Thelma and Uncle Harry lived in the same 1960's housing development as my parents. It continually annoyed my mother that her little sister lived in a newer, larger house. I didn't understand Mom's jealously of her sister and was happy my relationship with Annie was nothing like her conflict-riddled relationship with Thelma.

For me, my big sister was my everything. I'd missed her nearly every day for the past decade. Annie carrying me on her hip, calling me her "real baby doll," are my first memories. She knew she was our parents' favorite, but instead of reveling in it, she tried to compensate by lavishing her affection on me. When our grandma died, Annie was the one to break it to me. I was seven, too young to be at the hospital, and my parents had evidently thought me too young to understand death. Annie, at fifteen, was old enough to be by Grandma's side. She'd said Grandma had asked her to tell me that she loved me and that she would have done anything to stay with me if it had been in her power. Annie promised she would never leave me, but it sure felt like she'd left when she moved away for college when I was ten.

I walked home after helping Aunt Thelma and the rest of my aunts with cleanup. That it was only the women who worked on Thanksgiving had not escaped my notice, but I wasn't going to "rock the boat" within my family. Growing up in the house of an alcoholic, I already knew "how to pick my battles" and "stay in everyone's good graces"—three of my mother's favorite old saws.

I brushed my teeth and went straight to bed. I was excited about what tomorrow's date might mean, and I had a ton of homework to tackle, but Thanksgiving afternoon all I wanted was a darkened room and a date with my pillow.

I lifted my head on Friday morning about nine—I had slept for seventeen hours, a new Sarah Bolling record! I pulled my old robe over my flannel nightgown, not an easy thing to do since both were flannel. It made me think of the flannelboards we'd used in Sunday school and I laughed out loud when I pictured myself in my nightgown, holding a staff, stuck in the middle of a flock of cottonball sheep. I was hungrier than I had been in days, so I scooted my scuzzy slippers out to the kitchen to scrounge for breakfast. My dad was at work and Mom had gone Black Friday shopping, although I can't remember if that's what it was called in the 1970's. I poured a big bowl of Cheerios and topped it with half and half. Mom always filled a thermos with the morning's leftover coffee—I poured myself a cup, but the smell turned my stomach. I dumped it in the sink.

Jon wasn't expecting me until 6:30, so I had the whole day ahead of me. I'd taken all Thanksgiving Day off as a gift to myself. Today I had to study and write. My internal life was in a confusing uproar, but that was no excuse to let my grades slip. Whatever happened personally with Jon, I wanted to do well in his class for both my sake and his. If anyone learned of our personal relationship, I wanted there to be no reason for him to be accused of favoritism. Ever.

I took a bath and washed my hair. That was something I hadn't planned on. I'd washed my hair on Wednesday and I normally only liked to wrestle with it once a week, but, like my clothes from yesterday, it smelled of overcooked food. We hadn't even had Thanksgiving dinner at home and the air smelled like turkey and dressing. I shuddered to think of what it must have smelled like at Aunt Thelma's place. My new sensitivity to smells was aggravating—a nagging reminder of the problem I'd have to face again in January.

My mom came home in the afternoon and had me help her carry bags from the car with strict instructions that I was "not to open any of them." I obeyed, although there was one bag from the Three Sisters store in the Mall that I really wanted to investigate. Having already put down my pencil to give her a hand, I joined Mom for a late coffee break.

We were creatures of the Upper Midwest— morning and afternoon coffee breaks were almost a religious ritual. As I filled the kettle for tea, our standard afternoon substitute for coffee, Mom cut small pieces of the apple pie she'd brought home from her sister's house. Aunt Thelma never wanted to keep sweets around. No one had the heart to tell her it was too late for that rule to do her much good. Perhaps, because of Thelma's weight problem, Mom watched her weight carefully. It was one way she could outshine Thelma. For me, at least right now, weight wasn't an issue. No matter what I ate I stayed around a hundred pounds. I figured if I started gaining weight in December I could just blame Christmas treats like everyone else.

I'd already told Mom I was going to meet a friend that evening, so not to expect me for dinner. My family had pizza on the Friday after Thanksgiving. We'd been doing it for so many years I thought it was as much an American tradition as turkey on Thursday. I was probably in my teens before I figured out Thanksgiving Friday pizza was not part of every household menu. I started wondering what Jon might serve me that evening.... I shook my head as to physically dispel the thoughts and went back to my books.

—6—

I'd had to check the street map in the phonebook to locate the address Jon had given me in his note. It was on a street that I had never heard of, on the edge of town, tucked behind an old industrial and warehouse area. The streetlights were dim, making the winter stars appear even brighter in the November sky—at 6:30 it had been dark for nearly two hours.

Jon's house was compact, but cute, like a shabby storybook cottage. It had an arched front door with a funky little porthole and a barren green window box hung under what I assumed was a living room window. The house needed some paint and exterior maintenance, but I figured it was a rental; those being things Jon wouldn't be responsible for I didn't judge him harshly. As I walked up the narrow front walk, I gave myself the pep-talk I'd been giving myself all day when my mind had drifted from studying to thinking about what this evening might entail: *I am in control, I am in control, I am in control....* I wasn't scared, I was excited, but I needed to stay in control—my life was crazy enough.

I knocked on the hobbit-ish front door and waited. It was still above freezing so I hadn't bothered to button my coat after leaving the overheated car. I was wearing the outfit that I had chosen earlier that day

which included rust-colored, un-waled corduroy pants
that laced at the fly. They had stupidly wide legs and
were true hiphuggers. Because of the funny fly there
were no belt loops. I hoped I wouldn't step on one of
the floppy legs and de-pants myself, which I had done
on one occasion already, a victim of fashion. On top,
I'd chosen a simple dark blue turtleneck sweater long
enough to just cover my torso. The outfit was soft; the
pants were like velveteen and the sweater felt like
cashmere—luxury from Montgomery Ward with thanks
to Mom's employee discount.

Jon opened the door and took a deep breath.
The sound he made was not a whistle, but an inverted
whistle, the sound made by a quick intake of air. I was
sure no one had ever given me so much pleasure with a
simple sound. He swung the door wide and I stepped
into his faux colonial living room. He helped me from
my heavy winter dress coat and hung it on a spindled
hall tree in the corner.

The room was like his office, packed with books
and decorated for comfort. All of the early American
furniture might have made the room look old, but it
didn't. To me, it looked timeless. Jon asked if I liked
Van Morrison as he put a record on the turntable. It was
Morrison's *Street Choir* album, one I wasn't familiar
with. Jon suggested I sit on the couch while he worked

in the kitchen. The kitchen door was open and we spoke over the music while he chopped vegetables.

The stereo paused between songs as Jon set hors d'oeuvres on the coffee table. Just as the lively strains of "Give Me A Kiss" began to pour from the speakers, he took my hand and asked, "Dance?" I had never been so happy that I'd been forced to study social dance in junior high gym class. I surprised myself with my moves, but they probably had more to do with Jon's lead than my skill. He jitterbugged with the grace and ease of someone who had been taught by an expert. The song ended, and while I adjusted my pants, he motioned to the coffee table and apologized for his appetizer.

He explained he had wanted to make me shrimp cocktail, but couldn't find anything but canned shrimp at the grocery store. He said he'd had no idea canned shrimp were a third-of-an-inch long and sopping wet. I stifled a giggle as I dipped the tiny shrimp into a small bowl of cocktail sauce. I didn't know what a shrimp cocktail was supposed to look like, but I knew enough to know that this wasn't it. I thought, "Hmm, maybe this guy isn't so smooth after all."

Jon's meal seemed to be choreographed to the Van Morrison album, because as "Call me up in Dreamland" was ending, he asked me into the kitchen. I watched as he checked the red sauce and put the uncooked spaghetti into a large pot of boiling water. Jon turned from the stove and took me lightly in his arms as the first strains of the sultry "I'll Be Your Lover, Too" drifted in from the living room. He reached around me and unsnapped the latch of the large silver barrette that held the end of my single braid. With a move I barely noticed, he slipped the barrette onto the kitchen counter. My arms were still at my sides as we swayed to the music and he slowly undid my braid from twist to twist, the whole time looking down into my eyes. I could barely breathe.

As Van Morrison sang of his woman's many charms, Jon reached the top of my braid at the nape of my neck. He caressed that always tender area with the tips of his fingers and then gently put his hands on my shoulders and turned me so that he was facing the back of my head. With his arms once again around me, he nuzzled his face in my hair. Even though it had been hours since I'd washed it, my hair was still damp. The musky scent of my shampoo rose in the air and mixed with the steam rising from the stove.

Jon whispered he had wanted to hold me from the moment he had first looked into my eyes two weeks earlier. As I felt his clothed erection push against the small of my back, he smoothed my hair aside, bent, and kissed my neck just below my right ear. I heard myself as I quietly gasped. It was the sound I imagined I'd make while sinking underwater for the last time.

—7—

The Van Morrison record ended and so did the romantic mood in the kitchen. As I tried to catch my breath and regain my composure, Jon stirred the sauce and checked the al dente consistency of the spaghetti. He wasn't abrupt and didn't seem annoyed, but I felt I had somehow done something wrong. I had been sure we were heading for the bedroom, pasta be damned. As I began walking toward the living room I reached behind my head to re-braid my hair. Jon turned from the stove and asked me not to. "Leave the room or braid my hair?" I asked.

"Both," was his one-word response. That's when I noticed the small table in a nook of the tiny kitchen. It was covered with a red gingham tablecloth and set with silverware, a glowing candle, and an open bottle of chianti ensconced in wicker.

I told him I would be happy to leave my hair down if he could forgive wayward strands of it in his spaghetti. As I fastened my upper hair back with my barrette, I muttered that my hair was a little like me— "hard to control and with a mind of its own." Jon laughed, and said those were the two attributes that made both hair and people interesting.

He drained the pasta and doused it with olive oil. I think he had planned on serving me, but I asked if I could dish up my own plate. It always embarrassed me to be served more food than I could eat, and I remembered him teasing me about not eating all of my chow mein during the only other meal we had shared. He retrieved an iceberg lettuce salad from the refrigerator and French bread from the oven. I filled my plate, careful not to let my hair swing forward into my food, and walked to the table. Jon served himself and joined me.

"Chianti?" he asked as he put his plate on the table and motioned to the heavy green juice glasses sitting on the kitchen counter. As I nodded yes, my mouth already full of French bread, I thought it odd but strangely endearing that a man who owned a red checkered tablecloth didn't own real wine glasses. We toasted to the evening and sipped the chianti. It wasn't long before Jon noticed my wine was going down slowly and made me a cup of tea.

After the leisurely meal, we pushed our chairs from the table and moved to the living room. As Michel Legrand played on the stereo, we sat on the old couch leaning into one another and talked for hours. There were no more dances, no more amorous advances. Other than being snuggled next to one another, we could have been talking in the commons lobby on campus.

We talked about our mutual love of colonial and early American history and what we liked to read for fun. Jon's bookcases were full of the works of philosophers who I had heard of, but hadn't studied. He also had a surprising number of books on mathematics and physics for a historian. He liked Russian novels and had a row of Dostoyevsky, Nabokov, and Tolstoy. I told him I had enjoyed the little bit of Dostoyevsky I'd read, but I found it challenging when the characters broke into French.

I had studied French in high school, but still found the constant language changing in older novels troublesome. Jon said he spoke French and found it useful when studying American colonial history. He told me he thought I would eventually find it beneficial, especially if I remained interested in historic research. As for Russian novels, he said anything worth reading was translated into English—the French was just for show. It always had been.

Music was a subject upon which we didn't always agree. While we had established that we both liked Van Morrison, Jon also liked Michel Legrand. I had never in my life met a person, or even imagined a person, under age forty who listened to Michel

Legrand. When I said I liked folk music, and especially early Dylan, he insisted I was too young to be so enamored with the genre. Jon said while he thought Bob Dylan's poetry was excellent, he sang like a toad. I told him we were just going to have to agree to disagree on Dylan's music. I thought Dylan was a genius.

I asked Jon about his collection of colonial furniture. He explained that none of it was real, he couldn't afford the real stuff, but he enjoyed finding second-hand high quality knock-offs. His tables and chairs, desk, bed, and drawer chests were all mortise and tenoned maple and walnut. He told me colonial replicas had been in and out of style over the last hundred and fifty years, so there was a lot to choose from. He said that he liked the aesthetic and appreciated the quality. He called his collection his "fauxlonials," a combination of the words "faux" and "colonial." I told him I liked his new word, but I doubted it would ever make its way into a dictionary.

Around two in the morning, I re-braided my hair, Jon helped me into my coat, we kissed, and I drove home on empty streets not understanding the night's turn of events. I'd been sure at the beginning of the evening that Jon was seducing me. I wasn't shocked or offended—it was sort of what I'd expected, maybe even hoped for, when I'd accepted his invitation. But, it had all changed so quickly by the time we sat down to to eat. Had he changed his mind? Had he sensed something about me? I wasn't sure about anything that had just happened—except that I was falling in love.

—8—

On Saturday, Jon called me at home to say that he'd had a great time on our date. After some awkward pauses, he also admitted that he knew I was confused by his apparent change in ardor earlier in the evening. He apologized for revving things up to the boiling point while the spaghetti simmered—he said he "hadn't meant for things to go so quickly." He told me he respected me and didn't want either of us to get hurt by rushing our relationship.

I nervously told Jon that I'd like to talk with him, but my family's only phone was in the living room and my mother was home, making a private conversation difficult. As I was suggesting we meet in person to talk about anything of significance, Jon broke in and asked me to come to dinner again that night. I was so happy, and relieved, that my "Yes!" erupted with, perhaps, more enthusiasm than I'd meant to reveal. I was afraid when we'd started our phone conversation he was trying to extricate himself from our budding relationship. I quietly thanked god that I usually had full use of the family car in the evenings so I could get away without any questions from my parents.

I dressed for the gas station that afternoon in a sweater and my best jeans—a little nicer outfit than my normal work sweatshirts and tattered painters pants. Unfortunately, no matter how clean Millie (Rob's wife) and I tried to keep the convenience store, it always smelled of old motor oil. I drove to Jon's after work with my window down hoping to air-out my sweater, but when he greeted me at his front door with a companionable hug I'm afraid I still smelled like "*Eau de Valvoline.*" If he noticed, he didn't say anything.

Tonight Jon was dressed in jeans, T-shirt, and a plaid flannel shirt, its sleeves rolled to his elbows. I'd never seen him so casual. He looked younger than he did in his dress clothes—more like a classmate than a professor. I hung my coat on the corner hall tree and followed him to the kitchen.

The ingredients for chili were scattered across the metal edged countertop, but even more noticeable was a Windsor armchair, old newspapers spread beneath it, filling the center of the kitchen floor. Beside the walnut chair sat a steaming pail of soapy water and several wet rags. Jon explained he had just purchased the chair from a local junk shop. "I'm giving it the first good bath it's had in quite a few years," he said as he motioned for me to sit at the little table. He apologized for not having cleared the kitchen before I arrived. He said he always got excited by new furniture finds and liked to start cleaning and polishing as soon as he got home—time had just slipped away.

He started to move the old chair toward the back door, but I asked if he was done washing it. I said, "If it's ok, I can keep scrubbing it while you cook." Jon said he'd like that and gave me a crash course: Wooden Chair Cleaning 101.

He made chili. I pushed up my sweater sleeves and finished bathing the Windsor.

And, we talked. We talked while he stirred the chili. We talked while I set the table. We talked while eating dinner and washing dishes. We moved to the living room and curled together on the couch. And, we talked.

I had not realized I was so starved for conversation. My parents rarely spoke to me, but when they did it was about the weather or who got to drive the Dodge next. I'd never had much in common with most kids my age, so I had no close friends in the area. By living at home I hadn't gotten to know any likeminded people on campus. The few new friends I'd made during the McGovern campaign had scattered when school started in the fall, and, of course, Brian was out of my life. I really was alone.

Jon seemed to understand my situation—he had told me that he'd always felt like he'd never quite fit in with his peers, either. As a kid he had been advanced several grades, so he was younger than the others in his class. He said he had learned to focus on his studies and ignore the rest. At USD he was a popular instructor, but a loner—partly because he lived in Sioux Falls, but mainly because there weren't many other young, single professors.

When I told Jon I thought I should probably be heading home, he asked me if I would come back on Sunday. He said he wanted to make scalloped potatoes and his recipe fed an army. I told him I couldn't promise to eat an army's worth, but I'd never met a cooked potato I hadn't wanted to eat. I said I'd be over after work, so to expect me bout the same time wearing the same cologne.

Sunday evening was much like Saturday, except dinner had a less spicy main course. Jon made excellent "escalloped" potatoes. We had a pleasant argument over whether one should use the "e" when referring to the casserole. Jon said he would call the potatoes "escalloped" in the future as long as I promised never to call a "potato" a "potahto." I gave him my solemn vow (really, who calls a "potato" a "potahto" other than the Gershwins?).

When we moved to the living room after cleaning

the kitchen, Jon put Dylan's *Freewheelin'* album on the stereo. I was surprised and told him so. "I thought you hated Dylan—it amazes me that you own one of his records."

"I didn't own any of Dylan's music until this afternoon, but since you think he's a genius I thought I should educate myself." As "Blowin' in the Wind" ended, Jon said, "I've just learned to love this next song, 'Girl from the North Country.' The first time I heard it I immediately thought of you."

We sat next to one another on the couch and I listened with new ears to a song that I knew by heart. I'd never had a guy tell me he thought of me when he heard a song—truth be told if any of my former boyfriends had said such a thing I would have thought it a cheesy come-on. But Jon, having purchased the Dylan album to please me, made me believe his words. When the song ended I said, "Thank you. It's a pretty song, but I've always thought it sort of sad." Jon countered with, "Ahh, but, poetic. And so beautifully Northern, just like you." I leaned over and kissed him on the cheek. He turned and kissed me on the mouth, but it wasn't the kind of kiss that led to more.

He pulled away and told me he had been thinking about our first date again. He said he didn't believe that his strong feelings toward me would change, but he wanted to give me time to think about a relationship. He asked me to consider all of our differences and what they might mean if we were to get more involved. Jon suggested we wait until the month anniversary of the railing disaster to see how things developed. He called it our balcony anniversary. It sounded like something right out of *Romeo and Juliet*, but the actual day of the anniversary was December 7th. The significance of the date was lost on neither of us. I hoped ours would not be "a day that would live in infamy."

—9—
December 7, 1972

At the end of our weekly Thursday meeting to plan my interim trip, Jon had asked me if I would mind picking up our dinner that evening. He said he had preordered Chinese food from a little place on his side of town, but was going to have to stay in Vermillion later than he'd expected. He said the food would be ready by 6:30, and he should be home no later than 7:00. In normal Sarah fashion, my first question was, "Is it paid for?" I didn't want to be embarrassed by not having enough cash to cover the bill. He assured me that everything was taken care of. "All you have to do is go to the counter and tell them you're there for the order and give them my name."

I hadn't worn anything special to school that day, just my usual jeans and turtleneck topped with a flannel shirt. For the evening, which I hoped would be special, I wanted to dress up. I had two pair of pants that weren't jeans, so I chose the pair that I hadn't worn on our first date. I'd sewn them from olive green wool and lined them with a silky fabric that I knew would feel soothing against dry winter skin. I selected a white sweater, long gold chain necklace, and gold bangle bracelet to accompany the pants. The outfit looked good and I thought it made me look a little older than I did in my normal casual clothing. I didn't do anything special with my hair. As I brushed and re-braided it, I remembered Jon's arms around me while his hands deftly undid my heavy plait. I wanted to feel that again.

I pulled up to the Canton Café at 6:40. The restaurant wasn't much to look at—it was the corner unit of a newish strip mall on the west side of town, but its reputation for good Chinese food kept it popular. I'd cleared a space on the back seat of the Dodge for the food and found a blanket in the trunk to throw over the bags to try to keep them warm. Winter was both the best and worst time for hot takeout food in South Dakota.

The Asian woman at the cash register smiled as I walked through the door, as if she'd been expecting me. My first thought was that Thursday must be a slow night for takeout if ours was the only order. When I told her I was there to pick up an order for "Leggett," she asked me to follow her. I thought she must have been mistaken about what I'd said, but followed her anyway. She led me to a circular opening, a moon gate, at the back of the restaurant. There, to my surprise, Jon was waiting for me.

The small meeting room was empty except for a dining table and two chairs. In the center of the red clothed table sat a beautiful bouquet of white roses with Christmas greenery. Jon helped me with my coat and gave it to the hostess. I couldn't quit shaking my head and telling him I couldn't believe what he'd done. He said he hoped I didn't mind that he'd lied to me to get me to come to the restaurant, then stated, "There is *nothing* on campus important enough for me to be late for this date with you."

With those words, the food started to arrive— wonton soup, egg rolls, moo shu pork, egg foo young, chicken lo mein, and on and on.... I was overwhelmed at first, but Jon assured me I didn't have to try it all. He confessed that the only way to get the private meeting room for the evening was to order a minimum of twenty dollars. In 1972, twenty dollars bought a massive amount of Chinese food. Jon had already arranged to have the leftovers packaged to take to the history department offices the next day. Dr. Sargent had recently purchased a radar range for the break area and Jon said he and the rest of the Humanities building staff were having fun playing with it. He told me he liked the idea of our secret date scoring points with his colleagues.

Just before 8:00, the server brought our fortune cookies on a red plastic tray. I asked Jon if he had ever heard about the custom of adding "in bed" to the end of a fortune cookie saying. He hadn't, but he liked the idea. He said, "You first."

I roared with laughter as I read my fortune to Jon. "Today is an auspicious beginning—in bed." With a joking lascivious smile and raised eyebrow, Jon said that he couldn't have chosen a better fortune for us. But, when he broke his cookie to check his fortune, he chose not to read it to me. He crumpled it and dropped it on his plate. I never asked him what it said.

While I wrapped the roses back in protective tissue paper so that they stayed warm, Jon took the bags of cardboard-boxed leftovers to his pickup to stay cold. Jon's truck was parked far down the long side lot from the restaurant. He hadn't wanted me to see it and spoil his surprise. We took my car back to his place so we could ride together—I drove while he held the vase.

"The flowers are lovely, Jon, but I can't take them home. I haven't told my parents about us and I don't know how I would explain where I got them. Can we just enjoy them at your place?"

"Of course. Joint custody is fine as long as you plan on coming to visit them often—like every day until all the petals have fallen off... and the water evaporates... and the glass vase turns back into sand."

If Jon had further seduction scenes planned for the rest of the evening, our rush to the bedroom ruined them. As soon as the flowers were set on the coffee table we started undressing one another. Our coats and shoes hit the living room floor as we tumbled into the bedroom. We had been talking for weeks—it was time for another kind of communion.

Just after midnight I told Jon that I had to leave even though I hated to get out of his warm bed; I needed to drop him back at the restaurant to get his pickup and then get home to my own bed—Friday morning was coming too quickly. He kissed me and said he understood as he rolled from the bed. He told me to take my time getting up, he'd run out and start my cold car.

Alone in the house, I stared in the dresser mirror and I smiled with tears at the corners of my eyes as I thought of the past hours. I'd been having sex since I was seventeen, but I had never felt like I did that night. To say it was magical sounds trite; it was transcendent. Jon had made love to me as though he had known my body forever. I floated in unfamiliar reverie as I dressed and re-braided my hair.

When I came from the bedroom, Jon was already back in the house unwrapping the roses we had left neglected on the coffee table. When I told him, again, how beautiful I thought the flowers were, he looked at me with loving eyes and said, "A rose tho beauteous be, pales my love, nye t' thee."

"Thank you," I replied, "Did you just compose that on the fly?"

"No, but I'm flattered you think I could have. It's by Philip Blythewood. He wrote it in 1728. And, unfortunately, just like the history professor I am, I remember those details but not the rest of the lines. Ahh, but the first ones are perfect—you are beautiful, Sarah."

Jon's pickup was the only vehicle in the lot at 12:40. I asked if he'd like me to stay while his truck warmed, but he said no. He thought I'd like to get home to my bed, and he was right, but I hated to leave him in the cold. He undid his lap-belt and slid across the bench seat. As we kissed goodbye in the parking lot of the Canton Café, Jon told me he was falling in love with me. They were words I hadn't expected, and I didn't know how to respond. I only managed to stammer "goodnight" as he stepped from the car.

Once again, I drove home on empty streets not understanding what had just happened. I didn't understand how a man as perfect as Jon could love me, and I wondered if I would ever be at a place in my life when I could say those words to him.

—10—

The weeks following our date on the seventh were much like the two previous weeks, other than where we did the majority of our talking. I'd drive to Jon's place after I closed up the gas station on Monday, Wednesday, and Friday evenings, and invariably race him to the bed shortly after coming through the front door. We would make love, then Jon would usually go to the kitchen and bring back a snack: buttered toast or a sliced apple. By that time, I would have put on my glasses and rearranged the blankets and pillows. We would stay in bed and talk—sometimes for hours if I didn't have to get home to study. We talked about mundane things, like what had happened to us that day, but we also talked about what was happening in the state and the world. We talked a lot about books and history. Nerds in love—we were the definition.

America's Founding Fathers, along with the documents they had penned, were Jon's academic specialty. He was particularly interested in George Mason, one of the more obscure patriots. He thought that Mason's contributions to the Declaration of Independence and Constitution had long been overlooked, primarily because he had signed neither document. Jon loved to talk about Mason and told me that someday his dream was to write the definitive biography of the man.

I envied Jon, I was still trying to narrow my focus; I was interested in too many things. I liked art and old buildings, but had chosen not to study art history because I didn't want a major that was traditionally feminine. I enjoyed historic research, especially timeline building. I liked the idea of putting things in order to determine cause and effect, but I wasn't sure how I was going to make a career from that kind of research.

Jon had once asked me if I had always known I'd go to college. I told him not always, but ever since my last few years in grade school it had been my plan. I explained that Annie had left for Brookings to study psychology when I was ten. She would come home at breaks so excited by school and raving about her wonderful professors, "Dr. This" and "Dr. That." I was confused by the title and asked why she was taught by doctors, not teachers. She explained that her teachers, her professors, weren't medical doctors, but Doctors of Philosophy, or Ph.D.s for short. They had studied for years to be called Dr., and she thought they deserved that honor. I told Annie that someday I wanted to be a professor. I wanted to go to college and get a Ph.D. I wanted to be called Dr. Sarah Bolling. I wanted to make her proud.

"Annie hadn't laughed at my childish bravado. Instead, she'd helped me. Annie did everything she could to make my dream come true. She helped me pick my high school classes so I'd get all my college prerequisites. She taught me how to play to my academic strengths, so I could keep my GPA high, and she even coached me before I took the ACTs."

I told Jon that Annie had given me a bad time when I'd chosen the University of South Dakota over her alma mater. And, that she wasn't excited when I decided to commute to school, but she understood my desire to save money—helping me pay my bills was something she couldn't do. As a social worker for the State of Massachusetts, she didn't make much money, and it was expensive to live alone in Boston.

"Would you mind if I tell Annie about us?"

Jon knew I hadn't mentioned our relationship to anyone yet, nor had he, as far as I knew. He said he would be happy to have her know about us, and he was looking forward to the day when he could meet her. He laughed and said he owed her a big thank you—by helping me get into college, she had unwittingly helped him find me.

Jon told me he had always known he would go to college. His parents were highly educated and they expected nothing less of him. "What I didn't know until I was at MIT was that I would major in history, and I'm still surprised I'm a history professor. MIT is an unusual place to study history, but I'd been there two years by the time I declared it my major and I didn't see any reason to leave. I had some excellent professors and Boston is a great place for history. That's one of the reasons I'm so excited about your interim project—you are going to have so much fun exploring the city."

Jon said he'd stayed in New England for grad school. I already knew his Ph.D. was from Yale—his framed diploma hung on his office wall. "Where would you like to go to grad school, Sarah?"

"Oh, I'd love to attend an Ivy League school, but it's probably only a pipe dream. My grades will be good, but I'm still not much of a standardized test taker, and, honestly, I don't have much going on in my life to make me a likely candidate. I don't think a recommendation from Rob and Millie at the gas station is bound to get me very far."

Jon countered my doubts, "Ahh, don't worry too much. We should be able to parlay your interim project into something to impress an entrance committee. I still know some people at Yale, and you'll need to get to know Dr. Sargent better—he's a wealth of information and contacts. He'll be happy to help, too."

One evening after I'd mentioned living in my Grandma Bolling's house when I was young, Jon asked me how well I knew my grandparents. He'd just read that the education department at Stanford was doing a study to see if a student's interest in pursuing a degree in history was in any way linked to their relationships with older adults, especially older relatives. He said he had never known his grandparents, but he found the concept interesting.

I told him I remembered a lot from my days with my grandma, but my Grandpa Bolling, who had been a carpenter, had died before I was born. I explained that it was shortly after Grandpa died that my parents and Annie had moved into the old house with Grandma. My mother had always said it was to help Dad's mom, but as I got older and learned about my father's problems after coming home from the Pacific, I came to think it may have been the other way around. Either way, I'd spent most of my time with my Grandma. Mom and Dad both worked, so I'd been Grandma's little girl.

She was the adult I remembered bathing me and putting me to bed every night. She had loved my funny hair and spent hours every Sunday afternoon washing and untangling it. She'd work on the wet clumps close to my scalp and distract me with stories about growing up on the family homestead east of Sioux Falls. She told me about adventures with her younger brother, like building a raft to float in the slough next to the barn, and riding a calf because they were too little to climb atop the family horse.

"Since Annie's eight years older than me, during the school year Grandma and I were alone a lot. We did everything together. I learned how to crochet and tend a garden before I could read. Grandma showed me how numbers worked while we made cookies, and how to write my ABCs while she wrote letters to her brother."

Then, I told him about my favorite lessons. "Grandma had a big old upright piano—I loved it. My parents didn't want me to touch it—maybe they thought listening to Annie practice was enough torture—anyway, Grandma taught me on the sly."

"Grandma had always played by ear, but with Annie's piano books we both learned to read music. I practiced daily and took it pretty seriously for a little kid. The best compliment my mom ever paid me was when she walked into the kitchen after work, heard *me* playing in the front room, and called out, '*Annie*, I have never heard you play so well. You are really getting good!' Grandma just smiled at me and held her finger in front of her mouth in the universal sign for *hush*. It remained our secret."

"Well, Sarah, I think you should probably talk to the Stanford History Project researchers—you may have just proved their theory." Then Jon asked if I still played the piano.

"My folks got rid of Grandma's piano after she died in '59. That's when we moved to the house where we still live. I've barely touched one since then. Someday, when I have money and time, I'm going to buy myself a big old piano and try to remember everything Grandma Bolling taught me."

—11—

On Saturday the sixteenth I borrowed the Dodge for the day and took Jon on a ride around Sioux Falls. I'd been telling him about some of my favorite places in the city for weeks. Sometimes he could picture them, but a few places he had never heard of. I was going to remedy that.

Our first stop was Taco John's on 41st Street. The little franchised taco stand was the first place that I had ever eaten a taco and I thought it was fantastic. I left Jon in the car, and ran in to buy our feast: two tacos, a chili frito, an apple grande, and two Cokes. We sat in the car in the crowded parking lot eating our faux Mexican lunch as the windows fogged over and started to drip. Jon said that he had never tasted anything like it, and he had eaten tacos in California. I was afraid to ask him what he meant—I didn't think it was a compliment.

After wiping down the windows with my scarf, we took off on my planned route. I drove him through Tuthill Park and past my old high school. Then I took Cliff Avenue back to Falls Park so he could see the waterfall the city was named for. From there we drove past my grandparents' old house where my family had lived with Grandma Bolling until I was seven. The white boxy house was just north of downtown.

We drove past the Catholic cathedral and I told Jon about my Grandfather Bolling moving to Sioux Falls to build the round forms used to cast the concrete pillars in the massive church. A few blocks from the cathedral, we passed the Pettigrew Museum, a place I loved visiting when I was a kid. Most children would have preferred the zoo, but not me—I could spend hours poking around the stuffy building and examining the petrified wood on its exterior walls. As we continued east toward downtown, I showed Jon the old quartzite Carnegie Library, pointing out the windowed corner that housed the reference materials, another of my favorite haunts once I hit my teens.

Jon seemed entertained by my hometown trivia. I'd always thought of Sioux Falls as a rather large city. For Jon it was the smallest place he had ever lived. He said when he'd first come to South Dakota to interview for his position at the U, he was amazed by the open spaces and shocked by the lack of people. He asked me not to laugh and told me he had assumed when reading the population of Vermillion that it was a suburb attached to a city. When he saw that it was a small town attached to cornfields, he'd decided if he were offered the professorship he would live in Sioux Falls. He said he enjoyed the anonymity living in Sioux Falls gave him (and now, us), but, like me, was getting tired of the commute.

By the time we pulled into the river ramp, snow was starting to fall. We buttoned our coats and walked up Phillips Avenue to J. C. Penney. Jon was looking for a Christmas gift for Dr. Sargent and I still needed to find something for my parents. Not many young people came downtown after the Western Mall had been built, so that made Penney's the perfect option for us—it was less likely we would run into anyone from the University.

We were in the first floor men's department next to the escalator when a little girl approached us to ask for Jon's opinion about a necktie she was choosing for her father. She must have thought Jon looked like a daddy. In typical Jon fashion, he took his time with her. He asked her questions about her father: What did he do for a living? Did he have any pets? What color did he like the best? After about a ten-minute deliberation they settled on a red tie with silhouettes of little Scottie dogs woven into the pattern. I had so much fun watching the two of them together. Jon was the most attentive and kindest man I had ever met.

Jon found a silk tie and pocket square for Dr. Sargent, which he planned to present at the faculty

Christmas party in Vermillion that night. My plans for the evening weren't quite as much fun. I'd be staying home studying for my last final exam of the semester.

While Jon paid for the tie set and had it gift wrapped, I ran to Dickinson's Bakery on Main Street to buy my parents a box of chocolates. I hadn't had any luck finding my folks gifts at Penney's—I was such an unimaginative shopper. By the time Jon and I met up again it was getting dark. As we walked to the car carrying our packages, the Christmas lights strung over Phillips Avenue twinkled over our heads. Powdery snow sifted down around us. I couldn't remember ever feeling such contentment.

—12—

I swallowed two aspirin and curled up in the corner of the couch while Jon filled a hot-water bottle at the kitchen sink. After I'd closed the gas station on Sunday evening, I'd driven to his place. My head had hurt all day, but I wanted to hear about the faculty Christmas party. As he placed the flannel wrapped rubber bottle at the back of my neck, he teased me about being hungover. He said he was the one who had gone to a wild party the night before.

I was incredulous. "Wild party? You went to a *wild* party at Dr. Sargent's house? You're kidding, right?"

He said that he was, but he thought some of his colleagues, or their wives, might have been in some pain that morning. From what he had seen over the past few years, professors knew how to drink. He asked if I had ever seen the film *Who's Afraid of Virginia Woolf.* When I told him no, my parents thought I'd been too young to see it when it was released in 1966. He said, "Ahh, I sometimes forget your age." I told him that was fine with me. Sometimes I did, too.

He asked if I thought my headache was a migraine. I told him no, but that I got migraines every now and then. I said I thought today's headache was from eye strain and general stress. I hadn't talked much about my schedule, but I'd turned in two papers and taken three tests in the past week; one of the papers and one of the tests were for Jon's colonial history class, so obviously he knew about them. I suggestively commented, "After tomorrow, old man, you'd better watch out; I'll be done with my finals. I'm going to feel so good and have so much extra energy you won't be able to keep up with me."

He retorted, "Great! You can cook and clean while I grade papers and tests."

I stuck out my tongue slightly and replied, "You know that's not what I meant. If my head didn't hurt so much I'd beat you with your own sofa pillow."

Jon went to the kitchen and brought back a cool washcloth. As he placed it across my forehead he asked, "What's the difference between a regular headache and a migraine?"

"For me it's the intensity. With a regular headache I can function. It's not fun, but I can work or go to school. With a migraine I just curl-up in pain and try not to move. I want a dark room—no lights, no smells, no sounds, no motions. I'm really thankful I don't get them often."

He asked if I'd ever heard of ocular migraines and wondered what they entailed.

"I just have light sensitivity—I don't think my

migraines would be considered ocular." But, then I told him something I had never told anyone but my mother. "When I'm coming down with a migraine I hear voices in my head. It sounds like a crowd of people all talking at once. I've gotten used to it, but when I was a kid I was so scared by the voices all I wanted to do was press my hands over my ears and scream until they went away."

"Oh, Sarah, that sounds awful. Can you make out what the voices are saying?"

"No, it's kind of like everything that's ever been said in the space I'm in is being said all at once—words are sort of layered on top of one another. It's just jabbering, totally indistinguishable. I was in school— fourth grade—the first time I heard them. I called my mom to come get me; when I told her about the voices she just got angry with me and ordered me not to ever talk about them again. She told me that people would think I was crazy. Do you think I'm crazy, Jon?"

Jon sat down on the couch and put an arm around my shoulders. He rearranged the cool cloth on my forehead and said, "No, Sarah, you're not crazy, but I think your mom might be. What sort of adult puts a burden like that on a little kid?"

"A woman who's more concerned about what other people think than how her kid feels. I figured that out a long time ago." I fell asleep in Jon's arms. When I awoke twenty minutes later, Jon was still by my side, but my headache was gone.

—13—

Now that classes and finals were over, Jon and I had made plans to actually go out for dinner to celebrate our first Christmas together. We'd ventured outside his house walls a few times in the past month to shop or pick up food, but most of the time the risk didn't seem worth the reward. Now that the semester had ended, neither of us was quite as concerned about being seen together in public.

The twenty-third was to be our Christmas Eve. Jon had made reservations at a restaurant on the outskirts of town just past the shopping mall where my mom worked. The exterior of the new building was brick and built to look old; the interior décor had an old print shop vibe. We'd heard it was expensive, but Jon insisted that this was a special occasion. Along with being Christmas, it was the beginning of the most downtime either one of us had had in months. Also, I was leaving in less than a week—so, I suppose it was a goodbye dinner, too, although I wasn't ready to think about that.

I had no gift for Jon. I was a terrible shopper, and I never knew what to give people. It sounds like an excuse, but Jon really did seem like the kind of man who had most everything he wanted—well, everything that I could afford. On his living room wall he'd hung a plaque with a quote by Daniel Defoe, "All our discontents spring from the want of thankfulness for what we have." I thought it summed up Jon's spirit so well. He was happy, thankful, and not at all discontent. He had what he wanted and he wanted what he had.

I thought the best gift I could give him would be fantastic memories from our upcoming night together, enough to hold us both through the lonely months ahead. We had never spent a full night together, but tonight would be different. I'd already asked permission to keep the Dodge overnight. I'd said that I was going to stay with a friend home from college—technically not a lie. I told my mother that I'd have the car back by noon on Sunday.

My prep for our big date started on Saturday morning. Alone in the house, I bathed with care, shaving every inch of my body I thought might need it with a new blade in my old brass safety razor. I moisturized my winter skin and washed my hair that Jon loved so much. After grooming I spent time readying my wardrobe. I was trying for perfection, not something I usually thought about when it came to my appearance.

Late afternoon finally arrived. Before I dressed, I did my hair. If I braided it when it was wet it took over a day to dry. Today I'd left it down so it would dry more quickly, but it was still damp at the nape of my neck. I bent forward, brushed it upward, and twisted it until it twisted back on itself forming a large loose bun. Because of my hair's unusual texture, it took only three old fashioned hairpins to hold it in place. As I pictured removing the hairpins and shaking my blonde mane loose over Jon's recumbent body, I realized that my hair did have some positive attributes.

My dress wasn't new, but it was pretty. Annie had left it at home when she moved to Boston. That it had been a little large for me last year was a plus this December. It was made of soft red wool, lined with satin. The cowl style neckline was high, but the skirt made-up for it. I had re-hemmed it, and it was thigh-high short. Pantyhose would have been the logical accessory with a mini skirt, but I hated the idea of trying to stage my seduction while untangling myself from their unforgiving grip. I still had one pair of extra long nylons and a garter belt left from pre-pantyhose days. The crazy South Dakota weather was warmer now than it had been in early November, so the thought of nearly bare legs and high heels was tolerable.

I chose not to wear a necklace over the high collar of the dress for the same reason I'd chosen not to wear pantyhose. I wanted no fumbling later. I slipped my thick gold bangle on my wrist, threw on my dress coat, and left the house.

Jon met me at his door in a dark blue suit. He was wearing a tie that I'd said I liked on the day we met the little girl in Penney's. It was a paisley print in reds and navy; it was flashier than his normal conservative stripes and geometric weaves and I knew he'd secretly purchased it to please me.

"You look snazzy, Jon. I haven't seen that suit before."

"Well, I only wear it for special occasions—it's my interview suit."

I slipped my arms around his waist underneath the blue wool coat and whispered, "Don't worry, I promise you, you've already got the job and I'm pretty sure you can expect a good evaluation at your next performance review."

"Ahh, Sarah, you had better unhand me, or I can guarantee you... we won't make it to our eight-o-clock reservation."

We left my parents' sedan parked on the street and took Jon's old truck. It wasn't easy for me to climb in, but Jon helped me up. It felt like a real date being in his vehicle with him driving. I had once asked him, "Why a pickup truck?" He explained that a person who likes to buy used furniture has to have a way to transport it. He said he would have preferred a car for his commute to the U, but he could only afford one vehicle. He thought that someday he'd own both a car and a truck, but, for now, his little pickup had to serve double duty.

We were seated after a short wait. The restaurant was dark and romantic, and, for a change, food smelled delicious to me. I didn't want Jon feeling as though he had wasted money on me, so I ate enthusiastically. Seeing this, Jon decided we should splurge and have dessert. We split the special holiday dessert, a huge piece of cheesecake with cherries. It was delivered to the table topped with a snowflake fashioned from white chocolate. Jon gently lifted the sugar coated creation, holding it to my lips for me to take the first bite.

After dessert we moved to the lounge. Paneled in dark wood with built-in bookcases, it was a bibliophile's dream. Rows of old books, occasionally separated by antique bookends and objets d'art, covered the shelves. We chose a small table in a far corner, where the waiter eventually noticed us and lit the candle centerpiece. Jon ordered warm drinks I had never heard of: cappuccinos. They came topped with whipped cream and tasted like grownup hot chocolate. As we held hands across the table, my gold bracelet sparkled in the candlelight. I slipped off my shoe and slid my silky toe up Jon's calf just above his trouser sock. This time he was the one who made the sound of a person going underwater for the last time. I was starting to feel confident in my chosen role as a seductress.

Jon cleared his throat and asked if I might be interested in heading back to his place for the rest of our date. At this point I was sure my plan was working. While Jon retrieved our coats from the coat check, I stopped by the restroom to check my hair and make-up. I wanted to look my absolute best for our drive home and all that I'd envisioned once we passed through the door at Jon's house.

We walked across the crowded parking lot, Jon's arm hugging my shoulders. It wasn't snowing, but the nighttime dampness caused ice crystals to shimmer in the light streaming from the streetlamps. I was euphoric, but, perhaps, a bit too full after the big meal and drinks. Just as Jon reached for the truck door a gust of wind whipped up my coat and dress freezing my nearly bare legs. I started to shiver uncontrollably.

As Jon hurriedly helped me into the truck seat, after what had been the most romantic dinner date of my life, I turned toward him. The panicked look on my face must have served as a warning, because he stepped backward at the precise moment I leaned forward and threw up everything I'd eaten over the course of the long evening. Most of my dinner landed on the parking lot blacktop, but the rest landed directly on the tops of Jon's polished wingtips.

"Oh, Sarah, honey—are you ok?" Jon took the scarf from around his neck and tenderly wiped my chin before using it to wipe his shoes. As he tossed the scarf in the back of the pickup he asked if I thought I was ready to have the truck door closed.

"I'm fine...you can close the door... I've got nothing left to lose," I whimpered, holding the back of my hand to my mouth. After getting into the driver's side of the truck, Jon pushed aside his coat and searched his pocket until he found his handkerchief. He handed it to me and asked once more if I felt all right. I muttered a muffled "yes," and took off my glasses, wiped my face, and closed my eyes as we drove back to his place in silence. I was humiliated and so disappointed that my planned Christmas gift to him was ruined. I felt like a complete fucking idiot.

When we got to the house, Jon asked if I would like to go home. He offered to drive me in my parents' car if I didn't feel up to driving—he would find a way home. He also told me that the last thing in the world he wanted was for me to leave if I felt good enough to stay with him. I shook my head; I didn't want to leave and said, "I'm fine, just embarrassed and guilty for messing up your shoes." He helped me from the truck, put his arm around me, and we walked to his back door.

As I washed off my smeared makeup in the bathroom, Jon gathered some warmer clothes and left them on his bed before going to the kitchen to make us tea. I didn't have anything with me but my toothbrush and silver barrette; I had planned on this evening being a clothing optional event. Jon's choice of clothing for me was perfect: one of his well worn plaid flannel shirts and a pair of black cotton sweatpants that cinched at the waist. I carefully stepped out of my seduction outfit and into his comfortable warm clothing, rolling the sleeves and elasticized pant legs to uncover my hands and feet. I pulled the pins from my hair, shook it out and braided it, then went to the living room to drink the tea Jon had set on the coffee table.

He had taken off his shoes as soon as we'd come in the kitchen door. I'm sure he meant to give them a more thorough cleaning when I wasn't around to be embarrassed by his actions. While I was changing, he'd hung his suit coat on the back of his reconditioned Windsor desk chair, loosened his tie, and unbuttoned his collar. He joined me on the couch with his own cup of tea, then wrapped an old quilt around me, settled my head on his lap, and stroked my hair. He said everything was going to be ok. He told me I hadn't ruined anything. Then he said, for the second time since we'd become a couple, that he loved me. I fell asleep with my head cradled on Jon's lap while Michel Legrand crooned "I Will Wait for You" in his sexy French vibrato.

—14—

At some point in the night, we had moved from the couch to the bed. I woke with the morning sun streaming through the window and Jon studying my face from his pillow next to mine. My hair draped my pillow and, though I was still wearing Jon's flannel shirt, I had lost the black sweatpants sometime earlier. There were no seduction scenes played out that morning, but we made love with a particular tenderness.

It was the morning of Christmas Eve, and, as we were eating our eggs and toast at the little kitchen table, Jon handed me a small wrapped box. I told him I didn't have a gift for him, so once again I was feeling guilty. He said not to worry, his gift was just a token— something he thought I might like to take with me to Boston. I unwrapped the box to find a beautiful glass paperweight in the shape of a heart. The bottom of it was fashioned to hold a picture, but it was empty. Jon went on to tell me that he was actually pleased I didn't have a gift for him because he had a gift idea we could share if I were willing. I thought he was going to propose we get a professional photo taken together to fill the paperweight, but that wasn't what he suggested.

His idea was a strange twist on "Truth or Dare." His game was called "Question and Request." If I accepted his gift idea, I was required to "truthfully answer his written question in writing" and to the best of my ability "fulfill his verbal request in person." I was to write my own question and make a verbal request of him. Since he was proposing the idea, he told me if I accepted the challenge he would give me time to think about my question and request—his were ready. I accepted immediately and told him I already had a question, but I would need time to think about a request. So, sitting at the kitchen table with our dirty breakfast dishes pushed aside, we wrote down the things we most wanted to know about one another but had been hesitant to ask aloud. We agreed not to look at the questions until we were by ourselves.

We enjoyed the rest of our morning together making plans for the few days that I had left. It had been so nice waking in the morning with Jon by my side; I would've loved to have spent another night with him before I left, but I knew it couldn't happen. One night had been risky enough—I had to stay in my parents' good graces. Even though I now hated to leave, I couldn't jeopardize my trip to Boston.

Later that morning, as I walked through the family kitchen dressed in yesterday's clothing, I was thankful that my dress coat covered my outfit. In all my planning for my overnight date I'd failed to think about bringing any casual clothing for my return home. I was thankful Mom didn't pay any attention to me as I hurried to my bedroom to open Jon's question.

I found out later his question for me was one he thought he could already answer, but wanted me to confirm. My question for Jon was, "How did you learn the art of seduction?"

Jon must not have spent much time with the other orphaned faculty members celebrating Christmas as was his plan for the day, because when we met for lunch on the twenty-sixth he handed me a typed manuscript on the art of seduction and how he had learned it. I gave him my answer to his question in a sealed envelope. We agreed that we should read our answers while we were alone. So, after a very tense lunch of tomato soup and grilled cheese, I left his place and went home to my lonely bedroom to read his response.

I remember all of his long essay. He gave me a large part of himself with his words and they became an important part of me. He told me that his teacher was a woman named Lydia, who had been twice his age when they met while he was in grad school. She taught him about love and seduction and explained while there was a difference, seduction when done correctly should never cause the seduced person undue emotional pain, and seduction without some level of affection should never be attempted.

She said there would be individuals in most people's lives who could bring them joy for a short time, but that everyone eventually found their forever person. Lydia told Jon at the beginning of their relationship that he was never going to be her forever person, but if he was a willing student and agreed to let her go when the time came, she would teach him the skills of a good lover.

His story, after introducing me to Lydia, became a seduction primer. One of the more interesting aspects of seduction he explained to me was that perfection was not a goal. There was a reason he had served me the hapless shrimp cocktail and there was a reason he did not own wine glasses. He said part of seduction was a perceived vulnerability; his was staged.

He told me he knew exactly what he was doing when he choreographed dinner to the Van Morrison album—he was seducing me. He said he hadn't been with a woman since he'd come to the U, but after we'd talked on Election Day, he couldn't get me out of his mind. He said the seduction was meant to hurry things along, but he realized midway through he cared for me too much to rush things. He told me again the was sorry he had played with my emotions and confused me.

He wanted me to know I was under no obligation to fulfill his Christmas request if I was feeling at all ill-used. He told me he loved me, but he wrote, "I don't know if I can say that I am your forever person, Sarah." He said if I so desired, he would become my independent study advisor, former professor, and nothing more. Or, if I wanted him out of my life before I went to Boston, he would see to it a colleague from the history department took his place as my advisor as soon as possible.

I was guessing after he'd read my answer to his question, he would withdraw his Christmas request and want to find me a new interim advisor.

Jon's question to me was, "Are you pregnant?"

I wrote:

Yes, Jon. I'm pregnant and I have been since September. When you asked me about contraceptives before we became intimate I told you I had it covered. I assumed you'd think I was on the pill. In truth, I knew I couldn't get pregnant because I already was pregnant.

The father has no idea. I will not tell him. He let me know I "wasn't enough" even before I had the opportunity to inform him of our predicament. How stupid I was thinking that he might be of help. This is my predicament and I am willing to deal with it.

I knew I was pregnant when I asked you to be the advisor for my interim project. I devised the project as a ruse to get away and make a decision on how to handle things. At this point I can't tell you if I'll be coming back from Boston after the interim term.

I still don't know what I am going to do, but I am leaning toward having the baby and giving it up for adoption. When I started thinking of the pregnancy as "my" predicament, rather than a shared responsibility, I started thinking of the baby as mine. While I have nothing against women having abortions, and having one would be the

*most sensible solution, I haven't decided
if it's the right route for me. I'm waiting
until I can talk with Annie about my
options.*

*While I didn't think you needed to
know about the pregnancy to approve my
project, I feel I should have told you
before we became lovers. You gave me
time and opportunity; I gave you silence.
What we've had together for the last
month has been the best thing to have
ever happened to me. I never meant to
hurt you and I would hate to damage
your reputation at the University. If you
would like me to find a new advisor, or
just disappear from your life, I will. I'm
sorry for misleading you.*
Sarah

Jon waited to call my house until later that evening; he
had wanted to give me time to read his long answer. I
stood in the living room looking through tears at the
lights on the Christmas tree while he did all the talking.
He told me he felt I had done nothing that required his
forgiveness and he had suspected early on in our
relationship that I might have been pregnant, but he

continued to pursue me anyway. He asked if I could forgive him and then made his Christmas request, "Will you go to the campus with me tomorrow?"

All I said was, "Yes, yes," then hung up the receiver.

—15—

I read Jon's words over and over that evening, especially the place where he wrote he loved me but stated, "I don't know if I can say that I am your forever person, Sarah."

Those words had hurt when I'd first read them. I did love Jon, and I thought I would love him forever, but evidently he didn't feel the same way about me. I thought of Brian's words, "You aren't enough. You aren't who I want." It stung. It felt as though Jon was, in some way, saying the same things to me—he loved me, but I wasn't enough; he was still looking for someone better.

However, as I carefully reread Jon's words and thought about what he'd said when he'd called that evening, I started to see things differently. Jon was careful when he spoke and when he wrote. He communicated precisely what he meant. Jon hadn't written that he was not my forever person. He'd written, "I don't know if I can say that I am your forever person."

Not being able to say something is different than not being something. I couldn't tell Jon I was pregnant, yet I was. I couldn't say to Jon that I loved him, though I did. Perhaps there was some reason Jon couldn't say that he was my forever person. Maybe it was because Jon didn't know how I felt about him. Even though he had confessed his love for me several times, I had never told him I loved him. He had also suspected I was pregnant with another man's child. I'm sure that gave him doubts about my feelings. How could it not?

Tomorrow I would tell him. Tomorrow I would request what I hoped he wanted to hear. If I was wrong, I would have to live with the humiliation and rejection. But, once again, I felt I had nothing left to lose.

Jon picked me up at my parents' house on Wednesday. My mom and dad were both at work so we were safe from detection. I don't know why, but I didn't dress up for this adventure. Maybe I thought it would look more natural if anyone encountered us on campus, or maybe, I just wanted Jon to remember the real, imperfect me while I was away. I wore my comfy loose jeans, the sweater my parents had given me for Christmas, and I'd braided my hair.

The drive to Vermillion gave us an hour to talk. The nice thing about having a difficult conversation with a driver is that you are both excused from looking at one another. As we stared at the flat interstate ahead, Jon told me that when he'd first read my question he was afraid it was an accusation and he had offended me by trying to seduce me. I told him I should have explained myself better. I loved seduction—I had asked him the question because I thought I could learn by studying his response. I told him the truth; much of what I knew about sex I'd learned by reading. I just wanted to be a better lover for him. I wanted to turn the tables and be his seductress. He kept looking at the road, but I saw him smile.

I asked him why, if he already thought I was pregnant, had he asked me that question? He told me he wasn't completely sure of his motivation, but he thought it was because he wanted me to know I could confide in him. He said, again, he loved me, and my secrets were safe with him. I told him I had wanted to tell him I was pregnant, but I felt I'd waited too long. I was frightened that if he found out about the baby he would feel betrayed. As an errant tear rolled down my cheek, I admitted I had kept my secret because I was afraid of losing him.

As we took the exit toward Vermillion, I looked over at Jon and said the words I had been holding inside for so many weeks. "Jon, I love you."

The campus was deserted when we arrived, as we had hoped it would be. Jon parked behind the Humanities building and let us in the back door with his pass key. Neither of us spoke once we entered the building and we walked, almost on tip-toe, to keep our footfalls from echoing down the empty hallways. We were trying to be stealthy, but I also think we were just talked out.

When we finally got to Jon's office, he opened the door, took both my hands, and playfully pulled me in. He closed and locked the office door then turned and lifted me onto the corner of his desk. He took my glasses, set them beside his phone, and began to kiss my face until I could barely breathe. Then, with me still sitting on the desk, he walked over to the old plaid chair I always used when we met in his office and sat down. It was my turn now, and he waited for me to make the next move.

I got off the desk and stepped out of my shoes. Very slowly, I pulled my sweater over my head. I slipped off my jeans and socks. I straddled Jon on the chair, my knees pressing into the cushion. I ran my fingers through his hair and down the sides of his beard, then gently kissed his beautiful golden-brown eyes. With my hands still holding his head, I kissed him passionately on his waiting mouth. Jon reached around me, unclipped my barrette and began undoing my braid.

We spent a long undisturbed afternoon saying our goodbyes.

Before we left his office, Jon asked me when I was going to make my Christmas request of him. I smiled and then asked him what I had been thinking about for the past twenty-four hours. "Jon, I love you and I always will. I request that you be my forever person."

His response was what I had convinced myself it would be. "I already am, Sarah. *You* just had to ask *me*." Then, he did something I hadn't expected. He went to his top left desk drawer and removed a small box. He knelt on one knee before the plaid chair where I was once again sitting, handed me a beautiful antique ring and asked me to marry him.

With the ring clutched in my hand, I leaned from the chair and wrapped my arms around Jon. He responded and held me so tightly that my feet left the floor as we both rose to standing. As he set me down I nodded my head, handed the sparkling ring back to him, then I held out my left hand. While he slid the ring onto my finger I finally spoke the words my eyes were already saying.

"Yes, Jon. I will marry you."

—16—

The gold ring had a center garnet surrounded by small, but fiery opals. It looked like a glowing eight-petaled flower with a blood red center. Jon said that he'd been told it dated from the eighteenth century, but had no way to prove it. I thought it was the most beautiful ring I'd ever seen, however, it was far too big for my finger. I kept it on my left hand for the drive back to Sioux Falls, but had to keep my fingers balled in a fist so that I didn't lose it. We decided Jon should have it sized and appraised while I was in Boston.

Jon told me he had questioned asking me to marry him. He said not because he didn't want to, but because he knew I had plans for a future somewhere other than Vermillion. He was frank. He said he didn't know what that would mean for us. I said I didn't either, but I understood if we wanted to live together, marriage was our only option. Anything else would both jeopardize his career in my very conservative home state and make my already tenuous relationship with my parents implode. Unwed couples living together did not fit with either the South Dakota Board of Regents or my parents' concept of propriety.

I told Jon that I didn't want to change my name. He said he'd never thought I would. He recalled our discussion about my childhood dream of being Dr. Sarah Bolling—he said there was no way he would take that from me. He wouldn't ask me to change my name or give up my plans to earn my Ph.D.

We agreed that we were getting married because of other people's rules, but that our marriage would be a partnership based on the rules we created. We figured we had a lifetime to get them right.

Jon planned on writing me daily while I was in Boston and he hoped I'd reciprocate. Since I was trying to be honest, I told him I wasn't sure that I could make that commitment. I hated writing letters. I wrote to Annie once a week and, while I loved getting her responses, I found writing a chore. Jon asked why; he said letters were just conversations on paper—fast and easy to write. I told him that wasn't true if the writer couldn't spell. He countered with, "But, you can spell."

"No, I can't," I said while shaking my head. "You've only seen my research and essays. I work very hard to present myself well. It takes me hours to edit and check all the words I think I might have misspelled. I can't write anything without a dictionary by my side. That's the reason my purse is so heavy. I've carried a Merriam-Webster with me since seventh grade—it's probably the reason that I knocked your class notes over the railing. Without the ballast of that damned dictionary my purse wouldn't have become a weapon."

Jon laughed and said he didn't care how I spelled in letters to him. I explained that *I cared*. If I couldn't write to my big sister without fear of embarrassment, I didn't think I could write to my fiancé, a professor, without second guessing myself.

Jon kept pushing. He asked how I dealt with essay tests and quizzes. I told him essay tests were hard, but after studying my notes, I'd list important words and study them like elementary school spelling words. I could usually spell the words well enough to get by on the day of the exam. If I blocked on a word's spelling, I tried to think of an easier word—much like stutterers replace the words they are struggling to enunciate with simpler words. Quizzes were my worst nightmare because there was no way to prepare. After my freshman year I tried to find out which professors gave essay quizzes so I could avoid their classes—it was my only way to save face.

I said one of the reasons I liked history was that while spelling was an issue for me, dates were not. If I read a date, I remembered it. I was constantly building timelines in my head, ordering facts as I learned them. Jon said he knew I was good with dates, and he also knew I was an excellent student. He told me he would not think any less of me for my innovative spelling. He explained it might even help me in reading primary source documents because some very famous people, like George Washington and William Clark, had been notoriously creative spellers. Jon then gave me a wonderful compliment. He said, "Sarah, you are one of the most intelligent people I know. I love the way your brain works."

He asked me if I would consider writing daily if he promised to destroy my letters after he'd read them. He said to be fair, he would ask that I do the same with his letters. He admitted that it might give him more freedom in his writing, too. Jon said our letters could be like pillow talk—fleeting, consigned only to dreams and memory.

I promised to write everyday and not worry about my spelling if we started the process by destroying our written answers to our Christmas questions. I didn't want to throw out what Jon had written to me, but I had read it so many times I knew it by heart. I also knew I didn't want what I'd written about my pregnancy to ever be seen again.

Jon said we had a pact. He asked if I had his written answer with me. I did. I'd folded it and put it in my already heavy purse for safe keeping—it was nestled beside my dictionary. We decided that when we got back to his place we would put our answers together and burn them—perhaps an overly dramatic gesture, but a romantic way to seal the deal.

—17—

The crumpled pages flamed up quickly. We'd placed a cookie sheet on the concrete stoop by the back door to serve as the foundation for our pyre. One after another orange-tinged ashes drifted skyward in the cold December air. I told Jon I was very happy it was a calm evening, both for our comfort and for the sake of his little neighborhood. I didn't think burning down the west end of Sioux Falls would be a good parting gift from me.

Jon and I went inside and cuddled on the couch to get warm. With the old quilt sheltering our entwined bodies, we talked about our wedding. Jon suggested we wait until late August. He said after second semester had ended, we could openly date all summer. It would look like a natural decision to wed before school started in August, albeit a quick one. I asked him, "What if I come back for second semester?"

"Don't take any of my classes, so if anyone finds out about us at least we won't have that situation to deal with. I suppose we would just go on as we have for the past month. I don't like sneaking around, but I can't not touch you if you're within my reach." For emphasis he tickled me under the quilt and kissed the top of my head.

Jon reached over and picked up the ring box I'd placed on the coffee table when we'd gotten home from Vermillion. As he handed me the ring he asked, "Should I send it to you in Boston after it's resized?" I told him "No, I love it, but I don't want to wear it until closer to our wedding." Then, in what I thought was a flash of brilliance, I suggested, "Why don't you keep it for the ceremony. It can be my wedding band—an unconventional ring for an unconventional marriage!"

His response was something he'd told me a few hours before. "Ahh, my Sarah, I love the way your brain works."

Jon drove me across town to my parents' house. I had promised to be home for dinner that night, and I still needed to finish packing. I thought about all the times I'd made that same drive late at night after being with Jon and how often I had been confused by my emotions. This evening was no different. My head and heart were in a crazy tango of elation, confusion, excitement, and sadness.

Jon pulled his little pickup to the curb half a block from my house. As he helped me down from the truck, I wrapped my arms around his inclined neck. Holding one another in an embrace filled with both love and loss, we kissed goodbye. I was the first to speak.

"I love you so much. I promise I'll come home as soon as I can."

When Jon responded, "I love you, Sarah, and I will forever," I turned and ran to the house before he could see the tears pooling behind my thick lenses.

Morning arrived after a long sleepless night. My mother drove me to the airport and saw me off. It was a Thursday and my father had to work, although I seriously doubted he would have come even if I'd left on a Saturday.

Mom parked the car and stayed with me, which I appreciated. I was nervous. I had never flown before and I was worried about having to change planes in Chicago, although I would have never admitted that to anyone. Mom did know I didn't like heights and she was trying to convince me it wouldn't be a problem for me if I didn't look out the little windows. The more she talked, the more I obsessed. I don't know how she arrived at her advice; she had never flown either. Maybe she had discussed it with Annie. Annie was the family adventurer.

I'd checked my suitcase at the ticket counter, but I was still loaded down with my winter coat, purse and book bag. The bag held my independent study papers, the carefully wrapped glass paperweight that Jon had given to me for Christmas, and a paperback copy of *Jonathan Livingston Seagull* by Richard Bach. As I looked around at my fellow passengers, the book appeared to be a popular choice, along with the thicker *The Winds of War*, which I'd already read.

My flight was called. As Mom handed me the book bag that had been on the floor between us, her last words to me were, "Give my love to Annie." I walked across the tarmac to the waiting plane realizing that Mom hadn't even bothered to say "goodbye" to me.

The stewardess helped me find my seat and took my coat to hang in the closet area toward the front of the plane. I think she thought I was a little kid. At five-foot-almost-nothing, it was a common mistake when people first met me. I'm sure that the fear in my eyes made me look younger than my years, too. I fastened the heavy lap belt and waited for take off.

My flight to the East Coast left on schedule at 8:45am December 28, 1972. I was twenty years old, close to four months pregnant, and engaged to be married to my history professor, however, at that moment, I tried not to think about any of those things. I was taking life one step at a time; the lockbox in my brain had always been my primary means of survival.

Annie met me at my arrival gate at the Boston airport. After hellos and hugs, she barraged me with a non-stop list of questions about my trip. The first thing I told her was that Mom sent her love; I knew if I forgot to pass along the message my mother would be upset with me and apologetic to Annie. As we walked to the baggage claim, I answered all of her questions. I told her I liked flying well enough, and even though I didn't like heights, being in the air didn't bother me. I told her I thought both take-offs and landings were the pits and that I was pretty sure I'd always feel that way. The Chicago airport was big, but I hadn't had any problems getting around other than I'd had to wear my coat, making me very warm by the time I'd reached my connecting gate.

Annie had done her usual big sister thing and led me by the hand while I talked. Before I realized what was happening, she'd retrieved my suitcase, and we were boarding the subway to downtown Boston. Though I had just walked through it, I had no idea what Logan International looked like or how we got to the exit turnstile.

We took the Blue Line under the Atlantic Ocean to State Street. Annie's apartment was a short walk from the stop—right next door to a family owned pizzeria named O'Riley's Calzones. Just down the street from her building was a Dunkin' Donuts, but I soon learned not to use it as a landmark. There appeared to be a Dunkin' Donuts on every other corner in Boston.

Annie's place was just as I'd expected it would be (other than always smelling faintly of marinara sauce), a cozy one-bedroom apartment on the third floor of a walkup. There were large, drafty, multi-paned windows that Annie hung plants in front of in lieu of curtains. We had decided from the very beginning that she was to keep her bedroom for herself, so she'd borrowed a sleeping bag from a friend for me to use. When I wanted to go to bed, I would line up the old cushions that served as her couch and lay the sleeping bag on top of them. In the morning, I rolled up the bag and re-stacked the cushions in the corner.

Annie had cleared off the large office desk that took up most of the space in the living room. It was my work space for as long as I needed it. She told me since she had the bed, it was only fair I should have a space of my own, too. I unpacked my book bag setting out my copy of the interim project proposal, a calendar, a pencil and the heart-shaped paperweight that Jon had given me for Christmas.

The last days of the last full week of the year were spent by our happy duo, our "band of sisters" exploring Boston in the winter chill. Annie had so much to show me. We walked the Freedom Trail and visited the USS Constitution in Boston Harbor—the ship was still decorated with a spindly Christmas tree that matched its bare rigging. When we got cold and tired of walking, we splurged on coffee and a water taxi to cross the bay back to the apartment. Clouds of seagulls chased the wake off the stern of the boxy boat. We laughed as the birds swooped and dove to catch the hunks of donut we tossed toward their pointed bills.

Along with Dunkin' Donuts' *regular coffee*, Annie introduced me to seafood. The closest thing I had ever eaten to seafood was Jon's pathetic shrimp cocktail and school cafeteria fish sticks. Annie's gastronomic tutoring let me know there was a whole ocean of delightful flavors to discover. For our first outing she took me to a little hole-in-the-wall joint near Faneuil Hall for fried lobster and seafood bisque. I decided seafood bisque was one of my seven wonders of the world.

It was all so new and exciting, and while it was wonderful to be with Annie again, I couldn't help but wish that I was experiencing it all with Jon by my side. I told myself someday he and I would explore the old city together.

By Saturday morning I couldn't put off the inevitable any longer. I'd enjoyed my first few days with Annie without burdening her with my problems, but it was time to face the situation. I told her about Brian and the pregnancy, then asked for her help. Though shocked, she held me, patted my back, and said, "Of course, Sarie, that's what big sisters are for." It was the response I had expected from her. She had been my confidant for years; she knew from our past experiences I couldn't have gone to our mother for help or advice.

Annie continued, "I know you knew what you were doing — accidents happen." The only reason she seemed even slightly upset with me was that I'd not written to her about my pregnancy. She said had she known earlier she could have been better prepared when I'd landed on her doorstep.

Later that morning when I told her about my engagement to Jon, she just shook her head. "Talk about burying the lead, kiddo! Who taught you to write? It appears you've been leaving all the most important events in your life out of your letters to me!" I couldn't disagree and, to make up for my dereliction of sisterly revelations, told her all about the wonderful man I was to wed in August.

—18—

Annie was an active member of one of the many women's consciousness raising groups around Boston in the 1970's. After only a few phone calls over the course of the weekend, she'd made a doctor's appointment for me on Wednesday, the third of January.

The very nice young doctor who examined me said I was healthy and everything seemed fine with the pregnancy. She said while I wasn't showing much yet, I should expect that to change very soon. At my size it was going to look like I was trying to smuggle a basketball under my clothes. I thanked her for her very graphic visual, but it didn't thrill me.

Annie, who had accompanied me to the appointment, asked about my options for terminating the pregnancy at this point. The doctor said what she had to say: abortion was illegal in Massachusetts and, if I was interested in having one, I should probably go to New York. She said unfortunately for me, if termination was what I wanted, I should have done it sooner. I was at seventeen weeks, already past the first trimester when abortions were relatively easy.

Annie and I left the clinic and went to a little café down the street. As we drank our regular coffees, she told me not to be too upset by what the doctor had said. I could still probably get an abortion in the area, it would just be more expensive and I might need a bit longer to recover. Of course, it would be illegal, but that wasn't a huge concern if I didn't let it bother me.

I blew on the steam rising from my coffee and asked Annie if she knew anyone who could help me find adoptive parents for the baby if I chose to give birth. The doctor had said I was healthy and the pregnancy was progressing well, maybe it would be the better option. I told her I didn't like the idea of missing second semester, but I wouldn't have the money to pay for it if I had the abortion. And, although I hated being away from Jon, we would still have to keep our relationship a secret if I went home in February. It might be better for him if I weren't around.

Annie said she'd already been making inquires. She had friends who had made private adoptions and she thought she would be hearing back from some of them soon. She said while the decision on how to proceed was totally up to me, she wanted me to know she'd hoped I'd choose to have the baby. She said she wouldn't even mind giving up her bed when I got too big to lumber up from the floor.

On Thursday a fat envelope arrived for me. It was my first letter from Jon, and from the size of the envelope I thought he had written me a book. As it turned out, his letter was only a few heartfelt pages, but he had broken all postal regulations and rules of good sense. He'd sent me $700 in cash—his savings.

He wanted to help me. He said that it had dawned on him that he could have been the father of my child. Not that he was, he understood that. But, had I accidentally gotten pregnant after he and I had become lovers, I would be in the same predicament I was now. He said, had that been the case, he would have insisted I take the money before I'd left for Boston. He felt like a cad that he hadn't thought of it sooner. The decision on how to handle the pregnancy was mine to make, but whatever path I chose, I would need money. He was completely open in his letter and said if I wanted to keep the baby, we could still get married in August or even before the baby was born if that was my wish. He hoped that he would be a good father.

I knew that last option was one many young women in my position would have jumped at, but I couldn't do that to myself or Jon. I wanted my degree, I wanted grad school, and I didn't want to start our married life with a baby. I was pretty sure Jon felt the same way, but he was willing to make the offer of fatherhood to give me the freedom to make that choice. He wrote that he wanted me to know I wasn't alone anymore—he would always be by my side.

I asked Annie if I could use her phone to make a long-distance call that evening. She said yes and offered to find something to do away from the apartment to give me some privacy for a few hours.

With a big cup of tea by my side, I dialed Jon's number. I pictured his beige desk phone ringing and him jumping up from his comfy reading chair in the corner of the living room to answer it. I figured he might guess it was me calling by the timing. I was right. He picked up the receiver and immediately said, "Hello Sarah. How's Boston?"

"Boston's great, *Carnac*. When did you become clairvoyant?"

He laughed, then said, "Ahh, yes, I divined that's what you'd say." After groaning at his pun and sharing how much we already missed one another, our discussion became far more serious.

I told him I had received his first letter and the money. With tears in my eyes, that I hoped he couldn't hear in my voice, I said his offer to be a father at this time in his life and career was wonderfully generous, but I couldn't do that to us. I thought he would be a fantastic father, and someday I would love to have his child, but he knew that wasn't what I wanted for myself in the next few years. I said, "Eventually I want everything: I want you, I want an education, I want a good job, I want a family, and I want lots of adventures for all of us. I hope you know you're marrying a very greedy woman."

He laughed sweetly and said he did—he was fine with it, especially since he noticed that he was first on my list of wants. He asked if I really thought he would make a good father. Jon wasn't a person who suffered from self doubt, so it surprised me that he had asked. I told him I couldn't imagine a man who would be better at fatherhood. I didn't tell him, but I thought about the time I'd spent watching him choose the necktie with the little girl in Penney's. He had been so patient and attentive; I couldn't imagine he would be any other way with our child.

I told. him about my medical exam the day before and that after long discussions with the doctor and Annie, I'd finally made a decision on how to proceed. "I'm going to stay here and have the baby. I won't be home until early June. Annie is going to use her connections to help find me an adoption program or maybe a lawyer who deals with private adoptions."

I suggested I send his money back. "I thought you might have it earmarked for a used car—you gave me the impression you're saving for one."

"Ahh, yes—well that'll be sometime in the future. I don't need the money yet, although I suppose I'll have to invest in new snow tires for the pickup sometime soon—after three and a half winters the old ones are just about shot. But, for now hon, just keep the money in the event something unforeseen happens and you need it."

"No, really, I'm ok. I have my savings and I'm sure Annie could give me a loan if I need a little more."

Again, Jon's response was that he loved me and wanted me to keep the money, but then he added, "If it turns out you don't need the cash, just bring it home in June."

"Well, that does sound like a smarter plan than sending it back; the only stupid thing I've ever seen you do was to put that much cash in an envelope and send it half way across the country."

Jon laughed and said, "Ahh, so, you've evidently forgotten the scolding you gave me in November about driving to Vermillion on icy roads." I told him that was pretty stupid, too, but that decision was made from inexperience, not the willful flaunting of U. S. Postal Regulations. He replied he knew mailing the money wasn't wise, but he didn't know of any other money transfer method that wouldn't have identified me. He was trying to respect my privacy.

Our conversation turned much lighter as I excitedly told Jon about all the things Annie and I had done over the days I'd been in Boston. We would've loved to have talked all night, but I was concerned about running up Annie's phone bill. Jon understood. He said he'd just received my first letter and had been waiting to open it before he went to bed. "It'll be like we're still talking, and I'll get to take you to bed with me—this phone cord isn't long enough." He asked if I had written more letters. In a horrible French accent I replied, "*But of course!* One a day, totally unedited. Have you written to me every day so far?"

"*Mais bien sûr, mon amour,*" was his response, then he added, "You're going to love tomorrow's letter."

"Oh, please don't let it be in French."

— 19 —

Along with our pillow talk letters which we faithfully destroyed, Jon and I wrote to each other once a week regarding my project. Those were the letters sent to and from the University. I told him of my progress and included my daily journal entries. While not typed, my letters to the history department were neatly handwritten and carefully edited. I checked all spelling, dotted all i's, and crossed all t's. His official letters to me were typed. They were formal, but filled with encouragement and the names of people and institutions for me to contact. He'd gained access for me to library archives and the catacombs of art museums across Boston: The Museum of Fine Arts (MFA), The Gardner Mansion, and the Fogg at Harvard—a true academic gift.

I had almost always been good at compartmentalizing my life and soldiering on. I had managed through the chaos of last semester to keep my GPA intact. Now that I knew how I was going to handle the pregnancy, and was feeling sure of Jon's love for me, focusing on my work was easy. My research paper was humming along and I was having fun working on it. Almost daily I found interesting paintings and tidbits of information on colonial painters that delighted me.

Some of the bits of info I could use for my project, but others I squirreled away for the future. I thought historic research was akin to mining for gold, and I was getting rich.

Life got even better for me in the third week of January when Annie told me about finding the Tillersons. Annie had been intent on finding her "niecephew" a good home (I laughed the first time I heard Annie's combo word. It made me think of Jon's combination of "faux" and "colonial.") The Tillersons were a wonderful couple in their mid-thirties who wanted to adopt a newborn. They had money and offered to pay all my prenatal and hospital expenses. The couple had said that both Annie and I would be a welcomed addition to their child's life. I think they pictured us as entertaining aunties or maybe even babysitters. Annie loved the idea of staying connected; I told them I wanted a clean break, but thanked them for their kindness. Secretly I was thrilled Annie would be keeping her eye on the family.

My doctor determined my due date to be the first of June; the Tillersons started getting their baby's nursery ready.

Second semester at the University was scheduled to begin the second full week of February. I had contacted the Registrar's office and informed the powers that be that I would not be coming back until next fall. I didn't offer an explanation. In my official letter to Dr. Jon Leggett I apologized that I would not be returning in the spring, but that my independent study project paper entitled "Realism in Colonial American Paintings of Children" would be sent before the due date of March 1, 1973. I very formally thanked Dr. Leggett for serving as my project advisor and *opening so many doors for me*. I said I was *looking forward to resuming my activities in the USD history department* in September. The letter was prim but full of innuendo.

I thought about our last encounter in his office and knew Jon would enjoy my comments. I even thought the letter might have merited an official office phone call from him. I imagined how much fun he'd have figuring out just the right words to entertain me while keeping everyone within ear shot in the dark. When I didn't get a call I remembered that the University gave a small break before the start of the second semester and I pictured him at what was to soon be "our" home writing to me with one of his favorite fountain pens.

February tenth was a cold day in Boston, but I was feeling so good and so happy with all the work that I'd already accomplished that I went for a Saturday afternoon walk followed by a regular coffee at the Dunkin' Donuts just up the street from Annie's. The shop was crowded; I got my drink to go and headed back. It seemed a little harder to climb the three flights of stairs to the apartment than it had on Friday. I figured the baby must have changed positions. My bulge was showing more every day, and, as I looked down at my protruding stomach thought, "well, at least I'll have a shelf for my coffee cup in a few weeks."

When I pushed open the apartment door, I could immediately tell from the look on Annie's face that something was very wrong. She was standing by the phone with her hand still resting on the receiver. The first thing she said to me was that she thought I should sit down.

"Is everything ok with Mom and Dad?" I couldn't think of anyone else she would have heard from that I would know.

"Yes, they're ok, but there was an accident on the interstate. Jon didn't.... Jon was..."

I dropped my coffee and then dropped to my knees in front of the desk chair. I gasped, "Jon was what? How can you know that? You're wrong!"

She tried to hold me, but I flung out my arms, breaking her embrace. I kept saying, "You're wrong, you're wrong, you're wrong."

Annie asked me to listen. She said that she had just been talking with our mother. It was Mom's habit to splurge once a month and phone Annie to hear her voice. After they'd talked a while about other things, Annie told me that Mom had asked her if she knew the name of my interim project advisor. Annie managed to get her arms around me and said, "Mommy said one of the history department's professors had been killed in an accident on Interstate-29 about a day ago." Annie said she'd asked Mom what the professor's name was, but that she couldn't remember and went to check the newspaper.

"Sarah, Mom read his name to me. It was Jon."

I still wanted her to be mistaken; I weakly stammered, "You're wrong, you're wrong..." But, by then, I knew she was right.

I quit talking. Tears streamed down my face. I sucked air in and choked air out. I wanted to die, too.

Annie helped me to her bed and sat me down. She pulled my boots off and swung my feet to the mattress; I fell sideways still wearing my coat. Hours passed as I sobbed and shook. At some point Annie must have put a record on the stereo in the living room because I could hear Dylan's voice through the open door singing "Girl from the North Country." I cried harder.

Annie came in after it was dark and helped me remove my clothes and put on my nightgown. She tucked me into her bed and laid down beside me on top of the bedspread. Although I didn't hear her, she moved during the night to my sleeping bag in the living room.

I woke Sunday morning. Snow was blowing against the window. I felt warm and sticky between my legs. I lifted my blankets to a congealing pool of dark red blood. I pushed back the bedding and tried to stand.

The next thing I felt was the sting of wet snow hitting my face as paramedics carried me to the waiting ambulance.

—20—

A standard D&C was performed. The doctor told me that I had experienced a spontaneous abortion in the early hours of the morning on February eleventh. The irony did not escape me—the abortion that I'd considered, and in the end had decided against, happened spontaneously.

I drifted in and out... Bags with blood, saline, and antibiotics hung from poles on both sides of the bed... I was flat on my back with IVs in my arms... The light in the room was bright... My head hurt so much that I could barely open my eyes... I heard Annie's voice, "Is she still hemorrhaging?"... "Yes."... The nurse seemed concerned, "Normally miscarriages aren't this physically difficult"....

Annie whispered to the attending nurse that I had just found out about the death of my fiancé. *My fiancé*—it was the first time I'd heard someone say those words aloud and they made the tears that had finally stopped, start again. They rolled from the corners of my eyes and dripped onto the hard hospital pillow. Crying intensified the voices and searing pain in my head. The nurse said that she would have the doctor order a sedative for me.... Blessed sleep.

Annie was my constant companion while I was in the hospital. My only other visitors during my three-day stay were the Tillersons. They were kind to me, but visibly mourning the death of their baby. Once again, I felt guilty. I felt that I had failed them, so I suppose that was part of the guilt, but I also felt guilty that I couldn't mourn the baby. I resented the baby. Had I not been pregnant, I would have been in South Dakota with Jon. We could have had more time together. Maybe he wouldn't have even been on the road the day he died, because he would have been lying in bed with me. Painful fairytales of the life we would have led filled my brain when I was awake. I just wanted to sleep.

Before the end of the third day, the hospital obstetrician came to tell me what I could expect of my body in the future. He told me that getting pregnant again might be difficult because I had a tipped uterus. The doctor explained that, if I did get pregnant, carrying a fetus to term would be next to impossible—I had what was medically termed an "incompetent cervix." He said any future pregnancy would need to be followed closely and would most likely require complete bedrest starting in the second trimester. There was also the possibility that I would require internal suturing and a C-section delivery for a subsequent pregnancy. I didn't care. I would never have Jon's baby, so what did it matter. Nothing mattered.

The only thing that was positive about any of the hospital stay was that the Tillersons offered to pay all my expenses. They didn't have to—they really were wonderful people. I hoped that someday they would get the baby they so desperately wanted.

Annie took me back to her place and put me in her room. She tried her best to make me comfortable and set the paperweight that Jon had given me for Christmas on the bedside table. It would have been our first Valentine's Day as a couple. I fell asleep holding my empty glass heart.

Annie stayed with me for the rest of the week, but she needed to get back to work. She arranged for my airline ticket, packed my bags, and even found an old college friend from SDSU to help me through the Chicago terminal. On February seventeenth, she took me by cab to Logan International, saw that I got seated on my flight, and gave the stewardess orders to take care of me. She sent me back to our parents in Sioux Falls. They had no idea what was really wrong with me.

—21—

A few days before I flew back to South Dakota, Annie had called Mom and Dad. She'd told them, that shortly after she'd talked to Mom on Saturday, I'd come home from Dunkin' Donuts with a headache. We had thought I was coming down with a migraine, but by Sunday we'd realized it was a full-on case of the flu. Annie told them I'd been so sick that I had passed out. She'd moved me into her bedroom to nurse me back to health. She said I was still very weak and she didn't feel she could take any more time off work to be with me. So, as far as our parents knew, that's why I was coming home from Boston—to recover from the flu.

Annie had also taken the initiative to call the history department at the University to tell them that I would be back, but that I had been very ill and would probably need an extension on my interim project. She told the receptionist that she'd heard from our mother that Dr. Leggett had died—she thought he'd been my project advisor. Annie asked if there were some other professor she could talk to because she was hoping that he or she could call me in a few weeks if I hadn't contacted the department. She repeated, I had been very ill, and a call to prompt me might be in order. Annie was put through to Dr. Sargent, the head of the history department.

Dr. Sargent told her he was very sorry to hear that I wasn't well, but he was happy that I was going to be back in South Dakota. He said he was afraid I would be taking the death of Dr. Leggett hard because he and I had worked so well together on the interim project.

Annie later told me the thing that had surprised her most about their talk was that Dr. Sargent had wanted to talk about Jon. Annie said he told her that losing Jon was going to create a huge hole in the department, even though he had only been there a short time. He said Dr. Leggett was quickly becoming one of the best young professors he had seen in his nearly forty years in higher education. Annie told me it was so nice, yet very painful, to hear Dr. Sargent talk about Jon knowing how I felt about him. She said she'd wanted to cry, but realized that it would seem odd to the professor, so she tamped down her emotions. Before Dr. Sargent hung up he promised Annie that he would call me in a week or two.

A week after I'd returned home, my parents' living room phone rang. I was rarely leaving my bed, so when my mom answered it she had to come rouse me.

She told me that there was a professor from the university calling to talk. In my sleep and grief-induced confusion, I thought it was Jon. I ran to the phone. When I heard Dr. Sargent's voice reality returned.

He repeated to me some of the things he'd said to Annie. He apologized several times that no one from the department had thought to call and tell me about my project advisor's death. I did cry as he spoke about Jon, but I don't think Dr. Sargent thought it odd. He knew I'd considered Jon my mentor, much the same way Jon considered Dr. Sargent his mentor. The professor asked me to come by the history department later that week to discuss my research project and figure out a new timeline for its completion. He wondered if I would be trying to get a late start with the second semester since I was back in the state. I told him I didn't think so. We made an appointment for Thursday.

The drive to the University was the first time I had been out of the house since I'd gotten back to South Dakota. Before I left Sioux Falls, I drove past Jon's house that clearly wasn't Jon's house anymore. Only a few weeks had passed since his death, but the house looked vacant and there was a "For Rent" sign on the front door. I drove away, numb with the knowledge that it would never be "our" home, and found the back roads to Vermillion; there was no way that I was going to take I-29 and drive by the spot where Jon had died. From the photos I'd seen in the paper, I was sure that the ground would be scarred and burned. I thought about Jon all the time, but I couldn't face thinking about his death.

I brought my research and calendar to the meeting with Dr. Sargent. I had not prepared anything else. I hadn't looked at my notes since returning home — nothing was important to me. Nothing. It amazed me I could function at all. My mom had been trying to make me eat, and was constantly giving me fresh water when she was home, but that was about all she could do. Most of the time I stayed in bed and kept my room as dark as possible.

Professor Sargent invited me into his office and I sat down, dwarfed by one of the massive chrome and leather chairs facing his desk. He had been at the University for years; the books filling his shelves and the colorful abstract paintings and framed documents on his walls reflected his taste and spoke of his achievements.

He seemed shocked by the way I looked. He said something about being so sorry I hadn't been feeling well, that "the flu can really lay a person low," but I think he already knew that my illness was more than Annie had let on. We talked for half an hour, a lot of time for a busy man who really didn't know me. He asked me to get out my notes and calendar; together we planned a new timeline so that I could finish writing and get my credits. I told him I didn't want to think about starting classes again for a while. I wasn't ready for the stress.

Dr. Sargent said he understood, and that we could discuss my plans when I started to feel better. He then changed the subject to Jon. He told me once again how happy it had made him to have been Jon's mentor in the history department. He spoke of Jon's gifts as a lecturer and his rapport with students. He spoke of Jon's great promise. As tears quietly ran down my face, Professor Sargent asked if he might have the honor of becoming my academic advisor—he thought that I shared some of Dr. Leggett's fine qualities. I was puzzled, the man barely knew me, but I thanked him and accepted his offer.

I asked if he would mind if I walked down the hall to take one last look at the office where Dr. Leggett and I had spent time preparing for my independent study. He said that it would be fine, but that all of Dr. Leggett's items had been removed. I walked down the hall anyway. The only things left in the little office were the university-issued desk and chair. I ran my hand over the bare desk and, though I shouldn't have, I opened the drawers. They were empty—I had hoped that I might find the ring Jon had given me, but every trace of him was already gone.

As I turned to leave that far end of the hall, I saw a flash of color from the open door next to Jon's office. There in the broom closet sat the plaid wing-backed chair. I don't know how I got up the nerve, but I walked back to Dr. Sargent and asked him about the status of the chair. He said no one had wanted it, so it was probably destined for the dumpster. I asked if I might buy it from the department. Dr. Sargent smiled and said, "No, but you can have it." He then remarked on its size and asked how I planned on getting it home. I told him I hadn't figured that out. That's when he said he had a pickup and, if he could find some strong backs to help him, he could bring it to me in Sioux Falls.

—22—

Dr. Sargent was true to his word; on Saturday at 11:45 he drove up to my parents' front door in his Ford pickup with Clyde Dale, one of the department's work-study students, in the passenger seat. Clyde was a smart guy, but he resembled his unfortunate name. He had an oversized jaw and was about the size of a draft horse. Clyde greeted me with a quiet hello and said he didn't get to Sioux Falls often; it had been a scenic ride. I was still in too much of a daze to catch Clyde's attempt at humor. There is nothing *scenic* between Sioux Falls and Vermillion in the middle of the winter.

The professor said he was very happy to see me looking so much healthier. It was kind of him not to say "looking better," but I'm sure that's what he meant. When we'd met on Thursday I'd looked awful. I'd known it and hadn't cared. But, Dr. Sargent's words that day and finding Jon's chair had helped me come round a little.

(After getting home Thursday, I'd changed the sheets on my bed, taken a bath, and spent half an hour trying to get the leftover surgical tape residue off my body with rubbing alcohol. I'd left the adhesive gunk for so long it was starting to collect dark fuzz from my clothes and blankets. I noticed that the bruises on my arms from the IV needles were looking yellow and purple—a sure sign of healing. Thanks to the constant need for warm clothing, neither of my parents had noticed how bad my arms looked.

After Thursday's bath I'd washed my hair. I'd been re-braiding it occasionally, but it hadn't been washed since before Annie had told me about Jon's accident. As I combed the wet tangles with my grandmother's large celluloid comb I thought about how much Jon *had loved my hair*. I was starting to think of him in past tense.... I told myself I had to; as much as I had wanted to die too, I hadn't. I needed to put my grief away and learn how to face life again.)

When Dr. Sargent found out my parents weren't home and we would have no help unloading the chair, he was extremely pleased he'd brought Clyde. I was in no shape to be lifting. Dr. Sargent must have sensed it, because he was careful to ask me to help with only the light jobs, like opening doors and moving throw rugs out of tripping range. Clyde lifted the big overstuffed chair from the back of the pickup as easily as if he were lifting a webbed aluminum lawn chair and carried it into the house.

It took Dr. Sargent and Clyde less than five minutes to move the chair into the space I had cleared for it in my bedroom. Their next stop was Walt and Mary's, the buffet restaurant not far from my parents' home. A big lunch funded by Dr. Sargent was to be Clyde's pay for his labor. I'm sure that the professor knew, but wouldn't say, that Clyde was also relishing the four hours that this mission took. Clyde was a history major, the road trip offered him time for relaxed conversation with a brilliant historian. Dr. Sargent asked me if I would like to join them for lunch, but I begged off. As he and Clyde walked out the door, the professor told me he would call the following week to discuss my paper.

I knew I had the house to myself for the afternoon. Even so, when I went back to my bedroom I closed the door. Winter sunlight shone through the window warming Jon's chair facing my single bed. I thought about all the times I'd sat in that chair—our first meeting when I'd given Jon my interim proposal and all our meetings after that. I thought of the afternoon Jon and I had spent in his office the day before I left for Boston. In that chair we'd made love, he'd given me a beautiful ring, and he'd asked me to marry him. All I had left were memories.

With the words of Dylan's "Girl from the North Country" playing in my head, I knelt in the chair and ran my hands down the seat back and over the fraying arms. I slipped off the elastic-band holding the end of my braid and unraveled it twist by twist until my hair was free and flowing. As I rested my cheek on the warm chair back, my hand hit something metallic alongside the seat cushion. I knew immediately that I was touching my large silver hair clip—I hadn't seen it since the day before I left for Boston. I held the cold barrette to my pale cheek realizing Jon's hands had been the last hands to touch it. My tears came in waves until I couldn't cry anymore. I curled up in the chair, pulled the comforter from my bed and fell asleep in the low afternoon sun.

PART TWO

Late Winter 1973

—23—

The last frozen weeks of South Dakota's long winter passed as I worked on my research paper. I made the long back-road drive to Vermillion once a week to meet with Dr. Sargent, but by the time farm equipment was filling the rural highways, I'd convinced myself to drive I-29 even though it meant driving by the site of Jon's accident. Winter snows and early rains had erased every trace of the fiery crash that had taken him away from me.

My meetings with the professor were a godsend. He blocked off an hour every Wednesday for us to work on my project and discuss State-wide current events, history or anything else that he suggested from his pre-planned agendas. Those meetings helped me feel as though I were still part of the University. I don't know what I would have done had my part-time job at the gas station been my only reason to leave my bedroom.

Dr. Sargent did me a favor that I knew nothing about until he approached me with his plan after spring break. He asked if I would like to stay on track to finish my B.A. in 1974 and walk the stage with my original graduating class. He said that if I took summer classes, more independent studies, and registered for a large class load my senior year, it would be possible. He'd even created some scheduling options for me after having looked over the transcripts from my previous years.

I was touched he had taken the time to think about my future at the university. I had been planning on going back in the fall of '73, after working the summer to earn my tuition. I'd already given up the idea of graduating on time. But, with Dr. Sargent's suggestion, I started thinking about how I might afford the extra expense. It would be wonderful to stay on schedule, but I just didn't know how I could swing it. I still needed to pay my parents back for my airline tickets and I didn't want to borrow money—I knew I would be borrowing scary amounts once I headed to grad school.

I had the money Jon had sent to me while I was in Boston. It was tucked in my top dresser drawer under my socks, still in its original envelope. I'd promised to bring it back to him; its very existence made me feel guilty. I couldn't imagine spending it on myself. Instead, I'd been thinking about starting a history scholarship in Jon's name. It would be a way to keep him part of the university—I knew that I would never forget him and I didn't want people at the U to forget about him either.

I needed Dr. Sargent's help, but I hadn't screwed up the courage to ask. I wanted him to know about the money. I wanted him to know how generous Jon had been. But, telling our story meant revealing far more about Jon's and my relationship than I had ever told anyone but Annie.

I called Dr. Sargent and asked that he not make an agenda for our Wednesday meeting because I had some things I needed to talk with him about that didn't involve my project. Instead, he told me that an extra meeting might be in order to keep us on schedule and suggested we meet at his house in Vermillion at 5:00 the next afternoon. I happily agreed. Although nervous about our discussion, I was excited I would finally get to see his famous house, the site of the storied Platoon gatherings.

The next day at 4:50, I parked in front of Dr. Sargent's 1898 Queen Anne manse on a tree-lined street just a few blocks from campus. The exterior of the house was stone and brick, and an elaborate front porch led to heavy oaken double doors. I turned the handle on the old-fashioned mechanical doorbell and listened to its clattering peal. Even from outside the house it sounded loud enough be heard on every level of the multi-story structure. As I waited on the imposing porch I hoped I was making the right decision.

The professor welcomed me in. He was wearing a brown wool cardigan instead of his suit coat. Though still in a tie, he had loosened it and unbuttoned the collar of his white shirt. I had never seen him so casual. I hung my jacket on a peg in the small tiled vestibule and walked through French doors into a magnificent front room that had been made by combining the old foyer and front parlor. There was nothing Victorian about the interior of the old house. I stood with my mouth agape as Dr. Sargent explained that it had been remodeled in the mid-sixties after he and his wife, Margaret, had visited the Guggenheim art museum in New York City.

Stark white walls were hung with brightly colored abstract paintings and metal relief sculptures. He and Margaret had chosen to leave the soaring ceilings, beveled glass windows, and wooden floors—although they'd had them sanded. Wildly patterned Turkish carpets covered much of the light-hued oak. His upholstered furniture was leather and his tables glass and chrome. Shelves and stacks of books were scattered throughout the front rooms, and in every corner interesting items acquired during his extensive travels—things like African percussion instruments and brightly banded Sami *nutukas*—demanded attention. The house was a visual wonderland and Dr. Sargent shared it freely with both his colleagues and students, current and former.

He asked me if I would rather sit in the living room or at the dining table. I opted for the living room and took a seat in the corner of the couch. He had already made a pot of Earl Grey, but wondered if I would prefer something else. I said, "Tea will be fine." In truth, I hated Earl Grey, but I was not about to admit it. I was so nervous that I doubted I would be drinking much anyway. As he expertly poured tea into Mondrian patterned cylindrical cups, he apologized that he couldn't offer me more than packaged wafers as an accompaniment and sadly added, "I haven't had many home baked treats around since Margaret passed away." Only after we'd started drinking our tea did he ask what it was that I wanted to discuss with him.

I'd agonized over how to explain my situation to Dr. Sargent. I knew he had seen Jon's tremendous potential as a professor. After meeting with him for weeks I'd begun to believe that Dr. Sargent had already been grooming Jon to be his successor in the history department. I didn't want him to think any differently about Jon after I told him our story. But I wanted to tell the truth; I thought that after his kindness to me over the past months he deserved my candor. I wanted him to understand how I felt about Jon, and that I wanted the money Jon had sent to me to be used to keep his memory alive.

I set my tea on the coffee table, took a deep ragged breath, and plunged: I told him that Jon and I had been romantically involved, but not until after my interim project proposal had been accepted by the history department on its own merits. I also admitted to Dr. Sargent that I had originally conceived of the project as a way to get out of town—that I had been pregnant when I went to Boston and knew when I left that I might not be coming back for the second semester of school. I told him Jon and I had kept our relationship private for obvious reasons, but we'd planned on marrying in August before school started. Then I told him about miscarrying the day after I heard about Jon's death. Dr. Sargent looked remarkably sad. When he looked as though he was going to speak, I asked him if I might please keep talking.

I pulled Jon's money from my purse and set the envelope on the coffee table in front of the professor. I told him that Jon had sent the money to me while I was in Boston—I knew it had been most of his savings. I explained that Jon had wanted to help me, even though I had never asked him to. The money had been a surprise. After that, I told Dr. Sargent my plan. "I want to use the money he sent to me to start a scholarship in Jon's name." I asked Dr. Sargent for his help. I knew nothing about the mechanics of funding a scholarship, and I doubted that $700, although a lot of money to me, would be enough to start such a fund. I continued, "After hearing the truth about our relationship, will you still help me?"

I didn't know how to interpret the sad look in Dr. Sargent's eyes.

His first words were, "Sarah, I'm sorry."

—24—

"Sarah, before we discuss your idea for a memorial scholarship, I need to admit something—I had already presumed that you and Jon were involved in a romance. Let me assure you I did not presume this because of rumors, or anything that I saw pass between the two of you last semester. I knew because Jon told me of the relationship at the beginning of January. The only things that he didn't tell me were your name and that the baby you were carrying was not his."

Dr. Sargent went on to say, "Jon told me because he thought, as department head, I should know. Jon said that the student involved had left the area to make a decision on how to proceed with the pregnancy, a decision that she requested she make by herself, and he was prepared to leave the university and go to her if she needed him.

"Sarah, he told me that he loved his fiancée more than he ever thought it possible to love and that they planned on marrying before classes began in the fall. Jon said that if his marrying a student, possibly with a new baby, would bring an unnecessary scandal to the history department he would start looking for a new position immediately. He said he was sorry to have put me in a difficult situation, but that he wanted me to be prepared in the event he left suddenly.

"Jon never mentioned your name, Sarah. I don't think I suspected that the woman he spoke of so lovingly was you until the day your sister called the department to request that someone contact you to set up a completion date for your interim project. The day of our first meeting, when I saw you, I knew for certain."

He paused, then said, "What I thought then, and still think today, is that you are one of the bravest and most resilient people I have ever met."

I sat across from the professor and cried silently; when I tried to speak, Dr. Sargent turned his palm up to signal that he would like to keep talking. He told me his initial reaction to what Jon had told him had been disappointment. He was sorry Jon had gotten himself into such a difficult position and had put the history department in one, too. He'd had such hopes for Jon's future at the university. But, then, Dr. Sargent continued by saying, "Given a little time, my perspective changed. I went home that night and thought about the things Jon had said to me. My strongest impression of our conversation was how much Jon was in love with the student in question—you, Sarah. I started thinking about my love for Margaret and how I would give anything for another day with her."

Dr. Sargent said he called Jon the next day to tell him that he hoped there would be no emergencies that would require him to leave the University, but if there were, he would be granted a leave of absence. He said he'd told Jon he would like to host a reception for the happy couple at his home in Vermillion in September and if it included a baby shower, so be it. Dr. Sargent explained he was going to set the tone for the department. There would be no scandal.

As I continued to blink back tears, the professor said he thought a scholarship to honor Jon was a wonderful idea and he would be happy to help in any way possible. I could tell that the cogs were already whirring in his head. I asked if he would keep the envelope of cash and he put it in a compartment of the centuries old Chinese desk that sat against a wall in the living room. Ornately carved, it was another of the souvenirs from his travels on display.

Changing the subject, he asked, "Have you thought anymore about my ideas for you to stay on schedule with your studies?"

"I'd love to Dr. Sargent, but I don't have the tuition or a way to get to Vermillion. Without my carpool, I'd have to drive myself everyday.... and, since I share the family car with my mother, it just wouldn't work. Besides, I have to work this summer or I won't have the money I need for the fall. But, thanks for thinking about it—it means a lot that you care."

I bit down hard on my lower lip as I accelerated onto the interstate to Sioux Falls. I couldn't stop thinking about what Jon had done by telling Dr. Sargent about us and taking responsibility for a baby that wasn't even his. He could have tanked his chances for tenure or even gotten himself fired had Dr. Sargent been less understanding. It was hard for me to fathom how much Jon had loved me. I didn't feel I deserved his love— how could anyone feel that deserving.

I started to cry and had to pull off on an exit ramp halfway home because I couldn't see in the blackness of the countryside through my tears and fogging glasses. Jon had loved me, but he was gone. I'd done everything I could. I'd told Dr. Sargent the truth and given him the money. The wheels were in motion for the scholarship. It was time to put my grief behind me —I could think about Jon—I could still love Jon—but I had to stop mourning him. I had to lock the pain away. I dried my eyes and pulled myself together. Again.

The next afternoon, when we met for our regular Wednesday session in Dr. Sargent's office, he seemed happier to see me than I could ever remember. He was always welcoming, but that day he was almost giddy— slightly disconcerting to witness in a dapper older man.

He said before we started discussing our topics *du jour*, he wanted to make several proposals. He requested I write them down as he listed them, which I found comical since it was my habit to take copious notes during our meetings. I think he had just wanted me to have my head down as I listened to him speak, because he enumerated his requests and spoke uncharacteristically fast:

1. He had already made an appointment with University Foundation to discuss the creation of a memorial scholarship to honor Dr. Leggett. We were both to attend the meeting on Monday at 10:00am.
2. He asked that I spend Thursday thinking about the criteria for the scholarship and what I would like posterity to remember about Jon.
3. On Friday he wanted to meet with me to hammer out the details of our presentation to the foundation. He suggested Sioux Falls or his house in Vermillion mid-afternoon.

4. He asked for my forgiveness. When he'd been making plans for my precipitous return to my studies, he had forgotten to take into consideration my financial situation. He was sorry for his thoughtlessness.

5. He said he would like me to take back the $700 Jon had sent to me in Boston. He told me he thought nothing would have pleased Jon more than to see the first (unofficial) recipient awarded the Dr. Jon S. Leggett Scholarship be Sarah Bolling. With that said, he slid the envelope of money across his desk.

6. The last thing he did made my future life possible. He requested I move to Vermillion in June to take over the position of his live-in assistant for the upcoming school year. The position, which had been filled by a promising senior history student for the last ten years, included a rent-free apartment in his beautiful house and a monthly stipend of $100.

I looked up, once again with tears in my eyes and said, "Yes! Yes, to all six discussion points, Dr. Sargent. Thank you."

I put Jon's money into my patchwork purse, wiped my eyes, and we began our discussion of the final stage of my interim project.

—25—

To say that Dr. Sargent had given me an enormous amount to ponder would be to understate both "enormous" and "ponder." So many thoughts were competing for attention in my head, it was nearly as unsettling for me as the voices that clamored in my brain before I succumbed to a migraine. I quickly decided for self preservation I should tackle the subjects in the order the professor had proposed them. (I think he already knew me better than I knew myself.) I began preparing both my thoughts and emotions for the meeting with the University Foundation on Monday.

As Dr. Leggett's former student, what did I perceive to be his strengths as a professor? My first thought was that he was brilliant, but I realized immediately a brilliant mind does not necessarily make one a good teacher. I wanted people to know and remember that Dr. Jon S. Leggett had been, for a brief time, an important part of the University of South Dakota. His stay was too short, but he had already had an impact on the lives of his former students.

As for how I would like the scholarship used, I hadn't given it much thought. I suppose I was just thinking that a scholarship was a scholarship—it would go for tuition, books, and staying afloat. But, as I considered it more, and thought back to my time in Boston, I decided that if Dr. Sargent agreed, I would like Jon's scholarship to be used for travel. It would be a scholarship awarded to Juniors or Seniors to be used for further study in the place (or places) where the historic event they proposed to study had occurred, or where primary sources for the event (or subject) might be found.

As for the rest of the criteria and the dollar value of the award, I was at a loss. I knew Dr. Sargent was not going to let me down, and that he'd undoubtedly already been crunching the numbers. Those were details for us to discuss on Friday.

I had previously accepted Dr. Sargent's offer to become his assistant and move to Vermillion in June, but I hadn't told my parents as yet. I didn't think my folks would have any problems with me leaving home, as long as my mother deemed the position with Dr. Sargent respectable. She wouldn't want people talking about me, reflecting badly on the family.

I was excited by the prospect of living in Dr. Sargent's house. I had never seen the apartment, but it really wasn't important to me. What mattered was that I would finally be living in Vermillion. I wouldn't be losing two-plus hours a day on the road. I would have more library time, more study time, more time to talk with fellow students and professors. I could finally be part of Sarge's Platoon.

That evening, before supper, I told my parents about the job offer and what it entailed. Using my *good girl* skills, I asked their permission to accept the position that I had already accepted. I told them that if they would like to meet Dr. Sargent, he had offered to come to Sioux Falls the next day and I could arrange an introduction after they got off work. By the time we'd passed around the meatloaf, I'd gotten their approval. They had no interest in meeting with the professor.

The next day, while I drove my mother to work so that I could borrow the Dodge to get to Vermillion, she told me how happy she was about my new job. I was pleased that she understood what a wonderful opportunity Dr. Sargent was giving me, until she said, "I can hardly wait to look for a new sofa." Her happiness was about having extra square-footage in the house. She was already redecorating my bedroom in her head.

Dr. Sargent and I had a productive meeting later that afternoon at his house. This time, after meeting me at the front door, we went directly past the grand spiral staircase to the large dining room table that the professor had already prepared with his notes, a clean note pad, and a pot of Irish Breakfast tea, a better choice in my mind than Earl Grey.

He said my observations about Jon as an instructor were excellent, and that he'd already taken the liberty of contacting several other of Dr. Leggett's former students to get their impressions of his teaching style. He clapped his hands together when he read my suggestion that the scholarship be an award to help make travel affordable for history students and said he could think of no better purpose for the scholarship—he thought it would have pleased Jon immensely.

We spent the afternoon working out the details. I felt the back of my throat tighten and fought back tears when Dr. Sargent proposed the final criteria for choosing the scholarship recipient be the "belief that the project would be of value" to the student, and that the student "would prove a credit to the University's history department." They were the words Jon had used to describe my attributes just months earlier.

Dr. Sargent said he thought a good amount for the grant would be $350. Awarded twice a year it would match the $700 Jon had sent me. The professor said he would like to give $2,000 to start the fund. His hope was that with time and fundraising the scholarship would become an endowed fund that could serve students in perpetuity. Jon's name would forever be part of the University of South Dakota history department.

Our tea was stone cold, and we were making plans for our Monday meeting with the University Foundation, when Stephen Munce, Dr. Sargent's current PA, walked in from the kitchen. As Steve and I shook hands, Dr. Sargent mentioned that I was to be his new PA come June and asked if I might have a look at the upstairs apartment. Steve was agreeable, but offered to fetch more hot water for the teapot if we would give him a few minutes to straighten-up.

Ten minutes later Dr. Sargent showed me through the closed door at the end of the dining room. It opened to a small foyer at the side door of the house where there was access to a narrow winding "servant's" staircase. Off the second floor landing were three doors: one opened to a bathroom with a shower; the heaviest door led to a second story porch that faced the backyard; and, the final door opened into a large bedroom with equally large windows. The room was furnished with a double bed, a hefty desk and office chair, and walls sheathed in bookcases. In front of the floor-to-ceiling corner bookcases Steve had "straightened-up" by covering a mountain of packing boxes with a very ugly printed bed sheet.

My face was all glasses and grin—the room was perfect!

—26—

Our Monday meeting with the University Foundation and administration went as well as both Dr. Sargent and I had hoped. The professor presented the "Dr. Jon S. Leggett Memorial Scholarship" in a format so complete it could have been ready for publication that afternoon. He gifted his check for $2,000 and my anonymous $100 in cash to fund the scholarship for its first three years or six awards. He assured the financial folks at the foundation that the plan was to make this an endowed fund—it just needed to get started.

I turned in my final interim project paper on April 25th, the Wednesday before its due date. By this point it was a formality, but an important one to Dr. Sargent and me. I dedicated it to Dr. Jon Leggett, but knew that without Dr. Sargent there would have been no paper to dedicate. I felt I owed him for bringing me back to life, although he would have never taken the credit.

Dr. Sargent and I continued to meet on Wednesdays through finals week in mid-May. He had devised a scheme to get me independent study credit for the time we had spent together over the spring semester. I had always assumed that he'd planned our Wednesday discussions out of some sort of academic habit. In reality, he was already working to get me the credits that I would need to graduate on time.

In late May, I wrote another paper, entitled "What Becomes History?" It dealt with the February through May siege of the small community of Wounded Knee on the Pine Ridge Reservation by the American Indian Movement (AIM). The location of the occupation had been chosen to observe the 1890 massacre at that site. It was the brutal slaying of 300 Lakota by the U. S. 7th Cavalry—an event that had never been taught in my history classes. Dr. Sargent urged me to think about which voices we hear when we read history. He explained that too often the stories of the defeated, the disenfranchised, or those in the minority are either not recorded, or worse, not believed. He taught me that as a researcher I should task myself to look for those marginalized accounts, along with those of the statesmen and generals who had always been the sources of information.

With the paper I completed my "summer" independent study (proving that all official dates are not necessarily real). The professor helped me choose two more classes to take during the summer term and with Jon's money I paid the tuition for all three. I still didn't feel comfortable using the money, but I promised myself that I would save as much as I could over the next few years so that I could donate the $600 I felt I still owed. After that I planned on making yearly contributions of my own.

I didn't attend graduation ceremonies that spring, but Dr. Sargent told me later that the Dean of the College of Arts and Sciences gave a moving memorial tribute to Jon, mentioning that had he lived it would have been the close of his fourth year as a professor. He had started his career at the University the same year as the Class of 1973. The Dean finished by telling the crowd of the history department's newly created Jon S. Leggett Memorial Scholarship and said that further details would be forthcoming. Dr. Sargent gave me a copy of the dean's tribute; as I suspected, Dr. Sargent had written it.

On June seventh, with the help of my parents and a truck my father had borrowed from work, I moved from my family home to my new life in Vermillion. I had everything I owned in the back of that pickup: two suitcases with clothes; four boxes full of toiletries, office supplies, books, records, new bedding, old towels, and my clock radio; and, two final items too big for boxes, but perfect for a corner surrounded by bookcases—the family's old portable stereo and a slightly shabby, plaid, wing-backed chair.

That afternoon, Dr. Sargent gave me a more thorough tour of his house and then gave me *carte blanche* to explore all of its spaces on my own. Having spent most of my growing up years in a 1960's housing development, I'd never had the opportunity to explore a house of such history and proportions. The nooks and crannies on the upper levels were endlessly intriguing to me. While the main floor of the house had been modernized, the second floor and attic had changed very little in eighty years. Ascending the stairs was akin to time travel.

The wide white spiral staircase that began in the large front room on the main floor led to a stately Victorian second floor. Olive green Lincrusta (a textured wall covering created by the inventor of linoleum) swathed the grand foyer's walls and ceiling, while beautiful oriental rugs covered the parquet floors. Atop the center rug, overstuffed leather chairs graced each side of a square game table set with a perpetual chess match.

Off to the left, at the top of the stairs, was Dr. Sargent's study. The few times I'd been to his house I'd thought it strange that the professor didn't have an office on the main floor. Now I understood. The main floor was a public space. When Dr. Sargent read and wrote, he used his beautiful oaken study. On two of the walls, built-in bookcases flanked large windows; an onyx faced fireplace with a carved marble mantel graced the north wall; and, piled with books and papers, the professor's substantial oak desk filled the center of the room. At first glance the office appeared messy, but as I looked closer I could see Dr. Sargent's inherent sense of order.

The bedroom closest to the study was the professor's. There were two more large, windowed guest bedrooms on the second floor which had been updated only slightly by the addition of small private bathrooms so that guests needn't share.

On the first floor, Dr. Sargent showed me the rooms I hadn't seen during earlier visits: the kitchen, which I would soon know well, and the back parlor that was now a music room. A matte black grand piano sat behind the pocket doors on the west wall of Dr. Sargent's living room. The professor played, but his late wife had been the musician in the family. Dr. Sargent said that the Bösendorfer had been Margaret's pride and joy. She had given lessons to both children and adults in the area and performed regionally with fellow musicians. Dr. Sargent couldn't have missed the emotion in my eyes when I first saw the instrument, yet when he asked if I played, I belied my excitement and replied only that I had for a short time as a child.

He invited me to use the piano whenever I liked, then showed me Margaret's collection of music hidden away behind the sliding doors of modern storage cabinets that lined one wall of the room. Above them hung an impressive collection of colorful paintings by Willem and Elaine de Kooning. Dr. Sargent told me that he liked Willem's works, but Margaret had insisted that they buy an equal number of Elaine's paintings, which she preferred because they were more figurative (and she believed strongly in supporting the work of woman artists).

As soon as I found some free time later that day, I riffled through the cabinets and found adult beginner books among Margaret's collection of teaching materials. It wasn't long before I could play the easy classical sheet music once used as student recital pieces. I felt closer to my Grandmother Bolling than I had in years as I sat at the Bösendorfer grand playing the music she'd shared with me when I was her little girl.

—27—

Friday after breakfast, Dr. Sargent took me on a tour of Vermillion. Vermillion is just a small town on the prairie, and even though I had been attending the University at the edge of town, I had never seen its main street. I'd typically parked on the far north side of campus and gone to the buildings that housed my classes, the commons, and the library—I'd never even had enough time to fully explore the campus.

So, after showing me the features of his Cadillac and giving me the extra key, Dr. Sargent asked me to hop in for the very short drive to campus. As we motored slowly by the halls and dorms he told me their histories: when they'd been built, who they were named for, and when, in some cases, they were slated to be replaced. I saw shops and cafés on the south edge of campus that I had never noticed in my three years of study.

Dr. Sargent continued our drive-by tour downtown, passing the grocery store, drugstore, dry cleaner, and bank—all places I would become familiar with while performing my new PA duties. As we drove down the main drag, I finally saw the hangouts that my classmates talked of so frequently—the Char Bar, the

New Vars, and Carey's. I now lived within walking distance of them all.

After the working part of the tour had ended, the history lesson began. The professor drove me to lower Vermillion and explained how the whole city had been moved to higher ground after a devastating flood in 1881. I thought about what it would have been like to be caught in a flood. To have everything that mattered to you destroyed then washed away. I asked Dr. Sargent if he knew how long it had taken for the citizens of Vermillion to rebuild their lives. He said that only a quarter of the town had remained intact, so physically it hadn't taken long to move the structures. Then he added, "But, I'm certain that at some level the trauma of the event stayed with many for their entire lives." We both knew we weren't just talking about a ninety-year-old flood.

Dr. Sargent took the steep road cut into the edge of the river bluff back to the top of the hill. Bluff Cemetery overlooked the expansive Missouri River Valley. It was an old cemetery by South Dakota standards, which was evident as we drove past tilting markers and stately mausoleums with columns pocked by decades of prairie storms. Dr. Sargent pulled the Caddy off the narrow gravel road, and we walked a short path worn into the early summer grass to a large rose-quartzite marker. Its timeless design was engraved with the name "SARGENT." Two full names were carved beneath: Margaret Springer Sargent, Born December 28, 1905, Died March 19, 1969 and Benjamin Parke Sargent, Born February 8, 1905, Died

Dr. Sargent must have watched me as I read his name; when he saw my eyes pass to the word *Died* he said, "Died on the day I lost Margaret, or, so I thought." We stood in the warming summer air and he told me of his grief—the pain that had surrounded him for months after Margaret died and would still sweep over him in quiet moments. He told me he often spoke to Margaret and not to be alarmed if I heard him speaking when I thought we were alone in the house. He found it helpful and was fairly sure he wasn't going mad. We stood in silence by the grave, tears lacing our lower lashes. Dr. Sargent eventually broke the stillness by reading the inscription on the stone:

> Thy love is such I can no way repay,
> The heavens reward thee manifold I pray,
> Then while we live, in love lets so persever,
> That when we live no more, we may live ever.
>   Anne Bradstreet, 1678

"It's the last four lines of the poem 'To My Dear and Loving Husband.' When Margaret chose it, I was flattered, but I told her I thought it too one-sided to be carved on our shared marker."   Wiping his eyes, Dr. Sargent continued, "She laughed at me and said, not to worry. Most *normal people* wouldn't know the title of such an old poem and without it, the words would be assumed a mutual sentiment. In her usual fashion she quipped that since she was going to be spending eternity with a man, there was no way that she was going to give her final words to one, too. That was my Margaret."

As we turned to walk back to the car I finally asked what I had been thinking ever since we'd driven into the cemetery nearly an hour ago. It was a question I had tried to ask for months, but couldn't—the words would form on my lips, but the air to voice them wouldn't come from my lungs. Today was different. In a way, by taking me to visit Margaret's grave, Dr. Sargent had primed me to ask.

"Dr. Sargent, where's Jon's grave?"

I knew how Jon had died. I knew where Jon had died. But I didn't know what had happened to cause him to disappear so completely in the two weeks it had taken me to return from Boston. I had forced myself to find and read the newspaper accounts of the accident, but I'd never found an obituary. I knew the history department had held a small memorial service for Jon the week classes had resumed second semester, but I'd heard nothing about a public funeral. There was no information on an interment. Everything was done and settled within a mere two weeks—the man I loved had been swept away.

Instead of climbing into the Cadillac, we leaned against the hood in the shade of a large black walnut tree overlooking the valley. Dr. Sargent told me that as soon as the highway patrol had determined who the fire-ravaged pickup belonged to, the university administration had been notified. The U's president had called the professor with the news and asked that he notify Jon's next of kin.

"I was devastated, of course. But not just by the news. Jon had mentioned to me that he and his father hadn't spoken in years. And now I had been tasked with calling and telling this man of his estranged son's death."

"Do you know why they hadn't talked in so long?"

"I just know that Jon's mother had left the family during Jon's sophomore year in high school. He remembered her hugging him goodbye in the morning, not a normal occurrence in his teens, and when he arrived home that evening, she was gone. He never saw her again, nor did his father as far as Jon knew. He said after her disappearance, his father who had always been a distracted parent, became even more distant.

I didn't say anything, but I couldn't stop thinking about how selfish I had been with my complaints to Jon about my parents. Jon had been far more alone in the world than I was, yet all he did was comfort me.

"Sadly," Dr. Sargent went on, "and almost unbelievably to me, their final parting came from an academic disagreement. Jon's father is a professor at Stanford, a famous mathematician, who fully expected his talented son to follow in his footsteps."

Dr. Sargent explained that Jon had shown such great promise in math, that by the time he'd started college at age sixteen, he had already won several awards presented to the world's most gifted young minds.

At MIT, Jon had immersed himself in theoretical mathematics. He'd told Dr. Sargent that he'd become obsessed with proving an aspect of String Theory—one that hypothesized that time was layered, and, at fractures in those layers, time touched. He called it the Fractured Dimensional Supposition—it was a theory that made time travel possible. Jon told

Dr.Sargent that he had nearly driven himself insane in his quest to perfect the mathematics of the theory. It was only through the intervention of a history professor at MIT that he'd pulled himself from his mental quagmire and began to live outside his head once again.

"When to preserve his sanity Jon changed his major after his second year of college, his father quit speaking to him. Jon said that he was informed through his father's attorney that he was not welcome to come home until he returned to mathematics as his full-time academic pursuit. Jon never saw his father again." Dr. Sargent shook his head, and told me that he would never understand how Jon's father could act in such a manner. "Margaret and I couldn't have children—we would have given everything to have had a child like Jon." He continued, "When I reached the senior Dr. Leggett, he was cool and dismissive."

Dr. Sargent said that he'd received a call from Jon's father's attorney the day after he had notified the senior Dr. Leggett of his son's death. "I was informed that arrangements had been made to drive Jon's remains from Sioux Falls to Sioux City where they would be cremated before being sent to California. The attorney said there were to be no obituaries printed in local papers, and that a representative from their firm would be in South Dakota the following day to see that Jon's personal belongings were liquidated and his outstanding bills were paid."

"Sarah, it was as though they'd made him disappear. When you came to me this spring and suggested the scholarship in his name, you made him reappear. I will always be grateful to you for that."

I told Dr. Sargent that gratitude was unwarranted. Without his affection for Jon, and assistance to me, I could never have started the scholarship. If anything, for as hard as it had been to hear, what he'd just told me gave me some solace. It had given a little of Jon back to me.

—28—

As Dr. Sargent's personal assistant, I would be typing, filing, and proofing, plus running errands and performing some light cooking and cleaning. I realize it sounds somewhat sexist—it wasn't. Most of the professor's personal assistants had been male students; the duties did not change when a young woman served as PA.

Cleaning and cooking were not taxing because the Sargents had always had a full-time housekeeper. Mildred Gunther had been part of the household for years, and still did things the way that Mrs. Sargent had specified. Mrs. G came five days a week. On Mondays, Wednesdays, and Fridays she prepared lunch and dinner for us. She also created dinners that the professor's PA could easily prepare on the days she did not cook. On those days, Tuesdays and Thursdays, she deep cleaned the massive house. She had developed her own rotating work schedule, which I never quite understood, but the house was always spotless. Mrs. G was *usually* pleasant when encountered, but she kept herself nearly invisible unless you entered her kitchen.

Dr. Sargent was not a cook. He made a mean cup of tea. He could spread jam on toast. That was about it. He rarely entered the kitchen and that was the way Mrs. G liked things. I could tell that my interest in her kitchen was going to be a problem if I did not approach her correctly—she had already told me she was "happy to see that boy go!" referring to Stephen Munce, my predecessor. I decided the best way to handle Mrs. G was head on, so I explained why I wanted more kitchen access than other PA's had previously been allowed. When she heard my reason, she was willing to work with me.

I wanted to make cookies for Dr. Sargent. Not just any cookies, but cookies like the ones Margaret had baked for him. I trusted that Mrs. G had been around long enough to remember Margaret's baking, and I was right. She went to the far corner cupboard and pulled a recipe box from the middle shelf. In it were all of Margaret Sargent's cookie and dessert recipes. I was shocked—nearly half the recipes were for cookies and bars. I was ambitious, but not that ambitious!

It dawned on me that the family favorites would probably be toward the front if Margaret hadn't been a stickler for alphabetization. I was right again. The first four recipes in the box were her go-tos. Mrs. G confirmed that they were the professor's favorites: Oatmeal Raisin (with Walnuts), Cherry Winks, Snickerdoodles, and Great Chocolate Drops (descriptive of taste, not size). These were Margaret's parenthetical phrases, not mine. All four went into my cookie baking rotation, along with Chocolate Chip Cookies with Pecans, the only cookie I already knew how to bake.

A lengthy list of kitchen rules was quickly put forward by Mrs. G, along with an equally long list of punishments that I would incur if I broke them. Once I acknowledged her directives, she showed me where to find all the cookie-making utensils. She said if I wasn't "a bright nuff bulb" to remember where things came from, so that I could put them away properly, I should make notes until I learned. She said, "that Steve Munce fellow was 'bout a 20 watt-er."

I spent most of Saturday learning the kitchen. Saturday evening, I made my first ever batch of "Oatmeal Raisin (with Walnuts)" cookies. The smile on Dr. Sargent's face at Sunday's afternoon tea made me happier than I had been since December.

—29—

It was the summer of the Watergate hearings and nearly everyone, young and old, was glued to their TV watching Sen. Sam Ervin doing his "old country lawyer" routine. I always thought of Sam Ervin and his Harvard credentials when Dr. Sargent would say, "What do I know, I'm just a North Dakota farm boy." Yes, I would think to myself—a North Dakota farm boy, with a Ph.D. from Harvard and a John H. Dunning Prize for his first book. I learned early to never underestimate a self-effacing country boy.

Dr. Sargent and I spent several days in late August planning the official announcement of *Jon's travel scholarship*, as we had come to think of it. We wanted to make sure that all history majors knew of it early enough to make plans for January interim, yet would have enough time to change their plans if a travel interim were an impossibility if they didn't receive the award. Dr. Sargent decided that the Autumn History Department Picnic would be a perfect time to make the announcement. The professor would be sending out invitations to the picnic to all history majors—we chose to piggyback the information about the scholarship in the same mailing.

In late August, as I hand addressed 5x7 inch white envelopes to all the USD history majors and professors, I couldn't avoid the thought that they looked like wedding invitations. I didn't know if Jon and I would have sent invitations to our wedding. We may have just eloped, unless my mother had insisted we held a "proper wedding" for her friends to attend. While I couldn't picture a location, I could picture us. Jon would be wearing his dark blue suit with his red and blue paisley tie. I'd be in a gauzy white caftan with small white flowers braided into my hair. As Jon slid the beautiful garnet and opal ring on my finger, the officiant would pronounce us husband and wife....

I wondered if the professor had forgotten about how I might feel addressing those envelopes knowing he had offered to host a wedding reception for Jon and me at roughly that same time of year had life gone on as the three of us had expected it would last January. I didn't mention anything to Dr. Sargent, but I decided to do my best to make it a special day and celebrate Jon. The man I loved was gone, but a promising professor's gifts to his students would live on. Knowing I'd had a part in planning the scholarship, even though I didn't want that fact to be common knowledge, was a balm— just maybe not as much of one as I'd hoped it would be.

School started after Labor Day and the department picnic was held two weekends later. To say that I helped plan it would be incorrect—at this stage in its development, no one had to plan the Autumn History Department Picnic. The picnic was the same from year to year; only the players changed. The venue: the Prentis Park picnic shelter just a few blocks from campus. The menu: hot dogs and hamburgers grilled by Dr. Johnson wearing his custom-made bright red chef's toque. The program: the introduction (and occasional roast) of the professors, department staff, and all of the history majors in attendance.

The only change in the line-up this year was Dr. Sargent's brief memorial tribute to Dr. Leggett, followed by the introduction of the scholarship in his name. After he spoke, the professor invited me to the makeshift podium to tell about the wonderful aspects of traveling to study history and recount my memories of having Dr. Leggett as a teacher and advisor while I was in Boston. It wasn't easy, but I'd wanted to honor Jon and it seemed an appropriate way to do it. I'd practiced in the mirror for hours so that I could make it through the speech without crying.

As we threw things in the back of his pickup for the two block drive home, Dr. Sargent rehashed the afternoon. He was pleased with the comments he'd overheard from students regarding the scholarship. "Excellent job, Sarah," he said. A smile mixed with sadness and, perhaps, fatherly pride crossed his face. "I'm sure it wasn't easy for you. I meant for this day to be a much different kind of celebration for my two favorite young people."

Now I was crying. As Dr. Sargent patted the back of my hand resting on the tailgate, I wondered why I'd ever doubted him.

A few days after the history department picnic, students started dropping by the professor's house in the evening. It was an unwritten rule that one didn't arrive until after 8:00, and then only on Tuesdays and Thursdays. As I soon found out, there were many unwritten rules regarding Sarge's Platoon—the first among them was that Dr. Sargent's personal assistant was the unofficial leader of the troops—Second in Command, as the professor put it.

In the past, the professor's PA had always been a Platoon member before he or she was hired as personal assistant. I found myself in the unique position of running an organization about which I knew next to nothing. Dr. Sargent filled me in the best he could, but being a member of Sarge's Platoon was akin to being in a secret society where the rules were unwritten and constantly evolving. Very few of them were established by the professor directly—all of them were controlled by Dr. Sargent indirectly.

I was the gatekeeper to the living room, the Platoon's *sanctum sanctorum*. On Tuesday and Thursday evenings I let any history student through the doors who arrived between eight and ten. I could turn people away or request that they leave if need be. Intoxication or "too doped to speak" were the usual reasons for exclusion. If I asked a classmate to leave, he or she (truthfully, there was never a she) would be welcomed back into the fold on future evenings. If Dr. Sargent asked a student to leave, he could never return to the house. Very few students would allow themselves (or their friends) to be exiled—thus making my job easier.

Alcohol was consumed after 10:00, but only if the person bringing it brought enough to share with the whole Platoon. This rule worked beautifully to keep inebriation at the house under control—most of us were too poor to afford much more than a six pack of Old Milwaukee. Dr. Sargent always had coffee and tea available, and, during my tenure as PA, we usually had homemade cookies.

Over the summer my baking skills had increased—when the weather cooled, cookies happened almost weekly. Dr. Sargent, never greedy (and maybe enjoying variety), encouraged me to share the baked goods with my fellow students. By November I had a new nickname thanks to the guys in the Platoon— "Cookie." I hated it, but knew enough to not protest— they would have just said it louder.

One of my least favorite tasks on Platoon nights was making sure that the ashtrays never overflowed. I didn't smoke, Dr. Sargent didn't smoke, but at least half of the students and nearly all of the guests did: cigarettes, cigars, pipes, you name it. Nothing in that old house was fireproof—the oil and wax imbued antique Lincrusta covering the walls on the second floor could have been classified as an accelerant. I made fire safety a priority.

The currency of those evenings was conversation. Usually there was a natural flow that originated with the students, but on nights when a topic never gelled, Dr. Sargent would step in and give direction. He had an unending list of intriguing questions to prompt discussions. If we had started late, or were just getting warmed up at midnight, Sarge's

Platoon would adjourn to the saloon to keep the flow going. Sometimes I would join the Platoon at the Char Bar for one of their legendary screwdrivers—vodka mixed with powdered Tang—but usually I stayed back to clean up while Dr. Sargent headed upstairs to bed.

I don't think that I had ever appreciated the intelligence of most of my classmates until those thought-filled nights. In the classroom, our exchanges were somehow guarded or often seemed competitive. In Dr. Sargent's living room, debate was loud and lively, but it was built on respect for one another. The professor encouraged input from everyone, but demanded it of no one. We felt safe and built life-long personal and professional connections while washing down cookies with cheap beer or Annie Green Springs.

—30—

Golden leaves fell from the trees shading the back yard and tumbled down the street in the late autumn wind, prompting me to ask Mrs. G if she could find me an extra blanket or two. I could tell that my bedroom would soon be frigid. The same big windows that let me watch the seasons change did little to keep the cold at bay, and I was already shivering in dread thinking of the upcoming holidays without Jon. My memories of him were so intwined with Thanksgiving and Christmas.

Dr. Sargent saw me going through the motions and recognized the pain in my eyes. He asked if I wanted to talk as we shared our nightly cup of tea. I thanked him, but told him no. I didn't have the words for what I was feeling, but knowing that he understood meant a lot to me. I said the best thing he could do for me was to keep me so busy that I didn't have time to think: extra proofing, typing, errand running—anything to keep me in the moment and my brain on task.

Five students had presented proposals for Jon's travel scholarship before the November seventh deadline. Dr. Sargent said that they all had merit and that he thought that the committee had its work cut out for it. I had purposely not asked any questions about the scholarship lately. I knew of two individuals who said they were going to apply, but that information came in casual conversation—I hadn't pressed them for details. In fact, I'd changed the subject. I didn't want anyone to know that I had anything to do with the scholarship. I was still worried about people finding out about Jon's and my relationship.

When the winner was announced on the Monday before Thanksgiving break, I couldn't have been happier with the committee's choice. Clyde S. Dale was the first official recipient of the Jon S. Leggett Memorial Scholarship.

Clyde and I had become fast friends and, in a way, colleagues, since we both worked for Dr. Sargent. Clyde was top dog this year in the dog-pile of work study students employed by the history department. I didn't work for the department, but working for the department chairman meant that Clyde and I spoke almost daily. Clyde was as affable, competent, and intelligent as he was ungainly and LARGE. I don't know if his parents naming him "Clyde Dale" was prescient, but I decided it was just plain cruel when I found out that they had chosen a middle name for him that began with an "S." ClydeSDale—really!

Clyde planned to use his grant to travel to Vicksburg, Mississippi during the January interim. Clyde's growing area of expertise was American history from 1860 thru 1865. He was particularly interested in the major conflicts of the Civil War and was looking forward to using the scholarship to study the forty-seven-day siege of Vicksburg in the area where it occurred. Clyde was so excited when he heard that he'd won he'd bear-hugged everyone in sight, including me. I realized after he set me down that I had not been hugged in months. It felt good.

I celebrated Thanksgiving with Dr. Sargent and a few of the professors, spouses, and foreign students orphaned by time, money, or distance from their families. I had planned on going home for the break, but my parents had embraced being unencumbered and driven to Boston to visit Annie. They would be gone my whole Thanksgiving vacation. I suppose I could have gone back to the house in Sioux Falls, but I no longer had a bedroom or car and I thought staying in Vermillion would help keep my mind off last year.

The dinner was at Dr. Sargent's house, a continuation of a tradition that Margaret had started in the 1950s. Mrs. G prepared the turkey and enough of the usual fixings to constitute a complete meal even if none of the guests brought food. But they all brought food. I helped the professor enlarge the already big dining room table and set up two four-tops in the music room, along with a buffet table for serving.

Dr. Sargent greeted his guests at the front doors and I took their food offerings while they unburdened themselves of winter coats. As I moved platters and casseroles from the kitchen to the makeshift buffet in the music room, the growing mountain of food astounded me. Dr. Sargent made a comment about the buffet being a true groaning board, which made all his guests groan. Later I found out it was the same witticism he made every Thanksgiving, with the same witticism in response—another tradition.

Dinner lasted for hours. I did my best to ease some of Dr. Sargent's hosting duties. I was as familiar with the kitchen as he was, perhaps more so, after months of cookie baking. If a special dish or serving utensil was needed I could usually find it. The conversation flowed as freely as the wine, or with this group maybe it was the other way around; they were a naturally talkative bunch. After dinner I put away food that needed refrigeration, but the remaining spread stayed on the buffet to be picked at for the entire evening.

While I cleared the tables, part of the group, appropriately led by Dr. Singh, gathered around the piano. The music started with a tongue-in-cheek version of the U fight song and progressed to Rodgers and Hammerstein classics in four-part harmony. I hummed along as I moved to and from the kitchen.

The kitchen! Mrs. G's always pristine kitchen looked like a turkey had exploded within its walls. I was starting to panic until I realized that I had three days to clean, prompting me to throw down the dishcloth and join the singers just as they were hitting their stride on O-K-L-A-H-O-M-A!"

The last of the guests left around 11:00. Dr. Sargent was exhausted, but as happy as I had seen him in a long time. I was exhausted, too, and, to my surprise, happy. Instead of missing Jon, I had been thinking that he would have enjoyed this day thoroughly. Perhaps that's a form of missing, but it didn't make me hurt—it made me smile. When I tripped up to my room around midnight, I pulled the extra comforter from my bed and curled up in Jon's plaid chair humming "Some Enchanted Evening" until I fell asleep.

The next day, after sleeping in, I got down to business in the kitchen. By late afternoon it looked, to quote Mrs. G, "spick-n-span." I looked around the clean kitchen and thought about making the dinner that Jon had prepared for me a year ago, but it didn't take me long to realize how reckless that could be. So far my emotions were in check; I needed them to stay that way. I asked Dr. Sargent what he usually ate for supper on the Friday after Thanksgiving. He looked at me as though I were speaking a foreign language. He said that he had always just pulled turkey and fixings from the overstuffed refrigerator.

"Not this year!" I said. "This year, we're having pizza. Get your coat and keys—I'm treating!"

—31—

Dr. Sargent, per my request, kept me extremely busy during the weeks following Thanksgiving. With my study obligations and the professor's to-do list there wasn't much time to dwell on last year. Although, on December seventh, in the quiet time before bed, I lit a candle in my apartment bedroom and allowed myself to relive every nuance of that special night from a year ago.

I breathed deeply as I thought about our frenetic rush to the bedroom when we got home from the Chinese restaurant—how we pulled at each other's clothes until we tumbled onto Jon's four-poster bed nearly undressed, me on top of him. I'd kissed him like I wanted to devour him. After weeks of waiting, I was crazed with desire. Jon took my wrists and rolled me over. On his knees above me, he kissed me softly on my face, calming my frenzy. Then, Jon took control of the night.

Obviously, he wasn't the first man I'd had sex with, but Jon was the first man who had made love to me. I smiled as I remembered the deep crinkles at the corners of his adoring eyes as he held my face and told me he had known me since time began. I sighed as I remembered his beautiful slim hands caressing my body, smoothing the hair back from my forehead. I moaned as I remembered what it felt like to have him enter me for the first time—the feeling of being complete, thinking that I had found my other half.

As the candle burned out, I fell asleep wondering if I would ever feel like a whole person again. We had pledged to be together forever. Did that just mean I would miss him forever?

—32—

On a Tuesday evening two weeks before Christmas, Clyde followed me toward the kitchen during a small gathering of the Platoon. As I was turning to remind him that Dr. Sargent and I were the only people allowed in that space, he stopped and said that he had something he wanted to ask me in private.

"Cookie, would you like to go home with me for Christmas?"

My response came out an inelegant, "What the…what?"

"I can tell you're not looking forward to going to Sioux Falls. You're not all that hard to read, Cooks. I'd love to share my crazy family with you."

Clyde was an Iowa farm kid. I knew from talking with him that he had seven brothers and sisters; four older and three younger. He said that he had already cleared the visit with his mother and she was excited to meet me. I'd have to share a bedroom with two of his sisters, but I would have my own bed.

I thanked him and told him that I'd need to think about it. The invitation had been a big surprise. Then I told him that he still couldn't follow me into the kitchen and to go back to the living room before anyone noticed. Rules were rules.

Later, after the Platoon took off for the New Vars, I asked Dr. Sargent to wait for me while I ran up to my apartment. He was still in his favorite chair when I came back holding a bottle of B&B with a red velvet bow tied around the neck. As I handed it to him, I said "Merry Christmas," but I also laughed lightly and told him I was giving it to him early as a bribe; I needed his advice on a personal matter. He went to the bar cart in the dining room for snifters. As he poured our drinks I told him about Clyde's invitation. "You know Clyde better than I do. I want to know if you think I should go home with him?"

Dr. Sargent swirled his drink and was silent for a long time. When he finally spoke, he was very serious. He told me he thought going to the farm could be the best thing in the world for me, but, if I were careless with Clyde's feelings, it could be the worst thing in the world for Clyde.

I swallowed my last drop of B&B and coughed, "So, how do I tell Clyde that I'd like to accept his invitation, but that I'm not interested in him romantically? I'm going to sound like a presumptuous bitch."

The professor laughed. "While I can see how someone might think you presumptuous, Sarah, I don't think that anyone would ever think you a *bitch*." The last word being one I'm not sure he'd ever said, except, perhaps, when referring to a female dog.

I laughed and replied, "Oh, just ask anyone from the Platoon who I've barred from your house or torn into for not following rules—they might think differently."

Before we said goodnight, Dr. Sargent assured me that I would know the right things to say to Clyde. I wasn't so sure.

I called Clyde that night to make plans to meet the next day. We chose the small white café just across from the Law School. The cozy place had become one of my favorite haunts that winter. On cold mornings I'd often stop in before class to warm my hands around one of their big white mugs of ButterNut coffee. If it wasn't occupied, I'd sit in the little corner booth and finish reading the newspaper. Sometimes my mind would drift and I would imagine Jon across from me. Our noses red from the walk across campus, steam rising from our cups, the rustle of the newspaper as we turned the pages in the tiny wooden booth—it was a reverie I couldn't afford myself, yet there were days when those fantasies were my salvation.

I was having one of those sweet, painful daydreams when Clyde squeezed himself into the booth across from me. After giving him time to order, I awkwardly told him that I would like to spend Christmas with his family.

"I hope I'm not being presumptuous, but please don't think of me as anything more than a friend. You're a great guy, but I'm still...I can't... I'm not interested in dating anyone, Clyde. But I really want you as a friend. I hope that's enough."

I think Clyde had been spending too much time with Dr. Sargent, because he did to me just what the professor had done the night before. He swirled the coffee in his cup and sat in silence for minutes. When he finally spoke, he said, "The truth is, Cookie, I want you to come home with me for selfish reasons that have nothing to do with us. They have to do with my former girlfriend, Mary Kay. Her engagement was announced in the church bulletin at Thanksgiving. I thought maybe you could help me make her a little jealous."

I laughed and said I was relieved to know that we were just friends and flattered to think that he thought I could make anyone jealous. But I also told him that I didn't want to lie about our relationship and say that we were more involved than we really were. He said that I shouldn't worry about that—the more we insisted that we were just friends, the more the church ladies would talk.

"All you have to do for my plan to work, Cookie, is come home with me for Christmas and have some fun—time-honored small-town tradition will do the rest. By the day after Christmas the gossips will be discussing whether we'll be getting hitched in June or July."

On Saturday morning Dr. Sargent started packing the Caddy for his drive to North Dakota. When I came down to give him three tins of homemade Christmas cookies before he left, he told me that he had something for me as well. He handed me an envelope that I assumed was a Christmas card. It was, but it was also much, much more. I opened the Currier and Ives card to find a snapshot of Jon smiling back at me. I hadn't seen Jon's face in nearly a year—I could barely read the card through my tears.

Earlier in the week the professor had requested I take a roll of film to the drugstore. He'd found it in one of the cameras he was getting ready to take to North Dakota. "It appears that roll of film I gave you to take to the drugstore for developing had been in the Pentax a long time—since last year's faculty Christmas party. I had forgotten Jon had asked me to take his picture."

In the photo Jon was wearing his dark blue suit, the one that he had worn the night we went on our special Christmas date. He was smiling and looking directly at the camera. At first I assumed he was smiling at Dr. Sargent behind the lens, because it was an unfeigned grin—his eyes shone with fondness. But then, I noticed that he was wearing the red and blue paisley tie, the one he'd bought on that same day to surprise me. I realized that his smile was for me. Jon had asked the professor to take the picture so that he could give it to me. I was sure of it.

"If I'd had more time, I would have had an enlargement made for you, Sarah."

"Oh, no, the size is perfect! This is the best Christmas present anyone has ever given me." I was so happy I would have broken our unspoken policy about not hugging if the professor hadn't already been climbing into the Cadillac.

I watched and waved as he drove off. Then I went upstairs and carefully trimmed my only picture of Jon to fit into the heart shaped glass paper weight that he had given me on Christmas Eve morning a year ago.

—33—

Clyde picked me up on Sunday morning shortly before 10:00. We had purposely scheduled our departure to miss church in his hometown. He told me that we would be attending Christmas Eve services and figured that was enough church for the year. The plan was to show up at the farm in time for Sunday dinner, which Clyde promised would be delicious and plentiful. He told me not to expect a crowd at noon—"there will probably only be nine of us. The whole family won't show up until tomorrow." I thought about the concept of nine not being a crowd; my mother would have thought it a state dinner.

As we turned onto the driveway of the farm just north of Aurelia, Iowa, I couldn't help but think of the winter scene on the Currier and Ives card that Dr. Sargent had just given me. The Dale farm was a picture-perfect homestead with a large two-story white house and a huge red barn with a classic arched roof. Of course, this was a modern operation so there were newer out-buildings, too, but it was obvious that thought had been given to their placement. Fresh snow covered everything, frosting the evergreens that formed the first row of the shelter belt.

Clyde parked on the gravel pad back of the house

and we carried a load from his trunk to the kitchen. Betty Dale, Clyde's mom, wiped her hands on her apron and proceeded to hug her son as though she hadn't seen him for years, although I knew he'd just been home for Thanksgiving. After he'd introduced us, I got the same treatment from Betty and learned where Clyde had honed his bear-hug skills.

Clyde had been correct, we were "only nine" for Sunday dinner: his parents; his older brother, Dale (who went by the nick name DoubleD) and Dale's wife, Debbie; Clyde's three younger sisters: Patty, soon to be sixteen; Hillin (obviously, Hilly), just turned fifteen; and, Laurie, thirteen. I started to think that maybe Clyde's name wasn't so bad after meeting Dale D. Dale and Hillin Dale. At least you had to think about Clyde's name to get the joke, people had to stifle laughs immediately upon meeting Dale and Hillin if they used their given names.

After we cleaned-up the dinner dishes, Clyde's sisters took me upstairs to see the room that I would be sharing with Patty and Hilly. The threesome seemed so silly—I could barely remember being that young. I'm not sure I ever had been, but I decided as I climbed the stairs that I would give it a whirl—this holiday, in this place, I would be silly, I would play games, I would have fun. Mostly, I would try to forget.

I unpacked my small suitcase into the drawer that Patty had emptied for me, then Clyde whisked me off to visit his childhood. We drove by his elementary school and the combination junior-senior high school he and his former girlfriend, Mary Kay, had attended. He showed me the football field on the edge of town where he'd played during high school, and we drove past the church where he'd been baptized—the church where we would attend Christmas Eve services the next day. We got back in time for me to help Mrs. Dale, who insisted on being called Betty, fix supper (my idea), while Clyde took off to run errands.

Twenty minutes into meal preparations, Betty had me laughing so hard I was crying into the potato peelings. She'd told me stories about the things the kids had done while growing up. With eight children, she had a hilarious host of tales. While I stirred the chicken gravy, I thanked her for letting me join them for Christmas.

"Oh, Cookie, we are happy to have you. One more person really doesn't cause much more hubbub. When Clyde asked if he could bring a friend home the only thing that caused me any concern at all was the sleeping arrangements."

I thought she meant sharing a room. "Oh, I don't mind sharing a room with the girls. It'll be fun."

Betty was shaking her head and smiling. "I guess Clyde didn't tell you how he set me up? See, Clyde gave up his bedroom when he moved to the U so that the girls could spread out a bit—so, anyway, I asked him where he wanted his friend to sleep. When he suggested *with his sisters* I nearly spit my coffee 'cross the table. Ya understand, he hadn't told me you were a girl!"

"Sounds like Clyde. I bet he was thrilled you took the bait. He does things like that to me all the time at school. He's just lucky he's so funny, otherwise I'd probably kill him—well, maybe just avoid him like the plague. Of course, either of those options would make my life a lot less entertaining."

After dinner I begged off attending a house party with Clyde. I knew what it was like being with a group of old friends when you hadn't attended the same high school—I'd ended up in the middle of too many commons lunches that had turned into mini class reunions. Besides, I'd be meeting most of the same people at the local bar the next afternoon—I had already agreed to that encounter. I told Clyde to go and have fun; I was going to stay back and get to know his little sisters.

The questions started in the bedroom. Where had their brother taken me in the afternoon? What did we do? Was I Clyde's girlfriend? Was I going to marry Clyde? After explaining that we had just driven around and looked at schools and churches I told them, "No, I am not Clyde's girlfriend and I never will be, so I think that precludes marrying him." Laurie asked what "precludes" meant, but I think the other two sisters understood immediately. I told them that I liked their brother very much, but we didn't have romantic feelings for each other.

Maybe my answers helped convince the girls that I wasn't their brother's girlfriend—whatever the reason, they quit with that line of questioning. Now they were asking about me: What did I like to do? Did I have a boyfriend? Had I ever had a boyfriend? What kind of music did I like?—I told them that I was pretty boring —"I like to read and study, and lately I've been enjoying relearning the piano." When I said, "No, I don't have a boyfriend, but, I've had boyfriends in the past," I thought I heard Hilly mutter something under her breath.

None of my answers got much traction until we

started talking about music. I told them that I liked folk music: Peter, Paul and Mary, Joan Baez, and Bob Dylan — Patty made a sour face when I mentioned Dylan. I got a better response when I told them I liked some sexier artists as well, like Rod Stewart and Van Morrison. I think the word "sexier" got their attention. Patty asked if I would like to see their record collection — they had some Van Morrison albums.

I followed the girls' thundering slippered feet down two flights of stairs to the rec room in the basement, where a freestanding metal rack held the usual collection of family albums: musicals, country and western artists, a glut of Christmas albums offered as premiums by tire companies, and the precious records that the kids had pooled their savings to purchase. The Dales had two Van Morrison albums — *Tupelo Honey* and *Moondance*. *Tupelo Honey* was new to me. As I was reading the song list on the back of the album, Laurie yanked it from my hand and pointed to "I Wanna Roo You (Scottish Derivative)" — "This is a funny song" she said, "but what does roo mean? Does he mean like kangaroos?" The older girls just looked at me and shook their heads.

I told her that I didn't know for sure, but if we played it maybe I could figure it out. I couldn't believe the coincidence when I heard the familiar nasally growl sing, "Twenty-third of December." The rest of the song left me no doubt as to what roo meant. When the song ended and Laurie lifted the needle, I explained, "Roo is most likely synonymous with woo, and by putting the parenthetical 'Scottish Derivative' in the title Morrison is telling us that in Scotland roo and woo can be used interchangeably. I'm absolutely sure that the word had nothing to do with marsupials."

While Laurie stared blank faced, Patty added, "Oh, but I think it has a lot to do with sticking something in a pouch!" Laurie's empty expression didn't change, while the rest of us laughed.

We listened to the song again and then danced like water thrown on hot oil to the songs that followed. Patty quickly combed the albums for "dancing songs" and we spent the night jumping up and down to some of the liveliest songs that Van Morrison, Elton John, and Bachman-Turner Overdrive ever recorded. At about 11:30, Mrs. Dale yelled down the stairs, "Shut off that noise and go to bed." I'm not sure that I'd ever heard those words before; this was only my second slumber party.

As soon as I opened the drawer to get my nightgown, I could tell that someone had gone through my clothes—

they were folded, but not arranged in the way I'd left them that afternoon. Hilly was watching me. I don't know if she could tell that I was upset, but to her credit she spoke up, "I was looking at your stuff."

"Why would you do that?"

"We look about the same size, other than you're shorter. I thought maybe you'd have something I could borrow. My sisters and I share clothes all the time."

I told her sharing was fine, but she really should've asked my permission prior to riffling through the drawer I was using. Before I could say anything more, she said, "I saw the picture."

Against my better judgment I'd brought the heart-shaped paperweight with me. I wanted Jon's picture; I couldn't bear to leave it at home after having just received it. I asked Hilly, "Did you tell anyone about the picture?"

"No…" she slowly continued, "…but, I showed it to Clyde before he left for the party."

I swallowed back the metallic taste at the base of my throat and asked, "What did Clyde say?"

"He told me to put it back where I'd found it. He said that it was none of his business and certainly none of mine. He was pretty pissed at me for going through your things… I'm sorry, Cookie, I just thought Clyde should know if you liked someone else."

I don't know how I managed to mutter that it was "ok." But I did. I also asked her to please not mention the photo to anyone and never again go through people's things without their knowledge—if she did, she was going to be a pretty unpopular roommate in her future life.

After Hilly and Patty were asleep, I held the paperweight picture of Jon and thought about our date on this evening a year ago—how it hadn't gone as planned either, but how wonderfully it had turned out anyway. I whispered, "Happy twenty-third of December," kissed the glass heart, and fell asleep with it clutched to my breast. In the early morning hours, I wrapped the paperweight in my flannel shirt and tucked it in the interior pocket of my overnighter in the closet.

Christmas Eve day arrived bright and clear, and, just as Clyde had promised, it started getting busier around the house. Even though all of Clyde's older siblings and their families lived in the area, it was a Dale family custom for everyone to spend most of Christmas Eve and Christmas Day at the farm house. By afternoon, eleven more Dales had arrived bringing the house, and thankfully, the yard and barn, to a total of twenty raucous voices. As Clyde and I slipped out to go to the local bar to meet up with his friends, I was ready for a little quiet.

Clyde's car crunched down the frozen gravel toward town. We didn't speak for awhile; I don't know what Clyde was thinking about, but I was trying to get up the nerve to tell him that I knew Hilly had shown him Jon's picture. Finally, I just said, "Hillin told me."

He responded, "Did she tell you that I told her it was none of her business?" He paused, then continued, "It's none of mine either, but I want you to know, Cookie, he was a special person—we all miss him. Now, if it's alright with you, I think we should talk about something else, ok?"

When I thanked him my voice quavered, but I said nothing further about the photo. We talked about "something else"—I don't remember what we said, but I do know that Clyde never brought up my relationship with Jon. I don't know what he assumed, but Clyde Dale was not a dumb man—I'm sure that he had put two and two together. Along with seeing the picture, he'd helped Dr. Sargent move Jon's chair to my house in Sioux Falls. But, as far as I know, he never shared his suspicions with anyone.

We were among the first of the group to get to the bar. It must have had a name: Steve's, or Larson's, or something else equally nondescript, but it was the only bar in town, so everyone just called it "The Bar." It was a peeling wooden building with small windows, one covered with a neon Hamm's sign. Clyde told me that normally the bar and Main Street looked far more festive this time of year, but nearly everyone in the area had refrained from putting up lighted outdoor Christmas decorations because of the energy crisis. If President Nixon didn't want Aurelia lit up for Christmas, the patriotic citizens of the little Iowa town would comply.

Cigarette smoke and the stench of spilled beer greeted us as we walked into the dive. Someone had tried to add a little holiday cheer to the surroundings. A tinsel garland hung across the back bar. The silver roping, flattened and uneven, looked like a shiny gap-toothed grin hanging in front of the liquor bottles. Plastic poinsettias shoved into scummy pressed-glass vases dotted chipped Formica tables. It was a pretty sad excuse for a party destination...until it filled with people.

Clyde's friends arrived in waves. I tried as hard as I could to remember names. To them I was "Cookie," and, after our fourth pitcher of beer, I was usually referred to as "Clyde's Christmas Cookie." High school glory days had been rehashed by the group yesterday; today everyone was discussing the future. Almost to a person they were home from college for the holidays. Most were seniors, and the future was a big question mark for nearly all of us.

As we played pool on the beat-up table at the back of the room, his former classmates regaled me with Clyde stories. A few were hysterical, but most were about him being senior class president, homecoming king, and class valedictorian. Clyde told me that he had played football, he hadn't told me that even with his lineman size he was the quarterback his last three years on the team. I was learning about another country boy not to be underestimated.

As we drove home for supper before Christmas Eve services, I told Clyde I'd had a great time with his friends. He smiled his big toothy grin, "My friends really liked you, too, Cooks—they're all really poor judges of character."

"Thanks, Turkey. I should have guessed—they all seemed really fond of you!"

"Ha Ha," came Clyde's weak retort, followed by, "What do you think of your new "Christmas Cookie" moniker?"

"What do you think—I hate it! But I think we should keep it up for Mary Kay's benefit."

"Oh God, Cooks! You're brilliant!"

After a kid-crazy supper heavy on soup, cheese, pickles, cookies, and noise, Laurie asked me if she could do my hair and makeup for the Christmas Eve service. No one had ever made me that offer—not even Annie. Before I could decide whether to be excited or offended, Patty who seemed to understand Clyde's goals for the evening, encouraged me to take Laurie up on her proposal.

While Patty and Hilly readied themselves, Laurie did my hair. She brushed and braided it into two long plaits. She then wound them around my head, bobby-pinning them to form a twisted crown of golden hair. Laurie asked before she did my makeup if I could go without my glasses for the evening. When I assured her that I could not, she applied enough eyeliner and mascara to make my eyes shine through my thick wireframes.

I was just getting ready to slip into my white sweater and green wool slacks, when Hilly came from the closet carrying a beautiful winter-white Aran patterned sweater dress, the price tags still dangling from the sleeve. She said she had saved up to buy it for this night, but she thought it would look beautiful on me if I would like to borrow it. I could tell she was trying to make amends for yesterday, so I said yes. Clyde's sisters had just turned his *Christmas Cookie* into a princess. It had been a year since I'd paid much attention to my appearance—it felt good to feel pretty again.

Clyde handed me my coat as I came down the stairs to the foyer. Man of few words, he shook his massive head up and down and said, "Yup, Cooks, this should do the trick."

Clyde had to be at the church early, so we took his car and headed out before the rest of the family.

As we approached the church, the light coming from the sanctuary made the stained glass windows glow in a kaleidoscope of colors. The church that had looked winter shabby in daylight, looked like a jeweled box surrounded by white velvet in the star-filled darkness. It needed no extra Christmas lights to look festive.

Clyde parked beside an old station wagon; we went into the church by the back door and made our way to the choir loft where we were greeted by the organist. That's when I learned the reason for our early arrival. Clyde was the "special music" for the Christmas Eve service.

His errands Sunday afternoon had included a rehearsal, but he and the organist were still deciding which carols Clyde would sing while the congregation gathered. As his voice rang out on the first few notes of "O Come, O Come, Emmanuel," my jaw dropped. Clyde Dale was an operatic tenor; his was the most beautiful voice I'd ever heard in person. And I'd assumed we had come early because the pastor needed something heavy moved. I sat and shook my head at just how often I had underestimated my friend.

Clyde would be spending the service beside the organist in the choir loft, but he guided me down the narrow back stairs and showed me where the Dales sat in the sanctuary. There were no assigned pews in the church, but families used the same seats every Sunday year after year. Clyde also pointed out where Mary Kay's family would be sitting−he thought I might like to know; he was right.

As people poured into the room, the sounds of Christmas greetings and coats being shed filled the small sanctuary, but as soon as Clyde began to sing, all chatter and movement ceased, even among Clyde's nieces and nephews. A cheerful reverence settled over the congregation. I've never again felt as warm and embraced by a church as I did on that cold winter night surrounded by the Dale family. The opening of the service was so simple, yet so beautiful. I could feel tears sting the back of my nose, but managed to quell them before they could ruin Laurie's wonderful makeup job.

I thought about all the Sunday school classes and church services that I'd attended while growing up. I think my mom chose the big impersonal Lutheran church downtown because it was well known. We went because it was expected and gave us a proper answer to the commonly asked midwestern question, "Which church do you attend?" I was confirmed in ninth grade only to mollify my mother; I'd never felt religious, could never swallow the dogma or the impossible stories about a virgin birth and a heaven where we would once again see those we'd loved. How was I supposed to believe in something I knew couldn't be true? The problem was, as I sat in that country church on Christmas Eve, surrounded by love, I wanted to believe.

The service ended with candlelight and Clyde leading the congregation in singing "Silent Night." As the lights came back on, I turned to look at Clyde in the choir loft and caught a glimpse of Mary Kay with her family and the guy I assumed was her fiancé. I was convinced of it when he gave me a little wave and Mary Kay quickly elbowed him in the arm. The rumor mill was already grinding away.

At the coffee following the service, Clyde introduced me around the basement fellowship room as his friend, Cookie. I smiled, chatted, and ate gooey peppermint cake. We never said, or even inferred, that we were anything more than what we were—friends and classmates. Just as Clyde had said, we didn't need to. As we were slipping into our coats to leave, one of the church ladies put her hand on my arm and said, "Oh, so you're Clyde's Christmas Cookie! I've heard so much about you from my daughter, Brenda—all good, of course!... I understand the wedding is this summer???"

When Clyde and I were saying our goodbyes to the family on the day after Christmas, Laurie told us that if she had ever questioned our true feelings for one another we had put her question to rest with the gifts we had given each other. "You guys are just friends!"

I had given Clyde a book that Dr. Sargent had

recommended to me, *People of Paradox: An Inquiry Concerning the Origins of American Civilization* by Michael Kammen. Clyde had given me a very nice metal cookie scoop. My indignant retort to Laurie was,

"I'll have you know, my gift to Clyde just won the *Pulitzer Prize!*"

Clyde, arms akimbo and mimicking my cadence, chimed in,

"And, I'll have you know, Cookie makes cookies that *vary in size!*"

His parents were still laughing as they hugged us goodbye.

Clyde stopped his car at the side of Dr. Sargent's house and got my bag off the pile of his things in the trunk. He set it on the sidewalk and gave me a big Dale family hug. As he set my feet back on the concrete, he said, "Thanks for being my friend. You know, if you ever need anything—you should call someone else." After a comedic pause, he added, "Not really, Cooks. I owe you big time. You know I'd do anything for you."

"Back at you, Turkey...I had a great time. Your family's wonderful—I wish mine could take lessons, of course we'll never achieve your numbers."

Clyde quipped, "Cooks, all seven-hundred of'm

loved you—would probably replace me with you given half a chance." He continued more seriously, "Mom wants you to come visit anytime—with or without me. She told me she really enjoyed your company."

I told him I'd love to take his mother up on her offer. Clyde waited on the sidewalk until I'd unlocked the side-door. I waved as he took off for Interstate-29 to start the drive south to Vicksburg and the month-long   independent study the Dr. Jon S. Leggett Memorial Scholarship would be funding.

—34—

I quietly rang in 1974 with Dr. Sargent. We raised our glasses to the loved ones of our past and the adventures of our futures, with the professor assuring me that mine would be greater than his. I thought of last year, toasting in the New Year with Annie in Boston, then sitting at my desk after she had gone to bed writing a six-page letter to Jon. I wrote about how much I loved him and already missed him. I told him how excited I was about our futures, both apart and together. Later, as I cried myself to sleep in my half-empty double bed, on that first night of 1974, I vowed to Jon that I would keep on adventuring. I'd make him proud.

January was a busy month at the house. It was Dr. Sargent's custom to arrange an interim class for senior students that brought in lecturers from across North America to discuss a specific historic theme. Class participants were expected to complete the assigned readings by each lecturer before he or she arrived. It was challenging for any student, but I had the extra challenge of serving as auxiliary host to the visitors for the five to seven days that they stayed at the house in Vermillion.

Dr. Sargent had devised an interesting way to find the three to four lecturers needed for his class. He would find his first speaker, normally a friend or acquaintance from his many years as a professor and historian. The first guest speaker would suggest a topic from American history that they would like to speak to and then personally recruit the next speaker in the series with the promise that their times in Vermillion would overlap. This process continued with the second lecturer recruiting the third and, sometimes, the third recruiting the fourth.

This method of assembling lecturers worked wonderfully for all: Dr. Sargent didn't have to do all the recruiting and occasionally had the opportunity to meet new people. It also provided a time for scholars (often friends) from across the country to meet in a quiet setting for deep discussion. Sometimes lecturers would mix it up by inviting individuals whom they would like to meet or get to know better—sometimes speakers really livened things up by inviting scholars with contrary views from their own. Or, as Dr. Sargent liked to say in one of his tongue-twisting alliterations, "Contestation creates academic conversation of far more pith and intensity than consistent consensus ever has."

Dr. Sargent's interim class was how I met my first Pulitzer Prize recipient, although he had yet to win his award, and I, as yet, had nothing to disagree with him about. Dumas Malone left the relative winter warmth of his home in Virginia to spend the first part of January in cold, snowy South Dakota. Dr. Malone was considered at that time — and still — to be one of the foremost scholars of Thomas Jefferson. He was in his early eighties when we met and already having serious problems with his vision, although that didn't stop him from completing two more books before his death in 1986.

During his stay with Dr. Sargent, I often helped Dr. Malone up the circular staircase to the darker second floor. By the end of the week I'm sure that Dr. Malone could have found his room without my assistance, but we'd established a nightly ritual we both enjoyed. I'd sit at the chess table in the upstairs foyer while we chatted through the open door of his bedroom as he prepared his lecture notes for the next day. Dr. Malone's voice was soft and Southern, requiring his audiences (large or small) to listen attentively. Afterward, I would hurry downstairs, neaten-up the main rooms, then rush to my apartment to keep ahead of the assigned reading.

The interim progressed in a flurry of books, pots of tea, pipe smoke, and talk of America's founders—the men who thought a group of disparate British colonies could band together to overthrow the greatest power on earth. Dr. Malone had chosen the specific subject of Dr. Sargent's class, *The Development of the Declaration of Independence*. However, the late night discussions were often free-for-alls covering all sorts of people and issues. I was mentally and physically drained by the end of January when I delivered the last guest lecturer to the Sioux Falls airport to fly home, but I was also sorry that I would no longer have multiple distractions. It would soon be a year since the day Jon had died. I didn't know how to face the next few weeks; part of me just wanted to fall asleep and forget everything.

I slept away the first weekend in February. Getting up to use the bathroom took monumental effort. I was as miserable as the weather. Classes didn't begin again until the eleventh and I had no PA duties for the week— I saw no reason to climb out from under my pile of blankets. I remembered my New Year's pledge to Jon to keep on adventuring, but I hoped that he would forgive me. I just couldn't face the first anniversary of his death.

On Tuesday morning Dr. Sargent knocked on my apartment door. He hadn't been to my rooms since I'd moved in last June. He was shocked by the cold, but I think also by my condition. I hadn't looked in a mirror for days, but I had a pretty good imagination. The professor told me that both he and Mrs. G were worried about me — Mrs. G feared that I might be ill. Dr. Sargent told me that he was afraid I was suffering from something that couldn't be cured with penicillin. He was experiencing it, too.

Later, when he returned with a space heater, he asked, "After the room warms, will you please think about getting up and coming to the kitchen for something to eat? Nothing would make Mrs. G happier than feeding you her chicken soup, and I would love to share some of the birthday cake that the department presented to me yesterday."

I climbed from bed half an hour later. The bedroom was warming, but the bathroom was still frigid. I set the shower handle to scalding, watching as the room fogged over. I stepped into the steam and proceeded to take the longest shower of my life. I washed my filthy hair then dressed quickly in thick socks, heavy jeans, turtleneck, and sweatshirt. I placed the space heater squarely in front of Jon's plaid chair, plopped down, and spent the next twenty minutes combing through my wet tangle of hair before braiding it and heading downstairs to the promised bowl of soup and birthday cake.

I told Mrs. G that I was feeling better without being at all specific about my illness. Her response was, "Ya don't look it. Eat sum more soup." After my fill of chicken soup, I took a pot of tea that Mrs. G had prepared, along with two slices of Dr. Sargent's birthday cake into the front rooms to join the professor in front of the foyer fireplace.

As he took the plate from me, the professor confessed, "The cake was a surprise from the history department. I didn't want to celebrate my birthday this year—not ever again, really."

"Why, Dr. Sargent? Jon wouldn't have wanted that."

"Sarah, Jon wouldn't be dead except for me and my foolish desire for company on my birthday. I am the reason he was in Vermillion—I'd asked him to come spend my birthday with me."

The pain in Dr. Sargent's face made him look so much older than he had just a week ago. "I'm sure he came because he wanted to, Dr. Sargent. He came because he cared for you—I'm the guilty one. He sent me his money. He knew he needed new snow tires and he sent me the money anyway. He wouldn't have lost control if he'd had decent tires."

"Oh Sarah, you don't know that—we don't know if the accident was caused by his tires. Even new tires slide on ice. Jon's death was not your fault, and if you are going to say that he was in Vermillion because he cared for me, I want you to know that he sent you the money because he loved you. Do not blame yourself."

"I can't help it."

"Nor can I. Our minds want to understand our loss—that's the way of human beings. We are suffering, and his death was senseless."

"Well—don't blame yourself—or your birthday. Jon wouldn't have wanted you to, and neither do I. Please, let's just eat your cake and talk about happier times."

So for the next uninterrupted hour we talked about Jon. Dr. Sargent told me about their first meeting, when Jon was interviewing for his position at the University. I told Dr. Sargent about my first real interaction with Jon, when I knocked his lecture notes over the balcony railing in Nelson Hall. Dr. Sargent laughed. He said that he'd heard about the incident at the time, but he had no idea that I was the culprit. "Sarah, if I had known what a mishap maker you were, I may never have hired you to mind my papers."

I told him that I was fairly sure that without that mishap I would've never registered on his personal radar, because I'm not sure that Jon and I would have fallen in love.

"I would have been just another history student —a good student, but one who wouldn't have garnered too much attention. I've thought a lot about it, Dr. Sargent—you've given me this wonderful opportunity to work for you, and it's changed my life, but without Jon having loved me and told you about me, even cryptically, I would be back in Sioux Falls commuting to Vermillion and struggling to make ends meet."

Dr. Sargent said that he didn't believe that to be true. He said that the more that he'd gotten to know me, the more he felt that Jon and I were meant for one another. He said had I worked with Jon on my interim project, even without the railing incident, Jon would have fallen in love with me.

"I hope you're right, Dr. Sargent... I don't want to think about a past where he didn't love me."

When Dr. Sargent spoke again, he said that what I had just told him was the perfect segue to a subject he had been wanting to discuss with me. He repeated what he had told me several times in the past—that he thought of me as his daughter, the only difference was this time he said "beloved daughter." Then he made an

221

offer that continued to change my life; he told me that upon my graduation he wanted, with my permission, to set up a trust in my name so that, until his death, or we mutually decided otherwise, I would receive a monthly stipend. It would be enough to cover my expenses and pay for grad school.

To say I was surprised would be a historic understatement. I was, also, speechless.

Dr. Sargent continued, "Lest you think that I want anything from you, Sarah, be assured that I do not. My only desire is that you not worry about money. You have the mind to be an excellent historian, but if you have to spend the majority of your time working to keep a roof over your head, you will have neither the time nor the energy to study in the way that you should, or the way in which you would like."

He continued, "Margaret and I married young. Her money is perhaps the only reason I have a Ph.D. today—I know that it is the only reason that I am a wealthy man. One of my joys in life is being in a position to help promising young people. That's you, Sarah."

I swallowed hard and shaking my head asked, "But—but how will I explain—?"

He chuckled, "No one will care where your money comes from, and I doubt anyone will ever ask. If any person should be indelicate enough to ask such a question, don't answer. It is no one's business but your own. Margaret and I have always had our finances and legal issues handled by firms in Chicago. No one in Vermillion knows of my holdings or how I spend my money, except, of course, on what's obvious. You will not be the first student that we have helped financially —Margaret and I began supporting deserving students years ago; perhaps it was our *de facto* form of adoption. I am sure that if she were here she would want to help you just as much as I do."

Of all the words I should have said, all I could muster was a heartfelt "thank you" as I cleared the Mondrian china covered with birthday cake crumbs.

—35—

In early March, I'd told Dr. Sargent that, with his permission, I was going to give myself a year after graduation to explore and attempt to observe what I thought might be history in the making. I'd promised Jon I'd have adventures, and, with Dr. Sargent's offer of a monthly stipend, he had given me the opportunity to start early.

I had always felt that I was a few years too young to have experienced the life that I would have liked to have lived. I wasn't longing for the distant past like so many of my history major friends. I just wished that I could have been a part of the Civil Rights March on Washington in August of 1963, or the huge Moratorium March against the Vietnam War or, even, Woodstock in '69. They were events in my lifetime that I was certain would be a part of U.S. history, but because of my age and circumstances I could only read about them. I wanted to be a part of something that would go down in history.

To that end, I'd decided that I wanted to spend the summer of 1974 in a hippie commune. In the back of my mind I knew that it was a silly idea—going to study an experience was not the same as going to live the life, but I couldn't stop thinking about it. I wanted to see, feel, and taste a historic event before it ended. I was assuming that '70's communes and the back-to-the-earth movement would someday join the pantheon of American utopian societies that historians liked to write about.

Dr. Sargent told me that I need never ask his permission to lead my life however I saw fit, and, instead of dissuading me from my plan, he'd encouraged me saying he didn't think that it would hurt my chances to get into a grad school when the time came. He told me normally a little extra experience and age was looked upon favorably by most academic acceptance committees.

In late March Dr. Sargent called me into his office at the U to tell me that he had been informed of a unique opportunity. Strangely, he first asked me if I could knit. When I said, "Yes," he then asked me if I liked "handicrafts."

"Some..." There was no way I wanted the Platoon guys to find out about any of this. "Please, tell me why you want to know?"

Dr. Sargent knew of my interest in art; he had helped me narrow my educational focus to art, and how it interacted with history, particularly that of the

American colonial period. I hadn't let him know I could knit, crochet, embroider, and sew. I hadn't told him my first grade teacher had told my mother that I could cut so well she thought I must have been born with a pair of scissors in my hand (not something that my mother wanted to consider).

I was hiding from my hobbies—I was embarrassed that I enjoyed pastimes perceived as primarily feminine. I think that was one of the reasons that the "Cookie" nickname made me so uncomfortable. Part of me was pleased that the Platoon liked my baking, but part wished no one would mention it—it was such a *domestic* pastime. I was already bussing their dishes and emptying their ashtrays as part of my duties as Dr. Sargent's PA. They didn't need to know I could knit their socks as well.

Dr. Sargent finally quit his line of questioning and told me he had just received a letter from Dumas Malone telling him of an internship opportunity that had crossed his desk at the University of Virginia. The Abby Aldrich Rockefeller Folk Art Center at Colonial Williamsburg was looking for interns to help design, assemble, and write instructions for craft projects utilizing traditional techniques and materials to be used in future publications and educational programs. The selected interns would be employed during the summer and housed in a dorm at The College of William and Mary in Williamsburg.

Dr. Malone had told Dr. Sargent that he'd been impressed by my intellect and maturity when he was visiting in January and knew I was fascinated by colonial art and architecture from our evening discussions. He'd finished his letter to the professor writing, "It would please me greatly to recommend Sarah for a Williamsburg internship."

I knew I should jump at the chance—not only because it was a fantastic opportunity to get to the East Coast, but because it was such an honor to be recognized by Dr. Malone. Instead I asked Dr. Sargent if I could have a day to think about it. I was so conflicted. It wasn't just working with traditional crafts —it was working for The Colonial Williamsburg Foundation. I thought of Rockefeller's Williamsburg as a place of romanticized patriotism and idealized history —Disneyland for flag waving-adults—and I wasn't sure I wanted to be a part of it.

The next morning, before I could give Dr. Sargent my reasons for saying no to the Williamsburg internship, he said, "Sarah, I hope you will accept the internship." He continued in his measured way, "I ask this of you for several reasons, but primarily because I believe you will find it a rewarding experience that will eventually unlock many doors for you. A recommendation from Dr. Malone and a successfully completed internship at Williamsburg will help get you into a graduate program at any of the Ivy League schools.

"I know you were looking forward to travel and experiencing life in a commune, but this internship is only for the summer. You will have months to travel and *commune* after the internship ends if you still plan on beginning your graduate studies in the fall of '75.

"You will have your weekends free to visit Jamestown and Yorktown—they are both relatively close to Williamsburg. And, you must realize how close you will be to Monticello. I know how intrigued you are with Jefferson's masterpiece."

As I cleared our coffee cups from the dining room table, I told Dr. Sargent that I would stop by his office at the University to pick up the application form. It appeared that after graduation I would be on my way to Williamsburg, Virginia.

I could say "no" to anyone but Dr. Benjamin Sargent, and the money had nothing to do with the way I felt about the man. His reasons were in my best interest—I knew that. I wanted to go to a good school; I wanted Harvard. If taking this internship would get me there, I would take it.

Poor Dr. Sargent, both of his student assistants were suffering from senioritis and spring fever. Clyde and I had been students for the majority of our lives and we were chomping for the reprieve of summer and a change of venue. Clyde was even more of a basket case than I was; besides being accepted for the master's program at the University of Pennsylvania, over interim he had fallen in love.

Clyde's new love, Cathy Knox, was a librarian in Vicksburg. Looking for a quiet place to work on his interim paper, Clyde had found his way to the public library. His habit had been to take his books and notes to the library every morning before it opened and wait on the steps until Cathy came to unlock the doors. Clyde'd said, "I'd noticed Cathy, and that way she couldn't miss seeing me."

I didn't explain to Clyde that if he snuck into a building under cover of darkness it was unlikely that anyone would miss him—he was as noticeable as a two-story house being moved down the middle of a highway during rush hour.

After a week of quiet flirtation, Cathy had asked him if he would like to have lunch with her. Clyde said if Cathy hadn't had to get back to work he thought their first lunch might have lasted all afternoon.

They had dated until Clyde had to leave Vicksburg at the end of interim. In truth, and I was the only one to know this, they lived together when Clyde decided to stay South the first week in February after he'd had to vacate the furnished apartment he had rented for January. Clyde told me that leaving Cathy was the hardest thing he'd ever done. I understood what he'd felt, but I'd thought to myself—*there is something so much harder—I hope you never have to face it*.

Over Easter break in mid-April, Clyde made the long drive back to Vicksburg to ask Cathy to marry him. She'd said yes with the stipulation of a long engagement—she didn't want to move to Philadelphia and wouldn't dream of asking Clyde to give up an advanced degree from an Ivy League school. They would live apart, but make it work—others had; they could too.

I was happy for my friend—my best friend—I really was, but I was also so jealous of their relationship I felt as though I was being stabbed whenever Clyde said Cathy's name. Sometimes I think Clyde could tell it hurt me; other times, like when he'd just received a letter from Vicksburg, he was so over the moon wanting to share his happiness, he would forget how I might feel. I tried to be a supportive friend and continued to hide my pain, although I'm sure I didn't always succeed.

Had I not spent the last year at Dr. Sargent's, I doubt I would have bothered to attend my graduation ceremony. It would have just entailed another boring drive to Vermillion and my parents had never cared for pageantry; I think they would have skipped my high school graduation ceremony if Aunt Thelma wouldn't have been shocked by their absence.

Not so with Dr. Sargent! He wanted to see me walk the stage with my class. He knew how hard I'd worked to make up the semester I'd missed my junior year. He was the only one who knew how much emotional pain I'd dealt with in the last year and a half. He never failed to tell me that he was proud of me and all that I had accomplished.

As I crossed the stage to be handed my diploma, a cheer went up from the crowd. I was shocked, then realized because my last name started with a B, I was the first member of Sarge's Platoon to walk the stage that day. Yes, it was undignified, but it was tradition.

That ragged shout of "Way to go, Cookie!" meant far more to me than the Phi Alpha Theta stole over my robe. When Clyde walked the stage a short time later, I cheered louder than I'd ever remembered cheering— mainly because it was Clyde, but partially to cover the laughter that had erupted when his name (with middle initial) was read over the loudspeakers.

Dr. Sargent hosted a graduation party for all the history graduates and their families at his house after the ceremony—another tradition. He had always hired extra help for the celebration so that his PA, a graduating senior, didn't have to work the party. I was thankful, but it was still hard for me to not clear glasses and throw out abandoned paper plates.

My parents, who'd surprised me by attending the ceremony, surprised me even more by coming to the reception. They stayed at the party for about an hour. Dad had been kind enough to borrow a truck from his work so that they could drive two vehicles to the University. They left the family car in Vermillion overnight, giving me and my luggage a way to get back to Sioux Falls the next morning.

Clyde's family and Cathy were some of the last guests to leave the party. Cathy had taken her vacation time to come meet her future in-laws and see Clyde graduate. After a stay at the farm, she and Clyde would head back to Vicksburg for the summer—Cathy would go back to her job at the library and Clyde would continue working on his battlefield research. In late summer Clyde, after a quick trip back to Iowa, would be off to Philly.

The Platoon members stayed around to eat and continue partying for most of the evening, also tradition. At one point Clyde and I slipped away to my apartment so that he could help me move some things to the attic. Dr. Sargent had given me permission to store Jon's chair, my stereo, and several boxes of my stuff on the third floor. My parents no longer wanted to house my things at their place. When I'd made a comment that I felt a little like I was being orphaned, Dr. Sargent had told me that as long as he had a home in South Dakota, I would too.

The party broke-up with one last wild, boisterous march of the "Platoon to the Saloon," another tradition. Dr. Sargent shook hands and hugged all the graduate Platoon members as we passed through his front door—I was included for tradition's sake, even though the professor and I knew we would say our goodbyes the next morning. It was the first time in all of our months together that Dr. Sargent had ever hugged me.

I woke for the last time in the apartment at the back of Dr. Sargent's grand house. I stripped the bed and shoved the full size sheets into the top of the box I was taking with me to Williamsburg. I knew the sheets would be too large for a dorm bed, but I figured they could get me through the summer.

Mrs. G had come early to fix a special goodbye breakfast for Dr. Sargent and me to share. The professor told me it was a first—she was normally overjoyed to see his PAs leave. I felt a little sorry for Dave Bendt, a junior member of the Platoon who would be moving into my job and apartment at the end of the week. Breaking in (or being broken by) Mrs. G was one of the biggest challenges of being Dr. Sargent's personal assistant.

While Dr. Sargent and I enjoyed a large German pancake with rhubarb sauce and warm bran muffins, we spoke very little. I was sad to be leaving the professor, and he had let me know it wouldn't be the same around the house without me. He told me he would even miss my annoying habit of practicing the same piano tunes "over, and over, and over".... Somehow, the way he said it made me have doubts.

I hefted my suitcase and box of things into the trunk of the Dodge. With tears running down my face I hugged both Mrs. G and Dr. Sargent, who had come out to the curb to see me off. I knew that this wasn't goodbye for good, but it was the close of an important chapter in my life.

I looked at the freshly plowed fields as I drove I-29 toward Sioux Falls. Shoots of bright green corn were already reaching to the sun in endless rows. This part of the world, so generous with its bounty in summer, could be unfathomably cruel in the winter. It had taken the love of my life from me with its capriciousness; I wasn't sure that I could ever forgive it.

As I reached the edge of the city, I decided to drive past Jon's former house before going home. Different curtains in the windows made me think it had been rented since I'd last seen it. I parked across the street from the front door and stared. I could almost see myself walking up the concrete steps in my rust colored hip-huggers that Friday after Thanksgiving a year and a half ago. If I could only go back. If I could use Jon's mathematical theory, the one he'd abandoned at MIT, and go back to spend those weeks with him all over again…maybe I could have changed something and given us a future….

Had Jon lived we would be celebrating the end of the school year and looking forward to a fun, leisurely summer. I imagined him washing his pickup on the gravel driveway, while I planted red petunias in the flower box under the living room window. In my daydream, when I asked for the hose to water my new plantings, he laughed and turned the spray on me. I ran at him and we fell to the grass, rolling in each other's arms as the hose nozzle danced, shooting water in all directions.

I sat, my eyes swimming, until a car passed waking me from my reverie. I wiped my tears, blew my nose, and started the engine. My life here was over.

Two hours later at the Sioux Falls airport I boarded a plane to Virginia, knowing that I would never live in South Dakota again.

PART THREE

Summer 1974

—36—

An early summer storm over the Blue Ridge Mountains made the small commuter buck and roll as it made its initial descent to the Richmond airport. Lightning flashed in the night sky while the airline supper I'd eaten earlier moved from my stomach to my throat. I had flown just twice before, on my trips to and from Boston, and, while I didn't remember much about my flight back to South Dakota a year and a half ago, I was sure that I had never experienced turbulence like this. As far as I was concerned, this one event would be enough for a lifetime.

I looked around for reassurance and noticed that the woman across the aisle from me was enjoying the air-pockets with gusto, obviously helped along by the five tiny gin bottles lined up in the elastic of the seat-back pocket in front of her. As she hooted, "Gawd, this is better 'n a carnival ride!" the man in the window seat next to me clutched his rosary and talked to his God in a bit quieter tone. I was caught between dispositions willing to emulate neither.

When I saw the flight attendant walking down the aisle without a hint of alarm on her face I took it as a good sign. If this sort of turbulence was an everyday occurrence, one to be taken in literal stride, I decided I would attempt to do just that. Settling my jumpy gut was another matter.... I found the air sickness bag in my seat-back pocket and set it unobtrusively on my lap. The only good thing about the short turbulent flight was that it hadn't allowed me time to fret about my internship and all the unknowns in the days ahead.

The plane and I landed without incident in Richmond, where a former student of Dr. Sargent's met me to drive me to my new home at The College of William and Mary. Had I arrived earlier in the day I would have taken the bus, but my late flight had meant a night in the bus station awaiting morning transport to Williamsburg. Dr. Sargent wouldn't hear of it. He'd insisted, "Sarah, what are former students for if not to help other former students. Don is part of the Platoon— he will be happy to assist you."

"Don" was at least twenty-five years my senior and a history professor at Randolph-Macon College in Ashland, Virginia. We weren't exactly contemporaries, but during the ride I discovered why Dr. Sargent had wanted us to meet.

Dr. Donald R. Miller was happy to tell me about his days in Vermillion and what an extraordinary young professor Dr. Sargent had been. He said that he hadn't seen his former professor in a few years, not since he had been back to South Dakota for Margaret Sargent's memorial service, but that he and Dr. Sargent wrote frequently. He insisted he was always happy to be of service to his old friend and requests came too infrequently to suit him. He said, what I already knew, Dr. Sargent was far better at giving than receiving.

When I asked Dr. Miller about his family he told me about his wonderful wife and amazing daughter. He then went on to tell me about his hippie son, David, who lived in the rural Twin Oaks Community. Dr. Miller didn't seem too excited about his son's decision to join a commune. He said that he would much rather have had David "finding himself" in a college or university setting, but he thought David was content. He added that he was happy David had at least chosen to stay close to home—Twin Oaks was in Louisa County, Virginia, roughly half way between Richmond and Charlottesville.

I silently thanked Dr. Sargent, then inundated Dr. Miller with questions about the commune for the rest of the drive. He told me what he knew: what he had seen while visiting David, what David had told him, and what he had gleaned on his own. I could tell that Dr. Miller was the sort of man who needed to do his own research to be completely satisfied with the findings. I asked if he thought it would be alright if I wrote to David at Twin Oaks. He said he thought it would be fine, however I should address my envelope to "Max"—from what he could tell, no one but his family members called him David anymore.

Dr. Miller helped me wrestle my suitcase and well-taped cardboard crate into my assigned dorm at the college, wished me well with my future endeavors in Williamsburg, then headed back to Ashland. When I couldn't find anyone to show me to my room, I curled up on the stiff orange couch in the dorm lounge, shoved my balled-up jean jacket under my head, and spent a very uncomfortable first night in my new home.

Un-air-conditioned Brown Hall was to be my home for the next two and a half very hot and moist months. South Dakota could be hot in the summer, but I had never experienced anything like the humidity of Virginia.

Shortly after 8:00, a sleepy student aide showed me to my second floor dorm room. Hair that had loosened from my braid during the night stuck to the sweat running down the new crevices in my face formed by using my denim jacket as a pillow. I looked like I had just traveled halfway across the continent and slept fitfully in a sweltering building on a hard vinyl couch. Shit. I looked like shit. I dropped my suitcase in front of my room door just as Mel walked down the long hall from the communal bathroom.

Mary Louise Meister, nicknamed Mel ("from M. L., you see" she later explained in her patrician drawl), lived in the room across the hall from me, but had lived a life so different from mine that it was as though we had been reared on different planets. How we had ended up neighbors (and eventually, friends) is still hard for me to fathom. She stood a good head taller than me and moved her lithe body with the inner tension of a ballet dancer. Her shoulder length blunt-cut was never out of place, her makeup was always perfect. She seemed unfazed by the heat and humidity. Basically, she was everything I was not.

Mel said hello as she entered her room, then closed her door. We met again ten minutes later on the stairs as I tugged my box of belongings up each riser. She did not offer to help, but blithely said, "See you this evening." If it is possible to be in awe of a person and dislike them at the same time, I would say those were my initial feelings toward Mel.

I threw my suitcase on the lower bunk mattress, rooted around for my toiletries and something cooler yet presentable to wear. I needed food and a map, but I needed a shower more than anything else. I was to be at the Folk Art Center by 10:00 when my summer internship would officially begin. I had no clue what to expect.

—37—

A shower helped. Breakfast and a tourist map helped a little more. By 9:40, I was standing outside the Abby Aldrich Rockefeller Folk Art Center after a short walk from the dorm. Brown Hall was in a commercial area located between Colonial Williamsburg and William and Mary, which, I supposed, was why it had been chosen as the intern residence, although on some long sweltering nights I thought it had been selected to broil us.

With all the courage I could feign, I entered the double doors of the Center. It was blissfully air-conditioned! I introduced myself at the reception desk and was shown to the offices of the woman who would be my elusive supervisor that summer (I saw her three times after our initial interaction). She told me what my duties would entail, handed me a stack of books, then showed me to a nearly windowless lower level of the building. I was assigned a large work table in a white-walled office that already housed the other intern working on the project.

Jenny had started the week earlier, making her the *de facto* senior intern, which bugged me endlessly because she was still a student while I was the proud possessor of a newly minted university diploma. Jenny was a local and had volunteered at Colonial Williamsburg for years, so perhaps she deserved her senior status—it still bugged me.

Our supervisor had given Jenny orders to spend the afternoon introducing me to my surroundings, first the Abby Aldrich Rockefeller Folk Art Center and then the whole of ticketed Williamsburg—which she did after taking me to lunch in her parents' kitchen: egg salad sandwiches, potato chips, strawberries, and a doting mother. I quickly figured out why Jenny was so annoyingly sweet; the mango hadn't fallen far from its tree.

My job that summer was to get to know Colonial Williamsburg and the arts and crafts that made the Historic Area seem authentic. I was to do the same at the Center, with no worries about authenticity—folk art is nothing if not authentic. After studying the collections, Jenny and I were to identify those crafts that could be easily replicated by people in their own homes. We were then, and I quote, "to make stuff." Home crafting was becoming a popular pastime, and some of the honchos in the advertising and promotions department had decided that crafting and decorating instruction books under the Williamsburg umbrella would both sell well and promote the brand.

Jenny and I worked away the next two and a half months *making stuff*. We designed, created, and wrote the instructions and historical notes for the core of craft projects that the Center's staff used in following years for its educational programs and instructional books. By mid-July the office that had seemed so bare my first day was awash in brightly colored fabrics, yarns, and jars of paint. Jen's and my concept sketches covered the walls, along with quilts, hooked rugs, and wooden signs loaned to us for inspiration by the collections department.

Jenny invited me to join her family for dinner that first evening, but I told her I still needed to unpack and learn my way around Brown Hall. I was hoping I would find a kitchen down one of the long corridors in the dorm because I couldn't eat out every day and I did not want to become dependent on Jenny's charity. Also, Jenny was fine on her own, but when she was with her mother they were so cloyingly sweet to one another they made my teeth ache.

I strolled back to the dorm slowly, taking in my surroundings. Other than the heat making me feel as though I were in hell, I was in heaven. Williamsburg was more than I'd hoped for, and not nearly as hokey as I had feared. Now that I could look at the buildings and grounds without having to take notes on what Jenny was telling me, I could really appreciate what I was seeing.

I walked along the Palace Green up to the grand Governor's Palace then back down the street carefully examining the architecture of the houses to my right. My mind filled with thoughts of the people who had walked that same street two hundred years earlier, like Thomas Jefferson and George Mason, the statesman that Jon had so admired. I was feeling some of the same joy I had experienced when Annie and I walked the Freedom Trail in Boston. With a big history nerd smile on my face, I nearly skipped my way back to the dorm.

I left my room door open to the hallway to catch the nonexistent breeze and unpacked my few belongings. I'd been warned about the Virginia heat, so my clothes didn't take up much space: a few skirts and light-weight tops for work and my worn T-shirts and cut-offs for the rest of the time. Most of my suitcase had been filled with books, as was the cardboard box I had bounced up the stairs. I gave my diploma pride of place on the built-in desk, right alongside my clock radio. The glass heart with Jon's picture was still in my purse—I set it on the shelf at the head of the lower bunk and flopped onto the mattress.

I woke from my nap when I heard Mel gently knocking at my open door. As I lifted my sweat-soaked head, she asked me if I'd had a difficult first day of work. Her expression never changed, so I had no idea if she was mocking me or if she genuinely cared. I guessed mocking, but told her the truth; work had been fine, but the night before had been challenging and I wasn't sure if I would ever get accustomed to the South's killer combination of heat and humidity.

At that she smiled slightly and said, "I hope you do." Because of her lack of expression, again I couldn't tell if she was wishing me well or just hoping she wouldn't have to watch me drip all summer. I invited her to take the desk chair, and while I sat on the edge of my unmade bed we got to know one another as well as anyone gets to know Mary Louise Meister.

She said that she was oblivious to weather, "perhaps a phenomenon that occurs when a person has lived their entire life in all parts of the world."

Before I could ask why she was so well traveled, she asked if I was from South Dakota and how I had decided to make my first home after University a dorm room at William and Mary. Over the course of an hour she asked about my love of history, if I preferred AM or FM, and if I had left a boyfriend back in the "cool, dry hinterlands." Her questions were pointed, and I wondered how she already knew so much of my past until I looked around my room. She had read it like a book.

Mel eventually told me she had stopped to see if I would like to join her on her weekly trip to the grocery store. She explained there was a shared kitchen and laundry on the main floor of the dorm across from the larger lounge. She said the guys staying on the third floor had access to it, too, but so far none of her yogurt had been pilfered. She suggested I put a magic marker on my shopping list. She said it was best to treat dorm life (which she now knew was new to me) just like summer camp—label everything. I didn't have the confidence to tell her that I had never been to summer camp either.

After taking some time alone to redo my hair and make a shopping list, I met Mel and her olive green 1969 Aston Martin on Prince George Street. She said the car had been with her all through college. It was her high school graduation gift from her father; it didn't take me long to figure out that it was not a used car when she had been given the keys. I chose not to tell her that she'd seen my parents' high school graduation gift to me, too—the beige Sears Forecaster suitcase sitting on my dorm room floor.

Mel and I nibbled on our fresh groceries as we labeled and stashed things in the fridge and freezer. Thankfully, there were a few cubes in the frosty aluminum trays. As I iced my warm Coke I made a mental note to buy more trays and keep them filled. I remember thinking, "If I'm gonna make it through this summer, I'm gonna need a shitload of ice."

The male interns, i.e. the guys from the third floor, were in the lounge across from the kitchen watching TV. It was some stupid Monday night movie, but one of guys had suggested that since it was Monday they should call it like a football game. Their voices and ensuing laughter rang down the hall. Mel excused herself, but said I should go make myself known. Her high praise for her fellow interns was, "They're harmless."

Mel and I were the only women on second floor. Third floor housed five guys. Mel was right, they were harmless; loud, but harmless. After my year as second-in-command of Sarge's Platoon I was perfectly comfortable in a room full of cacophonous history majors. Truth was, I finally felt at home; while some of the guys may have been a bit more sophisticated than the history nerds I knew in South Dakota, they were still stereotypically familiar.

I pulled up a chair and joined in the play-by-play until we all gradually tired of it. During a kung fu rom-com you can only say, "the kick was wide right," "it's going to be a hail Mary pass," and" he's going all the way," so many times before it gets repetitious. The movie on its own was dreadful, and we were soon talking over it (no one ever turned off the TV—it ran all summer long).

We told one another about our internships. I was more than slightly envious when I heard about some of the projects. Scott, the guy from Berkeley, was helping map the location of a tavern from the early 1700s. Rodney, down from Penn, was working at the DeWitt Wallace Decorative Arts Gallery with the artists restoring and researching the origins of 18th Century English and American furniture. When I told the guys what I was doing, they feigned being impressed until Earl said, "So, you're crocheting Christmas ornaments. Like you really need a B. A. for that." Earl was part of an archaeological team working on a dig close to the edge of the Historic Area. My response was, "Well, at least I'm doing research…it seems you're paying a hell of a lot of money to Dartmouth to get credit for playing in the dirt." He shut up.

Later that evening, I tried out my new built-in dorm desk. I pulled my office-sized dictionary from the shelf above the desk and wrote three letters: one to Dr. Sargent to give him my impressions of my first day on the job and thank him for having the stipend sent directly to my bank in Sioux Falls; another to Annie to tell her how, as I walked down the streets of Williamsburg, I'd felt some of the same joy I'd felt when we'd walked the Freedom Trail in Boston; and the last, to David "Max" Miller to introduce myself and ask questions about the Twin Oaks commune. Williamsburg was fine, but I still wanted my commune adventure when my internship ended.

With all my proofing and spell-checking, it took several hours to write the three short notes. I thought about how Jon had asked me to write without proofing or censoring myself. Writing those letters to Jon had become the favorite part of my day while in Boston. It was so freeing to let him know my thoughts without second guessing myself, and I loved getting his letters where he had done the same for me. I'd destroyed them all, as we had agreed, but I would've given almost anything that night to have had one more "pillow-talk" letter. I still missed him so much.

—38—

Work occupied much of my time, but I also spent hours, especially at the beginning of the summer, hanging out with my new pals from the third floor and attending intern events. Mel and I, having already graduated, were not required to attend the official intern meetings. As far as I remember, Mel skipped them all. I, on the other hand, went to nearly all the early summer gatherings—I enjoyed getting to know my fellow history majors, and I liked the collegiate vibe and group activities.

Mel had told me she was taking a break from people (which sort of made me wonder what I was...). She'd attended boarding schools when she was young and had spent the last four years living on a campus. Conversely, up until a year ago, I had spent my life in self-imposed solitary confinement. I was reveling living in the company of history-loving strangers. That could be another reason Mel shunned the group—she had been an English/journalism major. Art history had been her minor. Her first love was fashion and, as a whole, we history types were not a fashionable bunch.

Mel's internship was with the costume department at Williamsburg. It was a way for her to fill her summer and pad her resumé before heading to a junior position at Women's Wear Daily in the fall. Her job at Colonial Williamsburg was part of an effort to bring more authenticity to the costumes worn by the living historians throughout the Historic Area. She was part of an ongoing study examining colonial art, writings, and period clothing to determine what individuals wore, and for what occasions they wore it: Did footmen wear lace? Were corseted bodices ever worn exposed? What colors were appropriate for daywear in the 1700s?

I would have thought that her love of fashion and writing made it a perfect internship for her, but she told me that she'd hoped for something a bit more hands-on. It seemed that Mel wanted my job. She wanted to make stuff—clothing to be specific. She had tried to talk her supervisor into letting her create costuming as part of her assignment, but had been told no. Her desire to prove herself to her boss was the main reason Mel and I became close that summer.

Mel asked me if I would help her by becoming her human dress form. She had bet her supervisor that she could design and construct a garment that could pass as an original piece from the 1770's. The experts in the costume department were to be the judges, so Mel knew the deck was stacked against her. She didn't care—she believed she could do it.

Mel wasn't planning on making just one garment, she wanted to make a dress with all the required underpinnings and accessories. It was to be made entirely by hand with authentic eighteenth-century materials and techniques. When I asked why she wouldn't make it to fit herself, she looked at me as though I had just asked her to juggle upside-down. She explained that to do so would take her twice the time and, moreover, she was not the size of a typical colonial woman. At a skosh over five foot and under a hundred pounds, I was.

It didn't take us long to know that we couldn't work in either of our second-floor rooms because of the evening heat and lack of floor space. We moved our operation down one floor to the smaller front lounge and stitched in front of a large box fan in one of the windows. Mel let me work on the muslin prototypes used to construct the patterns, but the silks and fine linens that she had so carefully selected for the finished garments were cut and stitched by Mel alone. She asked me not to be insulted, but she wanted the dress pieces to be sewn completely by her hands, as much for her own satisfaction as to stay true to the wager.

My primary memory of helping with the dress was of me standing on a wooden footstool while turning as slowly as a clock's minute hand. Every now and then I'd ask Mel if I could hop down to stretch my stiff legs and aching back. I thought her attention to detail might be killing me, and if I hadn't been so intrigued by her, I may have told her to shove her fancy dress up the tailpipe of her sports car. But, Mel was unfailingly interesting and often thoughtful in her own casual manner: she always included me on her grocery shopping runs and threw my few clothes in with hers when she did her laundry. Also, I suspected that she was the person refilling the ice trays.

Mel constructed the bodice stays first. As was eighteenth century custom, she'd also made a loose shift of white linen to be worn under the stays. All of the dress fittings were made atop these two garments. She would be kneeling with straight pins clamped between her lips while pinning tucks in the heavy silk muttering at me to, "kit setting-ur gunna' may da faric dice run." It took me days to figure out that she was saying, "quit sweating—you're going to make the fabric dyes run." I was thankful whenever I could shrug off the weighty silks to let her stitch.

While waiting, I'd quietly play the lounge piano in my colonial under-pinnings listening for Mel to summon me for the next fitting. I thought of the stays as a combination back brace and push-up bra. I felt far more like a saloon girl living in the Old West than a colonial lady to the manor born. The get-up inspired a few wolf whistles from the guys as they'd pass by the open lounge door on their way down the hall to the TV, but there was no way I was going to put on more clothing. Usually one piercing look from Mel would send the dorm perverts on their way.

Mel never spoke of herself during those evenings, but she taught me to think about fashion more seriously. We discussed how world events had changed fashion through the decades and, conversely, how fashion had occasionally changed world events. We discussed how furniture designs were adapted to accommodate women's gowns and how fashion influenced interior design. She spoke of her research and how studying the clothing worn by subjects in paintings gave historians clues into their lives. Looking at fashion through Mel's eyes made me appreciate it as a living part of history in a way I never had before.

—39—

Max Miller's answer to my first letter had come in early June. He said he was surprised our introduction came from his father, but he would try not to hold it against me—I was relatively sure that he was joking.

In his letters Max seemed wise beyond his years, not the confused kid his father had implied. He told me he had moved to Twin Oaks three years earlier, roughly the same time his classmates were starting their freshman years at colleges up and down the East Coast. Max said he'd graduated high school unsure of his future, but knowing that he wanted a break from school. He enjoyed reading philosophy and working with his hands. He said he thought he would have made a fine monk, had it not been for his dislike of both organized religion and celibacy. For now, he felt the commune was a good fit.

Max asked if I would like to come visit Twin Oaks for a day or two. To further entice me, as if I needed it, he told me how close the commune was to Monticello—just a hop, skip and jump from Thomas Jefferson's home. I loved the idea, but I had no transportation. When I wrote of my dilemma, Max said he understood—his offer was a standing one. Or, as he deadpanned in his letter, "If you find some wheels, I have a place for you to crash." It was too soon for me to think his joke funny, but he had no way of knowing that.

Mel and I would soon be done with her sewing project and, even though she still intimidated me a little, I felt I had the upper hand. After having spent hours as her animated dress form, wearing stays in the Virginia heat, I figured she owed me a favor. She could either loan me the Aston Martin, or better yet, accompany me on my adventure to Monticello and Twin Oaks. To help convince her to come with me, I shared Max's letters. Mel was intrigued.

Early on the Saturday morning of the first weekend in August, Mel and I headed northwest. Our plan was to drive to Monticello for a day of touring, then, in the late afternoon, go to Twin Oaks, just outside of Louisa, Virginia, for dinner with Max and his friends. Max had arranged our accommodations for the night and planned a grand tour of the commune and surrounding area the next morning. On Sunday afternoon we would return to Williamsburg. I was hoping after the trip I'd have a better idea of where to go at the end of the summer.

The Aston Martin roared as we wound our way through the green hills of Virginia toward Monticello. The day was warm, but for a blissful change the humidity was low. Mel looked perfectly in control as she passed through the gears of the sports car. No change there— Mel always looked perfectly in control no matter what she was doing. She was particularly happy that morning because the evening before she had put the finishing stitches into her eighteenth-century frock. It was magnificent. The following week, she would be presenting it to the staff of the costume department for their inspection. Even given her uncompromising judges, neither of us had any real doubts about the outcome of her wager.

Monticello was everything I had hoped it would be. Mel had visited the house and grounds in the past and said it was busier than she had remembered. I wondered if the recent Fawn Brodie book on Jefferson had increased visitor numbers—as if people could know the truth about Jefferson and the enslaved Sally Hemings by merely walking the grounds or looking at his alcoved bed. If only knowing the truth of historical events were that easy—no more working away in libraries and archives. Just show up at historical sites and magically know what had happened hundreds of years ago—wouldn't that be grand!

I listened carefully as the docent talked about the house and the gardens. I knew quite a bit at that point about Jefferson, but I was amazed when I saw the Entrance Hall walls in Monticello covered with the items he had chosen. There were maps and paintings, but also minerals, fossils, bones, and antlers. He'd included items sent to him by Lewis and Clark from the wilds of the West, as well as smooth marble busts of "Great Thinkers" carved in Europe. I thought back to the first time I saw Dr. Sargent's house and my amazement at his abstract paintings and the souvenirs from his world travels like the ornately carved antique Chinese desk. It seemed both he and Jefferson wished to entertain and educate their guests, while surrounding themselves with the things they loved.

As we'd walked through the house, the docent had said something that made me think more about what it meant to be a learned person in the 1700s. She said Jefferson's goal had been to read the entire canon of written word and he had learned several languages to do just that. In his day attaining that level of self-education was considered a possibility. The idea floored me—I had always been a good student, but there was so much I didn't know, could never learn. Only two hundred years had passed since Jefferson had lived at Monticello, but man's knowledge and the written word had expanded exponentially in that time.

Before we left Jefferson's home, I squirreled away a brochure and diagram of the house with a map of the grounds, hoping to get back while I lived at Twin Oaks. Mel had taken a few photos and promised me copies when she got them developed.

As we reached the turn to the commune, Mel spotted Max and erupted in an involuntary hum of pleasure that sounded as though it had launched from her solar plexus. At five-eight, he was shorter than Mel, but built like a bear in mid-summer: lean, broad, and powerful. He'd apparently gotten his smoldering good looks from his mother's side of the family, because he didn't resemble his pale Midwestern father one iota. Max's long hair was dark, just like his intense eyes. As he waved us around the corner, I couldn't take my gaze off the size of his hands—think Michelangelo's Statue of David proportions—basically, catchers' mitts.

Max's plan had been to jump in the back seat and lead us down the twisting gravel roads to the main compound, but when he saw the size of the the Aston Martin's back seat and looked about to change his mind, Mel quickly said, "Sarah will be happy to sit in back."

I curled up in the back seat as Max gave Mel directions. Aston Martins are not meant for gravel roads, and I'm glad we didn't have far to go. Mel, on the other hand, seemed ready to follow Max anywhere —if he'd directed us to the Atlantic Ocean via back roads she wouldn't have questioned him. It was behavior very unlike what I'd seen from my new friend in the past months.

Early Sunday morning I awoke to a note on the pillow beside me. It was on a heavy off-white note card, the kind Mel used all of her adult life for short messages. Other than the distinctive *MLM* monogram, all it said was, "Gone Out" in her perfect cursive. I don't think I would have worried about her, but it was nice of Mel to think that I might have. We were to have shared the double bed, but other than the card, her side had not been disturbed.

A few hours later as I walked to the dining hall, I saw a not so flawlessly coiffed Mel, still in yesterday's clothing, crossing an open grassy area on her way toward our shared room. She had her 35mm Nikon around her neck and an uncharacteristic smile across her face.

Max and Mel came to breakfast separately and greeted me and one another cordially. Max treated Mel no differently than he did me, but, if you looked at their eyes when they spoke, it was evident that they were more than simple acquaintances. I wondered if anyone had ever noticed a similar gaze between Jon and me. God, was I jealous again! It was just like I'd felt about Clyde and Cathy—I didn't want Max, but I wanted what I'd had with Jon. I wanted Jon back.

After breakfast Max showed the two of us around Twin Oaks. If Mel was already familiar with some of the places he took us, she didn't say anything. While we walked the dirt paths between buildings, she and Max discussed philosophical aesthetics—they may as well have been speaking a foreign language. At that time my knowledge of philosophy was limited to John Locke and the Enlightenment. If it wasn't an idea espoused in the Declaration of Independence, I was lost. Once again I was realizing how little I knew and how much I had yet to learn.

Just when I thought our tour of the grounds was ending, Mel asked Max if he would show me his work.

He had shown us the work areas of the commune and shared information about tasks that all commune members were expected to perform, so I was curious as to what Mel was referring. Max looked at her and said, "Only for you, Mel—only for you."

We took off walking across the field that I'd seen Mel crossing before breakfast. After about a fifteen-minute trek we came to an open valley with one of the most amazing structures that I have ever seen. Max had built a thirty-foot sculpture from castoff furniture, farm implements, and scrap wood from derelict buildings. It was shaped like the Eiffel Tower, wide at the base and narrowing as it reached for the sky. It's hard to describe the wonder of this work of art built by the twenty-year-old son of a disappointed father, but years later when I saw a Broadway production of *Les Miserables* the famous barricade scene brought back memories of that morning.

At its base, along with other objects, were a green patinaed cupola from an old barn, the rusted carcass of a Model T truck, and a massive Hoosier cupboard. The whole piece was an astonishing feat of engineering, as well as an impressive work of art. Every item had been placed so that the viewer's eyes were drawn to the apex of the sculpture. Every board was placed to cast an ideal shadow. Max had spent years working on it with the help of other commune members and grateful locals who appreciated having their rubble hauled away.

Max couldn't miss the joy and amazement on my face as I walked around the base of his sculpture. When I exclaimed, "My god, Max, everyone should have the chance to see this!" His response was "Thanks, Sarah, but that's not why I made it."

Mel and I left Twin Oaks around noon for the drive back to Williamsburg. I was happy with what I had seen and fully intended to come back for an extended stay at the end of summer.

—40—

Mel had thought of everything. From the cap on my head to the silk shoes on my feet. I was the perfectly dressed colonial woman. She and I began our preparations before dawn on the Monday after we returned from Twin Oaks so she could shoot her photos in the morning light. I'm not a huge fan of early morning, but I was grateful we could work when it was cooler outside and I didn't have to take any time off work.

Mel photographed me in the gardens of Williamsburg. We had piled my hair in an exaggerated bouffant with curled tendrils at the nape of my neck. The golden gown shimmered in the soft morning light, contrasting beautifully with the pale blue stomacher and petticoat. Mel had embroidered the ruffles at my elbows and fabric shoes with pastel flowers. Hidden in the pale green leaves and vines were the curves and loops of her initials in cursive—*mlm*.

Without my glasses I was nearly blind, so Mel had me take her arm as she led me to the garden. When I asked why I couldn't wear my glasses until we started shooting, she told me they were so heavy they made marks on my face. She didn't want anything to skew the illusion of the 1770s—not even pad dents on the sides of my nose.

After the photo session, while she was helping me unpin the stomacher and unlace the stays, Mel told me that this was her second early morning in a row. The day before, she and Max had gone out at dawn to photograph his sculpture. She said that, as far as he knew, hers would be the only photos ever taken of what he called Opus I. They had worked together to get the aspects and angles he thought best represented the work. Mel said that she would show them to me before she sent them to Max. She was having them developed overnight along with the gown photos.

On Wednesday evening Mel met me at my room door with the gown in her arms. From her face I couldn't tell if the wager had gone her way or if her costume critics had found some minor flaw in her design or handwork. Before I could ask, she pushed the dress toward me and said, "It's yours."

"Did… didn't they like it?" I stammered.

She smiled, "They loved it. They even offered to buy it from me."

"Mel, why didn't you sell it? It must have cost you a fortune to make, and you have so many hours wrapped up in it."

Mel's reply was the same as Max's had been the day before. "That's not why I made it. I made it for the experience and to prove a point. I don't need it anymore."

She went on to tell me that she thought I deserved it much more than anyone at Colonial Williamsburg. "Not just for helping me with my wager, but for introducing me to Max Miller. He's not like any man I have ever met, and whatever happens between us, well, it wouldn't have happened without you. Giving you the dress is the only appropriate 'thank you' I can think of. If you don't want it, *you* can sell it."

We hung the gown on its padded hanger from the top of my closet door. Mel helped me pin the stomacher, petticoat, and sleeve ruffles in place so that the dress looked like a single garment. We put the shift, stays, cap, mitts, hose, and shoes in one of my empty dresser drawers. Mel mused, "this must be a first for a girls' dorm—an empty drawer." She said something about me living a like a Shaker. "No, I'm just poor," I replied, even though, thanks to Dr. Sargent, my checkbook was fatter than it had ever been. Being cash-strapped was so ingrained that it would take time for me to think of myself as anything but a pauper.

At our celebratory dinner, Mel shared the photos she had taken of me in the dress. I barely recognized myself. It wasn't just the dress and hair—my posture was from a different century. The stays stiffened my torso and lifted my breasts. Mel had adjusted my hands, feet, and the tilt of my head for each shot, but the biggest change of all was in my eyes. Because my vision blurred six inches from the end of my nose, my gaze was at nothing. I appeared lost in a pleasant dream. I was a colonial Mona Lisa. Mel offered me some of the photos, but I chose only one. I thought she should have the pictures; I had the dress.

Mel also showed me the photos of Max's sculpture. Her pictures were magnificent and, while no photo could completely capture the awe of the physical structure, her shots came close. She gave Max most of the credit. She said as they'd walked around the sculpture Sunday morning, he'd described precisely the angles he'd wanted her to capture. He chose the play of the shadows and the position of the lens—she said she'd shot as he'd directed and agreed with everything he'd said. I told her while that may have been true, she had *taken* the photos, and they were splendid.

Max and I wrote a few more letters to one another, but they were primarily concerned with the workings of Twin Oaks and the logistics of my move. That August the majority of his letters to Brown Hall were to Mel. She and I started planning our post-internship adventure. I no longer had to worry about how I was going to get to the commune, as Mel was more than happy to drive to Twin Oaks again. So, my immediate future was planned.

Until it wasn't.

A week before the end of my internship I was approached by my supervisor and offered a permanent position at Williamsburg. The offer tore me in two; it was good news that I didn't want to hear. I'd been looking forward to my move to Twin Oaks. I thought it was my chance to be part of a movement—something I thought might have a place in the written history of the United States. But the offer from Colonial Williamsburg was a real job—not something temporary, not just something to help get me by, but a real post-college position in my field of study that paid more than I could have imagined.

With Dr. Sargent's assistance I was putting finishing touches on applications to three graduate programs. All were expensive, and even though Dr. Sargent had been reassuring, admission was not guaranteed. If I got into grad school, I would need money, and, if I didn't get into grad school, I would need a job. Also, as much as I'd thought about joining a commune, I still didn't know if it would be the *real* experience I was hoping for. I would be living the life to study it. How did that make it any different from any of the other things I studied? And, coming back to money (which it seemed I always did), I would have to pay to spend time at Twin Oaks, since I wouldn't be staying long enough to be considered a full-time resident.

In the end, I couldn't say no to the Williamsburg job.

With the help of Jenny's mother, I quickly found a cheap furnished apartment. The landlady was a friend of hers and explained that the unit had been abandoned unexpectedly by the former occupant. I paid three months rent, sight unseen, before it could be snapped up by a William and Mary student. It was close to campus, which meant it was close to Colonial Williamsburg—vitally important to me since I didn't own a car. Being furnished was another plus.

Mel and I moved out of Brown Hall on Saturday, August 24. After carrying my suitcase, cardboard box, and beautiful colonial gown to the first floor lounge, we loaded Mel's two suitcases into the Aston Martin. She had teased me about not having much—surprisingly, she had even less. After hugs and promises to keep in touch, I watched as she took off for the commune without me. Mel had to be in NYC to start her job at *Women's Wear Daily* in less than a week, but she was unwilling to leave Virginia without seeing Max again.

I was expecting Clyde Dale to arrive at the dorm within the hour. He'd planned to visit me at Twin Oaks on his way to school in Pennsylvania and deliver the warm clothing that I'd left in the attic at Dr. Sargent's house. When my plans changed, he'd offered to come anyway and bring my stereo and records as well. I was flattered that he would make the extra drive (Williamsburg was farther off his path), until he explained that the detour would afford him the opportunity to visit a few more Civil War battlefields during his move East.

Clyde and I shoved my suitcase atop his things in the trunk of the old Rambler. He threw my box of books on the backseat, then held Mel's massive dress while I settled into the passenger seat. Clyde carefully laid the creation, still pinned together, in my lap, where it billowed up and swallowed me whole. Clyde laughed as I disappeared under the golden silk, saying, "It's been nice seeing you, Cooks. Wish it could have been for longer." I pushed the dress skirt away from my face, faking a sputter, and told Clyde how to get to my new place only three blocks away on Scotland Street.

The key was where the landlady had hidden it that morning. Because the unit had been empty, the owner was doing me a favor by letting me move in a week early. I still hadn't seen the place. We trudged up the steep wooden stairs loaded with my stuff. Key in the lock, I shoved open the recalcitrant front door. High ridges in the living room's dirty green shag carpet were the problem. A gray Herculon couch that smelled like cat piss and a small air-conditioner installed in the window behind it were the only furnishings in the cavernous room. I quickly flipped on the AC and the unit roared to life.

"Whoa, Cookie, this is *quite* a place," Clyde said,

as he steadied himself after tripping over one of the folds in the filthy carpet.

"Thanks for stating the obvious, Turkey," I probably would've called him by a less friendly name had he not been carrying my stereo and records. "Set those down over there, and let's get the rest of the stuff before we take the *grand* tour."

After another trip up the rickety outside stairs, we dropped my things and Clyde's sleeping bag on the living room floor, then followed the matted traffic pattern in the shag carpet to a little kitchen.

An orange and brown kitchen print wallpaper covered the lower six feet of the walls; above that was a green and blue floral design from several decades earlier. Whoever had decided to wallpaper over the blue flowers had evidently not owned a ladder; they wallpapered to the top of their reach. Had the paperhangers measured to create an even line it might have looked intentional, but they'd chosen to cut the paper off in uneven strips so that it formed an ugly jagged border around the room about three feet from the ceiling.

The room was furnished with an ancient refrigerator, a rusting metal sink unit with lower cabinets, an apartment-size electric stove, and an ugly 1950s chrome and vinyl dinette set patched with peeling duct tape. Clyde just muttered, "It's good you like old stuff, Cookie."

The bathroom was off the kitchen. I invited Clyde to take the first tour of the facilities. He came out wiping his hands on his cut-offs. "Cooks, the drain is slow and your hot water doesn't work."

"That's ok," I responded, "if the air conditioner doesn't cool things down a little, I'll be taking cold showers anyway."

Clyde and I agreed the bedroom was the best room in the place. It had a full size bed, an old bureau with a foggy mirror atop, and a bedside table with a lamp. The walls were covered in blotchy off-white wallpaper printed with faded pink roses. The plaid indoor/outdoor carpeting on the floor didn't match anything, but appeared to be clean.

The room's main decorative feature was located above the bed, which was pushed into a corner of the tiny room. On the plaster wall a former tenant had carved "FUCK" in big block letters. On seeing the graffiti, Clyde motioned toward it and said, "Nice touch." We then began discussing what the carver could have been thinking. We decided punctuation would have helped us decipher the word, especially in its prime location above the bed: FUCK — was it a hopeful question (?), a forceful command (!), or, what I was feeling by then, a muttered statement of defeat (.)

Clyde and I had a fun weekend of exploration and catching up. He had lots to tell me about his summer with Cathy and I had all of Williamsburg to show him in a day—not nearly enough time for two history buffs.

We spent most of the weekend away from my new apartment. Given the choice of sleeping on the smelly couch or dirty carpet, Clyde chose to unroll his sleeping bag on the floor. He said he thought it was *possibly* as clean as the ground at the campgrounds where he'd been spending his nights, and while the inside air wasn't as fresh, the air-conditioning was nice. Clyde has always been a "glass-half-full" person.

Monday morning, August twenty-sixth, after saying our goodbyes, Clyde took off to find the site of Fort Pocahontas at Wilson's Wharf, and I stayed in Williamsburg to start my new job.

—41—

Work was trying. Had I still been researching, designing, and writing at the Folk Art Center I may have kept my spirits from the quicksand, but the job I'd been offered was in administration. At first I didn't know what I was doing; when I finally figured out the protocol after about three weeks on the job I realized that I hated administration. To top it all off, the other interns were gone. I was left working with older people who I did not know and who seemed uninterested in knowing me.

William and Mary was close, but I wasn't a student. Wandering around watching the undergrads made me sad. I wasn't one of them and never would be again. I had done a good job of exploring Colonial Williamsburg while I was interning in the summer—I didn't want to walk the grounds alone anymore. The magic of early summer had left me. Most of the time, when not miserable at my job, I was miserable in my miserable apartment.

I'd learned more about my place over the past few weeks. For one, I'd learned that it wasn't just my bathroom sink drain that was slow. I had to keep my showers short to avoid overflowing the shallow shower basin and flooding the apartment below mine. That meant washing my hair in the equally slow kitchen sink and showering like I was on a camping trip: wet a washcloth, suds up, quickly rinse in cold water, then towel dry. So much for relaxing showers after frustrating days of dealing with other people's problems (my definition of admin work).

And, even though they didn't help pay the rent, I had roommates. Roaches ate the crumbs in the kitchen and crickets ate the cotton crotches from my underwear collecting in the cardboard box I used as a laundry hamper. Every night before I went to bed I'd spray the kitchen baseboards with Raid. In the morning I'd slip on my Dr. Scholl's and sweep crunchy little carcasses into neat piles while my coffee perked.

I didn't own a phone or a TV, so in the evenings I would console myself with music. I'd set my parents' old stereo on the dresser in my bedroom and played my record albums over and over. I listened to Bob Dylan, Joni Mitchell, and Linda Ronstadt. I bought albums that Jon had owned. I listened to Van Morrison and Michel Legrand. I cried during sad songs and love songs, both. I cried as I ate my lonely suppers. I cried until I fell asleep atop my crumpled sheets.

I was lost and homesick, but saw no solution. I knew where I was and I wasn't homesick for anything that I could ever regain. I was quickly sinking into the place I had been just after Jon's death—I wasn't just remembering, I was mourning. Nothing and no one seemed important. That I could get up in the morning, dress, and go to my office was a minor miracle.

In late August about the time I'd started my job, before the malaise had settled over me like a dark cloud, I had purchased tickets to a concert by The Band to be held at the William and Mary Hall on September twenty-fifth. I'd actually splurged and bought two tickets thinking that by late September I would surely know someone to invite along. That didn't happen. On the concert day, I forced myself to use one of the tickets, hoping to forget for a night.

The Band was often Bob Dylan's backup band. While Dylan wasn't part of the concert, I had been really excited about hearing the group—I owned their album *Rock of Ages* and liked most of the cuts. I had a headache but stayed in the pulsing auditorium waiting for songs that I knew. Three songs into the concert they played the ear-splitting "The Night They Drove Old Dixie Down," followed by a new song by Robbie Robertson called "It Makes No Difference." As Rick Danko sang the plaintive words, I sat mesmerized thinking that somehow he knew everything I was feeling. When the song ended I fled the pandemonium of the auditorium.

I bought a bottle of vodka on my way home. I'd never been a big drinker, but I knew people drank to forget; I'd watched my father do it my whole life. Sitting at the kitchen table I mixed the warm alcohol with orange juice from my fridge. I spent most of the night writing a pillow-talk letter to Jon, pouring out my heart. I made it to my bed before I passed out—I was late for work the next day, but no one seemed to notice or care.

Letters to Jon and vodka became my nightly solace. I wrote down everything I was thinking. I begged him to fracture the dimensions of time and come back to me. Some days I just asked to forget: *"Jon, I know it's not your fault, but sometimes I hate you for leaving me alone. Some days it hurts so damn much having you filling my brain that I try to forget you ever existed—then some little thing will happen and everything about you comes flooding back to me. I end up thinking about our time together and dreaming about how wonderful our lives would've been if you hadn't died. I've replayed this endless cycle of forgetting, remembering and day dreaming so often that I don't know what's real anymore. Our time together was so short. I've lived over a year and a half without you, but instead of getting better, my pain is getting worse. Jon, please come back. Come hold me—make love to me. Promise me that forever is forever."*

I taped the scribbled pages to my bedroom wall. I had started by covering the word FUCK, above my bed, but after a week the whole wall was covered with notebook paper. I'd lay in bed and watch the autumn breeze coming through the window make the pages flutter. Their motion made me think of the day it all began, when I'd knocked Jon's notes over the balcony railing and his papers floated down like large white confetti.

By mid-October, my big sister was starting to worry about me. I know this because on October thirteenth, late in the afternoon, she showed up at my apartment door.

Annie told me that when my letters had quit arriving, she'd called Mom. She'd told Annie they hadn't heard from me for several weeks either. Annie'd then called Dr. Sargent at the USD history department to find out what he knew. He told her he knew nothing —he hadn't had a letter from me since we'd finished my applications to grad schools at the beginning of

September. He said he'd found it unusual, but thought I was just busy with my new position.

Annie had known better. She arranged for an emergency leave from work and bought a one-way bus ticket to Williamsburg. My sweet big sister came six hundred miles to save me. Over the next five days, she did my laundry, bought me groceries, and cleaned my apartment—starting with the bedroom wall. She convinced me to shower, put on clean clothes, and eat, then pushed me out the door to my office.

While I was gone, Annie sorted my albums after telling me, "No woman lives a life so filled with happiness that she can live on a constant diet of Linda Ronstadt and Joni Mitchell." She took what she considered *harmful music* and left me the albums that she could tell never made it to my turntable—*Grieg's Greatest Hits* and the recording made by my high school's marching band. I guess she didn't think that "In the Hall of the Mountain King" or Sousa's marches would bring me to tears.

The day Annie left for home she made me promise to take better care of myself. She encouraged me to start eating better and lay off the liquor. She suggested that I get out of my ugly apartment and spend time in the fresh air while it was still warm enough to enjoy being outside. She thought I should take a book with me in the morning when I went to work so that I could stop in a park to unwind on my way home.

She rewarded my solemn promise to do better with a letter—the last one Jon had written to me before he died. Annie told me it had arrived at her place the day I had come home from the hospital after I'd miscarried. She said that she'd left it on the bedside table for me to read while I was recovering, but that it must have gotten knocked off. She had just recently found it under the bed still sealed. She told me that she thought about not giving it to me because it could open old wounds, but she now realized my wounds were still fresh. Annie hoped Jon's last words to me might be healing.

February 7, 1973

Hi, Sarah,

This can't be a long letter because I'm swamped right now, but I have some things that I can't get off my mind. Don't worry, there's nothing wrong—but without you around to talk to I can't rid myself of the things rattling around in my head

*distracting me from the stuff I should be
doing. Writing's my substitute these days. I'd
much rather have your beautiful lips
distracting me, but that's for another letter…
I'll write you a long romantic one tomorrow
after I get home from Dr. Sargent's (it's his
birthday—he asked me to join him for a little
celebration).*

*I know you're hurting now with interim
coming to an end. Yes, I wish you could have
come back, but I think you made the right
decision. It hurts us both not being together,
but it's not going to be an uncommon
situation for us in the future—I think we are
just going to have to get used to it.*

*When you graduate, you and I both know
that your plan is to continue your education.
As much as I like USD, it's not the graduate
school you need—you are destined for ivy
covered buildings with illustrious pasts—I
am sure of it. I'm staying put. I'm happy
here with Dr. Sargent and I feel that my
future is here. After you have your Ph.D.*

286

your work may call you elsewhere. I understand this. We will figure it out.

What I'm trying to say is that, while being apart hurts, it's going to be alright in the end. We can make our separations work knowing that we are meant to be together forever.

You are so much younger than I am. You deserve the right to make your own decisions about your future. I took that power for myself when I was younger, but I had to pay a high price for it. I don't want you to ever feel bad about a decision you make to ensure your own happiness or self-fulfillment.

Above everything Sarah, <u>I love you.</u> I know that we are meant for one another and that our future is guaranteed, whether we are in each others arms or, as now, in one another's heart.

Yours Forever,
Jon

Author's Note:

The following four chapters, 42 through 45, were written in 1982. I am including them in the narrative just as they were written at that time other than changing the numbering so that they structurally fit within this more recent account.

Because these chapters were written as a free-standing narrative, as a reader, you may find some of the information repetitive; please forgive this small annoyance.

One of the tenets of historic research is to give the most credence to primary sources written nearest in time to the event(s) in question. So, holding to that dictum, I am giving you what I wrote about my experiences seven years after the fact, rather than forty years later like the rest of this memoir.

Sarah Bolling, 2016

—42—

Sarah Bolling
10/1/1982

Now that life has slowed down, I think it's finally time to write down everything that happened from October 1974 through February 1975. I don't plan on sharing this with anyone, but I want to commit it to paper before I start to forget the details. It is still hard for me to believe that what I'm going to write is true, but having lived it, I know that it is.

In the autumn of 1974 I was living in Williamsburg, Virginia. I'd taken a job with the Abby Aldrich Rockefeller Folk Art Center department of museum administration.

I hated my new position and was trying to decide whether I should quit and go to the Twin Oaks Community in Louisa, Virginia until the fall of '75 when I hoped to enter grad school.

I was still mourning Jon's death, or perhaps it would be more accurate to say, I was once again mourning Jon's death. For over a year (really, starting just several months after his death) I had tried to put my sadness away and focus on his memory. Sequestering my grief had worked fairly well as long as I stayed busy, but, with only a job I disliked to occupy my time, an apartment that was nearly uninhabitable, and no friends in the area, I couldn't think of anything but Jon's death and the future together that we had lost.

Annie, sensing my depression, had come to Williamsburg to help me. She was hoping to convince me to regain some joy in being alive. She brought along Jon's last letter to me, which she had found unopened under her bed more than a year-and-a-half after he had written it. We hypothesized that I had knocked it off her nightstand when I'd pulled Jon's heart shaped paperweight into bed with me on Valentine's Day evening after being released from the hospital. Annie's conditions to give me the letter were that I promise to take better care of myself and make some solid decisions about my immediate future. To that end, she suggested I start walking after work to get some exercise and clear my head.

Before she left, I agreed to her

terms and tried to take her advice to heart. So, on cool evenings that fall, I started strolling through the village again. Sometimes I would stop to read at a secluded bench near the edge of the Historic Area to delay returning to my depressing apartment.

On one such evening in mid-October, I looked up to see a man emerge from a copse to my north. He was dressed in full colonial garb: coat, waistcoat and breeches. Such dress was not uncommon in Colonial Williamsburg, however, the color and cut of his suit were unusual. Most of the men's costumes in the Historic Area were red and blue uniforms or the utilitarian leather aprons of craftsman.

He walked with a gait that I had seen before. As he passed, I set my book in my lap. He tipped his tricorn and looked me in the eyes. For me, it was as though a small electric shock passed through my body. I thought I saw a glimmer of recognition in his golden brown-eyes as well, but he did not break stride. He continued on his way; I remained on the bench in stunned silence, my book closed, until the sun set. I could have sworn I'd just seen a beardless Jon Leggett.

I tried to forget the encounter. I attempted to convince myself that my feelings of connection were nonsense, but I soon found myself walking Duke of Gloucester Street peering in shop windows. Williamsburg was full of historic reenactors: What role did he play? He looked like a Statesman, but I couldn't find him at the Historic Courthouse or the Capitol. I began worrying about what I would I do if I found him. Would I stand with my mouth open, speechless? Would he think I was a crazed stalker? I tried to tell myself that I was fortunate that I hadn't found him.

In late October, I gave up my search and went back to the secluded bench at the edge of the village. Days were getting shorter and, though it was much warmer in Virginia than in South Dakota at this time of year, darkness fell just as early. Soon it would be too dark and cool to sit outside after work.

I was reading Laurence Sterne's <u>Tristram Shandy</u> when he came over the rise. He approached. The smile that crossed his face let me know that my earlier fears were groundless. As he bowed slightly, reaching for my hand he said, "May I introduce myself; I am Jonathan Leggett."

I breathed deeply and replied, "My name is Sarah Bolling; I believe we have met somewhere in the past."

I knew something was amiss when he countered with, "Perhaps, Mistress Bolling; however, I feel certain that our paths have crossed somewhere in time. You have been calling for me and I have been seeking you."

We sat on the bench and talked until it was too dark to see one another. We parted with a promise to meet again the following afternoon.

* * *

We met at the park bench for the next three evenings. We soon learned that while we could see one another, anyone passing could see only one of us. A tourist wandering off the recreated streets of the Historic Area could catch me in rapt conversation with an empty bench. Jonathan was in an even more compromising situation being a well-known figure in the old colonial capital city of Williamsburg. He would often pause for minutes as we spoke to avoid appearing a lunatic to his fellow citizens.

Through our halting conversations we learned that we were living in the same city, but separated by two hundred years. For Jonathan Leggett, it was the October of 1774. We were desperate to be together again, yet we didn't know it was actually possible until a Wednesday evening when Jonathan took both my hands and pulled me toward him. That was all it took for me to pass through to his world. I found myself in Jonathan's arms as darkness fell in the eighteenth century.

I would have run away with him at that moment had it been possible, but I was wearing my 1974 office clothes: slacks, sweater, and embroidered jean jacket. I would have been inexplicable and we would have had nowhere to hide. I asked Jonathan to send me back, which he did by holding my hands and physically pushing me from him. It hurt, not so much physically, but emotionally, to make that transition. It seemed like an action of rejection; however, it was simply the means of time transportation that we both came to rely upon. As long as we were near our special bench, with a push or a pull, dimensions fractured, and two hundred years disappeared.

We made plans to meet on the following evening, October 31. We could enjoy ourselves in public and be totally inconspicuous. Jonathan was wary, but I assured him that we could do as we pleased in 1974 on Halloween night.

***

Jonathan strode toward me wearing his best suit of clothes. His light brown hair was pulled back in a low ponytail and he wore a tricorn made of beaver felt. When he reached the bench he bowed slightly and took my hands. I pulled him to my world. I hugged him as though I would never let go. It may have been a strange sight anywhere else; a young woman in a wool mini skirt with her arms around a Colonial gentleman, but this was 1974 Williamsburg. Our behavior may not have been expected, but it was acceptable. Jonathan asked if he were dressed appropriately for the evening's activities. I told him that his dress could not have been more perfect. I took his hand and we walked to my apartment.

***

We made love, leaving me no doubt that I was once again in Jon's arms. He knew me as only a past lover could. When we eventually dressed for dinner, Jon adjusted and laced the stays of my eighteenth century ensemble; it was one of the most sensual experiences of my life. I donned the beautiful gown that Mel had made the previous summer. As I twisted and pinned my hair into a loose bun, Jonathan amused himself by looking at my books and flipping the light switches off and on. I had made eight o'clock reservations at the Regency Dining Room at the Williamsburg Inn and I had requested that they notify our waiter that I would be paying the bill. I did not want Jonathan to be embarrassed by his lack of proper currency.

We walked down Nassau Street toward the Inn with my hand in the crook of his elbow. Jonathan remarked that the surroundings were familiar, but very different from the Williamsburg he had left a few hours ago. I had the fanciful thought that we looked just like a porcelain figurine that Grandma Bolling had kept on her dresser when I was young.

When we strode into the beautifully appointed restaurant, the other diners applauded our "costumes." My 1970s glasses were the only thing that took away total believability in our 1770's countenance.

After dinner we walked to the campus of William and Mary in search of a party to attend. We drank beer and danced to music blasting from dorm windows. The Band had played on campus in late September; because of that, theirs seemed to be the music of choice drifting across the quad most any time of day. On Halloween night the music from The Band's screaming guitars was amplified to head splitting level. Jonathan begged my pardon and requested that we return to my apartment.

If Jonathan was confused by the

students' costumes he didn't say anything. Later I realized that everything about that evening must have been disorienting to him: cars, street lights, recorded music, and wild dancing. It would have been like being born at the age of thirty in the middle of Dante's Inferno. I had the distinct advantage of remembering our 1970's past. Jonathan didn't remember anything because he hadn't lived it as yet. He only knew that he loved me, and, in 1974, I was his port in a sea of bewilderment.

We left my apartment just before dawn to send Jonathan back in time. We had spent much of the night making love and making a plan for our future; a future that meant I would be living in the past.

***

We met every evening during the following week to finalize details. I would pull Jonathan to my world and he would wrap his warm wool cloak around us while we huddled on our remote bench planning my disappearance.

On November 9, 1974, I moved to November 9, 1774. I had given my notice at work on the day after Halloween. I had written or telephoned everyone who might worry about me and explained that my current position in Williamsburg had not been a good fit; I was moving to Twin Oaks. My friends and family, especially Annie, were not surprised by the move, as it had been my original intention after completing my internship at the end of the summer. Of course, I told no one about Jonathan.

Jonathan had prepared the way for me in 1774, by arranging for me to lodge with a bohemian artist friend of his, Lydia de Treville. He told Mistress de Treville that I was the daughter of a little known relative of his late mother's. He said that I had been reared in the wilds of western Virginia by a father who was a merchant dealing with savages and fur traders. He believed me to be amiable, but he did not know further. He told me that Lydia had happily agreed to take me in as part of her household, but he also suspected that she did not believe him. After meeting her, I knew that part of her willingness to host me was because she assumed Jonathan and I were illicit lovers. It delighted her.

—43—

Lydia met us at her door and welcomed me with warmth. I told her that I was pleased that she could take me in on such short notice. She said that it was "no matter for concern." Her home was large and she often hosted guests for long periods of time.

Jonathan and I explained that I would be requiring many personal items, including clothing. I told her, "I fled my home with few belongings."

Lydia's eyebrow raised as she inquired, "In a ball dress?"

I said that it was my most valuable garment and I knew that it was my only irreplaceable possession. She inquired whether it had belonged to my late mother, "though exceedingly lovely, it is somewhat out of the present fashion." I cast my eyes down and responded, "Yes, but it's the only thing that I have to remember her." This was my first lie in my new home. I felt guilty; however, I also felt as though I had made it over a hurdle. I was familiar with keeping secrets; telling lies was another matter, but, to make our plan work, Jonathan and I would end up lying and breaking laws in two countries, as well as, two centuries.

Lydia wanted to host a gathering to welcome me to Williamsburg and introduce me to Jonathan's associates. Jonathan and I implored her to wait. I needed time to adjust to my new surroundings. Jonathan explained that the hubbub of the Capitol City was going to be hard on my nervous system, "being that she is accustomed to the solitude of the backwoods." It was decided that any large celebration could wait until Lydia's husband, Major John la Boularderie de Treville, returned north from the family home in Beaufort, South Carolina.

* * *

To pass my days, when I could not spend time with Jonathan, I attempted to read and embroider, but could do neither well without my glasses which Jonathan and I had agreed I could not wear in public. My nearsightedness posed enormous physical and emotional problems for me in 1774, but I was trying hard to adjust to my situation and not complain. I would have done almost anything to stay in a world with Jonathan.

Lydia thought me pleasant company and though she often found my behavior odd, she could not be dissuaded from hosting a small dinner party to honor my arrival after I had been with her for several weeks. She asked me if there was anyone in the area whom I was particularly keen to meet. I did not want to appear too excited, so I asked if I might have some time to ponder her question and talk with Jonathan.

In truth, I knew that I wanted to meet Thomas Jefferson. I had read Dumas Malone's first three books about Jefferson. Dr. Malone had painted a vivid picture of the man, but I wondered if it was as accurate as Fawn Brodie's portrait of him in her book, <u>Thomas Jefferson: An Intimate History</u>, which I had read just one month earlier.

Jonathan thought a dinner with Mr. Jefferson would be a fine evening. He had met Jefferson on several occasions. They were both educated men working within the government. Jonathan was of a lower social rank, being an employee of government representatives (not an elected official). He mentioned that he and Jefferson were the same age, both born in 1743. I didn't ask more questions of Jonathan. I wanted to see for myself what I thought of Thomas Jefferson, armed as I was with my twentieth century knowledge.

***

Lydia clapped her hands and purred, "Ahh, Mr. Jefferson. He is a delightful guest. I will see if he is available to dine with us. I have heard that he is in Williamsburg, but I do not believe his wife is with him, she recently gave birth… something I fear she will be doing very often married to her choice for a husband."

Lydia's comment, and the lift of her eyebrow, left me little doubt about her intimate knowledge of Mr. Jefferson, despite being at least twenty years older than he. Lydia said that she planned to invite another couple she thought I might enjoy meeting, John and Betsey Walker. Their inclusion would bring our dinner party to a very comfortable six. Lydia assured me that in such a small group I would have no trouble handling the challenges of polite social intercourse.

Even so, days before the gathering, I began asking Mistress de Treville what I should expect to be served, and if the foods would require any special implements. I had already embarrassed myself by using the sugar nippers to cut a pickle. I did not want to do something equally embarrassing in front of Thomas Jefferson or Mr. and Mrs. Walker. Lydia said, that while we would have many dishes, she didn't believe any of them would be foreign to my palate or experience with table utensils. She said to honor Mr. Jefferson's predilection for vegetables, she would serve less meat than she might for a different group of guests.

Lydia told me that at the table I should not expect to be seated with Jonathan, she would situate me beside Mr. Jefferson. She said that she realized that I was of a serious nature, and had been a quiet house guest, but now that I was somewhat more comfortable in my surroundings, it would be appropriate, even expected, that I be a lively conversationalist that evening. She said that she had seen my quick wit on occasion, and that her guests, especially Mr. Jefferson, would enjoy its employment. In Virginia flirting was a sport, and those who were proficient at it became welcomed guests at most gatherings.

***

What I learned from that dinner party was that Thomas Jefferson was

far more like Fawn Brodie's interpretation of him, than Dr. Malone's
portrayal. Jefferson may have been
tongue-tied around "the ladies" as a
young man, but by the time I met him,
he showed no fear of the opposite
sex. Of course, he was in comfortable surroundings. He knew Lydia
well (this became obvious as the
evening progressed). And, he and
John Walker had been schoolmates.
Jefferson had even served as one of
the best men at John and Betsey
Walker's wedding.

I had a harder time deciphering
the feelings of Thomas Jefferson for
Mrs. Walker. I had first read of
their scandal in Dr. Malone's book
Jefferson the Virginian. If I were
remembering correctly, according to
some accounts, Mr. Jefferson would

have still been in active amorous pursuit of Betsey Walker in 1774, even though, by that time, he had already been married for several years.

Betsey Walker was exceptionally beautiful and charming. She flirted skillfully with everyone at the table, except Thomas Jefferson. With Jefferson she barely spoke. While, he occasionally spoke to her, it would be a comment on his garden or the weather, not a statement to flatter or tease. It struck me as a case of studied avoidance, an undertaking with which I was all too familiar. I could tell that Lydia knew something was going on between Jefferson and Betsey Walker, and had invited the Walkers to add an undercurrent of intrigue for her own entertainment that evening. Lydia would have assumed me clueless to the rumors of the Jefferson-Walker peccadillo.

I was the only person at the table that Thomas Jefferson did not know, and he made it very apparent that he wanted to rectify that situation. He flattered me shamelessly, and with Jonathan's blessings I did my best to reciprocate. At one point in the meal, the men were beginning to banter about amusing limericks that they had heard. Lydia interjected. I thought that she might attempt to change the subject, but instead she added her own ditty, its tone even more suggestive than the poems the men had been sharing. When I laughed at her witticism, she asked me to share a verse of my own.

When I demurred, saying that I didn't know any, she insisted, saying that I should attempt one, that I had an unusual gift for words (I think she just meant that I spoke oddly). She offered to start it and gave me the line: "There was a young gent come from Breyer." I asked my table mates for a few moments while I composed. After they had eaten more bites of their almond pudding with jam, I recited my offering.

"In the spirit of your earlier rhymes, and with a bow to Tristram Shandy:

There was a young gent come from
Breyer,
Said to boast a nose quite long as a
spire.
He met a young lass,

She ventured a pass,
Assuring his long spire climbed e'er
higher."

Betsey raised her head lifting
her nose in the air, thinking that
the "lass had been snubbed" by the
long-nosed gent. The men and Lydia
erupted with laughter, understanding
my literary mimicking of Laurence
Sterne's humor.

After our meal (rice soup,
"sallats," oysters prepared in cream,
meats [beef, mutton and ham], well-
seasoned Brussels sprouts, and a
tureen of stewed root vegetables),
where I did not embarrass myself with
my lack of table manners (only my
limerick, I feared), we adjourned to
the music room. It was on the far end
of the entrance hall that ran the

317

length of the main floor of Lydia's home. Paintings by Mistress de Treville adorned the walls of the vast hall. I had spent hours during the early days of my visit studying her work, my nose nearly touching the brush strokes.

Lydia had requested Mr. Jefferson bring his violin that evening and had told me that it was her intention to hear us play together. I was worried about what I might play. I knew that most of the music I could play by memory was written later than 1774. Much by Mozart was written during the later eighteenth century, but I didn't want to play a composition shortly before it had been written. That would have created all sorts of issues. I thought that Antonio Vivaldi's "Four Seasons" might be familiar to Mr. Jefferson, so suggested we try a duet from the first concerto of the piece. He was delighted with my choice and we managed a very nice impromptu "Spring" on that cold November evening in Williamsburg.

Mr. Jefferson proposed that we play the sheet music that he had brought with him for the occasion, but I explained that I did not see well enough to read it by candle-light, especially from the distance of a shared music stand. I suggested that he, or others in our party, sing tunes that they enjoyed, and that after hearing them I would join in, playing by ear. So, that is how the evening progressed. We had a Colonial sing-along. I was impressed by Mr. Jefferson's virtuosity on the violin, and he by my skill on the pianoforte.

At the end of the night, after everyone had left but Jonathan, I asked Lydia and him to assess my conduct, to tell me if they thought I could meet more people. Jonathan said he couldn't have been more pleased and thought I had charmed Thomas Jefferson. After Jonathan left that night, Lydia came to me in private and said that she could tell that Mr. Jefferson was enthralled with me. In jest I said coyly, "But, he's a married man."

"And, that is a very good thing! Otherwise, Mistress Bolling, he would be at your feet, behaving like a puppy baying at the moon. Mr. Jefferson is persistent when he wants something… or someone." I wasn't exactly sure what Lydia meant, but thought I might be starting to understand the man's nature. It made much of what I had read in the past few years make more sense.

***

Other than the success of the dinner party, it seemed that I continually embarrassed myself while living in Lydia's home. I was an adult woman, but I had no idea how to care for myself as such in 1774. I was dreading getting my period nearly as much as I was fretting that it was already late. My history books had taught me nothing about women's hygiene. Lydia was entertained by my ineptitude, and graciously covered my many faux pas, but there were some things that I just couldn't ask her and other things that she couldn't do for me. Having servants to assist me with dressing and my daily toilet was a boon; nevertheless, it made me uncomfortable on multiple levels; the first being that they were slaves.

All of Lydia's household servants were owned by her husband, Major de Treville. From what I could see, Lydia treated the slaves as paid servants, and, as her house guest, I followed her lead. I found the system of slavery abhorrent, but I knew that it had been a part of colonial life for one-hundred—fifty-five years by the time I appeared in 1774. It wasn't courageous of me, but I did what I had been taught by my mother: I didn't rock the boat and I stayed in my host's good graces.

***

During my first weeks with Lydia, she had encouraged me to take strolls in town and walks in the gardens, but I soon found that I too often tripped because I could not see the uneven ground or debris below my feet. After one particularly nasty spill where I damaged a new gown and twisted my ankle, I quit leaving the house.

Playing music was the one thing that I could do to entertain myself as I grew accustomed to my new circumstances. Lydia's beautiful pianoforte had been constructed in Vienna and purchased as a gift by her husband. When others were present I attempted to play only tunes that would have been known in the mid-eighteenth century. When alone in the house with the servants, I allowed myself to play the modern music that I missed. Interestingly, Lydia never asked how a young woman from the hinterlands learned to play minuets. She had accepted that much of my behavior was inexplicable.

In late November, Jonathan found me at the pianoforte in tears. I tried to wipe them away, telling him it was nothing. He said that he knew me better than to believe that I would "weep for a trifle" and insisted I tell him what he could do to cheer me. I broke down and told him how frustrated I was with my life. Lydia was wonderful, but she could do little to ease my day-to-day anxiety. Life was difficult, and I was fearful for our future.

I didn't tell Jonathan of my most personal concern, but I did tell him that I missed things. I told him I missed foods — pizza, Cheerios, and Chinese takeout. I missed rock radio and recorded music. I missed the comfort of jeans and flannel shirts. I missed hearing from friends and family. I don't think Jonathan understood much of what I said, but he listened intently.

I told him what hurt the most was feeling worthless. Without my glasses nearly every activity that I had valued in my former life was impossible. I could barely write, reading was exasperating, and studying was out of the question.

Jonathan suggested that he bring me books to study in the evening in the privacy of my bedroom so that I could wear my corrective lenses. I told him it was kind of him to offer, but by evening I was so tired from struggling to see during the day that my fatigued eyes could not focus even with correction. I could not study by candlelight. To be a scholar in 1774, I needed to study the classics. I needed to know Ancient Greek and Classical Latin. My 1970's education had included only modern French, which I spoke like merde.

I closed my eyes while Jonathan wrapped me in his strong arms. I tried to convince myself that I could live this life. After all, it was 1774, in Colonial America; I was being given the opportunity to be with the man I loved and live during a period of history that would be studied for centuries. I was living my dream. It should not have been making me miserable, but it was evident to Jonathan that it was.

The next day, he offered to give up everything to join me in 1974. I

didn't know if it was the right
decision for him, but I gratefully,
and perhaps greedily, accepted.

—44—

On November twenty-ninth,
Jonathan and I traveled to the
future. We walked to the bench in
Williamsburg where we had met, joined
hands, and I pulled Jonathan into
1974.

We arrived at my old apartment
wearing 1774 travel clothing. We had
told Lydia de Treville that Jonathan
was taking me to see mutual relatives
near Charlottesville; it would have
looked ridiculous to leave in the
ballgown that I had arrived in.
Jonathan decided to wear what he
thought would be least conspicuous,
the brown suit that he was wearing
the first time I saw him. He topped
it with his great coat. Though I

liked his cloak better, I told him that his choice of an outer garment was excellent. Men's overcoats had not changed much in two hundred years.

* * *

With his shoulder, Jon (as I'd started calling him) broke the entry door on my apartment. I had left my keys on the kitchen table along with a twenty-dollar bill to reimburse my landlady for the inconvenience of having to clean out the abandoned unit. I changed into jeans and a sweater, grabbed the twenty, and we took off for the Goodwill Store to buy Jon a wardrobe.

In corduroy jeans and a plaid flannel shirt, his long hair untied, he looked like any older student on the campus of William and Mary. Jon had told me that he would have preferred a suit of clothing, but would take my lead in "sartorial matters." I explained to him that suits could come later once he had a professional position; for now, jeans, cords, flannel shirts, and turtlenecks were to be his camouflage.

Our next stop was the bank where I cashed out most of my checking account. I was so happy that I had stupidly left my checkbook in the bureau drawer at my apartment when Jonathan and I had bolted for 1774 at the beginning of the month. I was naive enough to think that it would be safe and, that when found, someone would give any remaining funds to a worthy cause. The checkbook would travel with me from then on.

That evening, while Jon walked the campus and surrounding area, I called my parents, Annie, and Dr. Sargent. I lied and said that I was calling from a pay phone in Louisa, Virginia, the small town close to the Twin Oaks commune. It didn't seem like too much of a stretch. It was where they thought I was, and, in a day, that was precisely where Jon and I would be living. Annie asked why I hadn't written to her. I told her that something must have been wrong with the address she was using because I hadn't received her letters. I comforted myself with the fact that it was technically not a lie. Dr. Sargent told me that he had been anxious to write to me, but was awaiting my proper address at the commune. Ever practical, Mom said

that it was nice to hear from me, but
that I should not be wasting my money
on phone calls.

On Saturday, November thirtieth,
Jon and I moved to Twin Oaks. Max
had made arrangements for a month-
long stay while Jon and I planned our
future. Jon's manner of speaking and
general behavior was unusual for
1974; conveniently, "unusual," was
the norm in communes. I was
confident that he could learn to
navigate the twentieth century while
being left in peace by our new
neighbors.

The first physical shock to Jon's
system was the motion of the large
bus that took us to the commune. He
said that the speed concerned him and
"created an illness in his stomach."
I told him he wasn't the only one

concerned with speed, very soon buses would only be allowed to travel fifty-five miles an hour as America attempted to conserve fuel. He stared at me in amazement; I don't think that he knew which of his questions to ask first.

***

Twin Oaks turned out to be a good place for Jonathan to transition, although it was often confusing for him. When we first arrived he received several compliments on his colonial great coat, as in "Cool coat, man." This caused Jon consternation. He often countered with, "on the contrary, it is a warm garment… man." Most people recognized his polite sincerity as an attempt at humor. Since I was an inveterate wisecracker, our new friends expected the same from my boyfriend.

One of the things that both Jon and I found interesting was that many of the people at the commune assumed he was from Canada. His manner of speech was unusual and he often broke into French during conversations. We started to realize that this might be his cover. Jon needed papers. As a woman in Colonial America, I hadn't needed documentation. Jon, however, was planning to work or go to college. He needed to prove that he was a citizen of some country in 1974. We determined that Quebec, Canada, would be our destination at the end of the month.

We spent a festive Christmas at the commune. We had said that gifts were unnecessary, but on Christmas Day I gave Jon a card and the only

photo of myself that I owned. In it
I was wearing the colonial ballgown
that I had worn on Halloween night
and, again, for our move to 1774.
Jon pressed it to his heart saying,
"I will forever cherish this token of
your affection." He apologized for
not having made a portrait of himself
for me. I told him that he needn't
bother, that I carried his picture
with me in a glass heart. He said,
"Yes, but in that likeness I have
whiskers and am not dressed properly.
Someday I shall remedy that particular situation."

   Then, he reached into the pocket
of his corduroy jacket and removed a
small box. "*Ma chere* Sarah, close
your lovely eyes." That said, he
slid a garnet and opal ring onto the
third finger of my left hand. It was

the same ring that he had given me nearly two years earlier, the ring that had disappeared with the rest of his possessions. This time it fit me perfectly.

When I told Jon I thought it absolutely beautiful, he responded by paraphrasing the line of poetry he had shared when I had complemented the roses he'd given me on December seventh two years earlier. "One *fair ring*, though beauteous be, pales my love, nye t' thee."

I told him his poetry was lovely, but that I thought he had misquoted it slightly. "Ahh, my Sarah, so you know of Master Blythewood's words." I had to admit that I knew only the first lines.

"Then I must recite the complete poem. In truth, it sounds as though

it were composed for you; I wish that
I were in such a manner gifted.
Please, think of these as my words:

One lone rose,
Tho beauteous be,
Pales, My Love,
Nye t' thee.

Thine eyes do shine,
So fair, so bright.
'Luminate they,
Min[e] darkest night.

Thy heav'nly crown,
Of golden tresses,
To min[e] hands only,
Brook caresses.

Tho we must part,
Thy kisses sweet,
Nourish me,
'Til 'gaine we meet.

Min[e] bonds to thee,
Shall I ne'er sever.
Min[e] adoration,
Thine forever."

—45—

Getting to Canada was much easier than either Jon or I had anticipated. Twin Oaks' sister community was Morninglory Farm, in Killaloe Ontario, Canada. And, even though divided by seven-hundred-fifty miles, commune members made the trip frequently. We were able to catch a ride with residents of Morninglory heading home after celebrating the Christmas holiday in Virginia.

When we asked our traveling companions if Jon would have problems crossing the border into Canada without documentation, they told us not to worry; they had friends who had been getting young men into Canada for years. I suspected that they were part of what was sometimes called the "second underground railway"— a loose union of people working to help men avoid military service in the United States during the Vietnam War. But I didn't ask unnecessary questions, and they paid us that same courtesy.

On New Year's Day, 1975, we moved to Canada to establish Jonathan's credentials. We lived at the Morninglory commune until Jon's forged documents were in order, then we moved to La Tuque, Quebec, Canada. This trip was not as easy for us; no one was going our way. The sojourn entailed two long, cold rides: first a bus to Montreal followed by a five-hour train trip north to La Tuque.

Jon said that if he were going to pass as a born Quebecois, he wanted to do it well. We had chosen La Tuque as his new hometown because it was remote. The only way to learn about it was to spend some time in the area. I doubted that once we moved back to the States anyone Jon encountered would have ever heard of La Tuque, but I was ready to do anything for Jon's mental comfort by this point. I was beginning to notice the unremitting pain and confusion in his eyes.

The community was what I had suspected it would be, a small town with a pretty train station and little else of charm. It looked like most towns in the U.S. Midwest, albeit the signs were all in French. We walked in horizontally falling snow from the train yard to the nearest bar, bought drinks, and inquired where we might stay for a while. The bartender suggested we check with the owner of *la pharmacie* just up the street. She said that the pharmacist had furnished rooms above the drugstore that he rented by the week.

We won over the druggist with our French, mine bad and Jon's dated. I knew Jon spoke English with some very odd twists. For some reason it hadn't dawned on me that his French would have the same issues. However, when our new landlord asked *"Es-tu marié?"* Jon responded perfectly to my ears, *"Non mais nous sommes fiancés."* For the second time in my life, I had a fiancé. With that statement, our very proper host opened the door to our new home.

* * *

Our room was small, but warm and

quiet. We had everything we needed for the time being. Jon was especially pleased when he found out that there was a public library just one street over from our new place.

Jon studied daily. I did too, but the selection of materials in English was lacking as far as I was concerned. In the afternoons, Jon would walk to a nearby café for bad coffee and conversations with the locals. I tried to follow their discussions, but my conversational French was no better in 1975 than it had been in 1774. When I occasion-ally heard people sniggering when Jon spoke, I just assumed his antiquated expressions had caused their chuckles; however, as I soon found out, it was something much more distressing for Jonathan.

Most of the time I sat quietly, queasy from the smell of burnt coffee and daydreaming about our future back in the United States. We would be going home soon. I needed it to be very soon.

***

The sixth day of February 1975, Jon and I entered a small plane on the tarmac of the airstrip at the edge of La Tuque. We were flying home, but it was not the homecoming that I had imagined since arriving in Canada. After days of tear-filled conversations we had decided to return to the Williamsburg of 1975 and then, at our secluded bench, travel back to 1775.

Over the past months, Jonathan had come to the realization that he could not live in my modern world.

The reasons were many, varied, and undeniable. It embarrassed me that some of them hadn't occurred to me. Or, perhaps, it was that I felt guilty: most of them had occurred to me and I had chosen to keep quiet.

Jon confessed to me that he was becoming increasingly unhappy with himself. He said that his goal of becoming a college professor within a few years was unrealistic. He admitted that he couldn't even have a discussion of events in a small-town coffee shop without embarrassing himself by his lack of knowledge. He felt he knew less of world affairs than a five-year-old child.

He also said that there was so much more to know in 1975. He prided himself on being a learned man. He had studied the classics, read the canon of Western thought. But, so much had been added in two hundred years. He could never know it all.

I tried to assure him that no one knew it all. He shook his head and said, "At one time, not long ago, I was getting close. Now, I am afraid to open my mouth in public."

What made me most ashamed of myself was what he told me next.

I knew that Jonathan was often employed by George Mason as a clerk. What Jon told me during our last week in Canada, that I hadn't known previously, was that he was often Mason's sounding-board and pen. Jon claimed, and I now believe, that many of the ideas in Virginia's Declaration of Rights, The Declaration of Independence, and, eventually, the Bill of Rights, were already topics of their discussions by 1774. Jonathan said that he felt it was his duty as a Patriot to go back in time to help Mr. Mason.

He told me that he had been a fool for love. He said, not for loving me, but for so willingly leaving Virginia when he could be helping with a cause vitally important to the future of civilization. He was thrilled that the United States of America had become a great, independent nation, but in an accusatory tone he asked, "Why did you not share other knowledge with me? Why did I have to read about such important, imminent events in a book in Quebec?"

As he spoke I understood that Jon needed to go home. What's more, I knew that he had been present and working with George Mason helping draft America's founding documents. I knew his thoughts, I'd been listening to his ideas for months by that point. There was suddenly no doubt in my mind that he had been part of everything that happened in the late eighteenth century in Virginia, even though I had never seen his name in my history books.

Love has no pride; I begged his forgiveness. I admitted that I had wronged him. I had withheld information. I confessed that I was so happy to have him back in my life that I was willing to do almost anything to keep him by my side. I told him that he was right; we should go back to 1775 immediately. I would learn to cope with my situation.

While Jonathan packed our few

things, I stopped downstairs and told our landlord that we would be leaving. He helped me call the airport and arrange flights to the U.S. Then I walked to the library to write two final letters: one to Annie with my news and one to Jonathan.

***

It took us a long day of flights and connections to reach the Richmond airport. I was exhausted, Jon was exhilarated. He had been watching planes, both large and small, since his arrival in 1974. He found flight an easier concept to grasp than the workings of a television or microwave oven. People had been dreaming of flying for thousands of years. But, while flying had been exciting, I sensed that going home to 1775, was the true cause of his elation. It was good to see him happy again. His life had a purpose that only he could fulfill and he was heading home to accomplish it.

We stayed the night in a hotel near the airport. In the morning Jonathan dressed in his colonial suit. I dressed comfortably for travel in dark modern clothing. I had sold my travel gown in November, shortly after we had arrived back in 1974, because it was too cumbersome to pack when we moved to the commune. Once we passed into 1775, our plan was to wrap Jonathan's great coat around me and rush to Lydia de Treville's house. We trusted that Lydia would ask no questions about my strange clothes, and that she would have something that I could wear, perhaps even the clothing that I had left in my old room at her house.

In our mismatched outfits, we took the early bus to Williamsburg and walked from the station to our secluded bench at the edge of the Historic Area. We sat in silence for a few minutes before Jonathan stood and took my hands in his. As he stepped backward pulling me toward him, I pushed at his hands and broke free from his grip. I ran from our bench, never looking back. In the cuff of his great coat was the letter explaining my actions.

—46—

February 1975

As I made my way from Jonathan's and my bench to the Williamsburg bus station to buy a ticket to Twin Oaks, my mother's admonition from my childhood kept cycling in my brain, "Keep your mouth shut or everyone will think you're crazy... keep your mouth shut or everyone will think you're crazy... keep your mouth shut or everyone will think you're crazy..."

I had no way to explain what I'd been doing for the past three months. I didn't understand it myself. I just knew that it had happened and, even though I couldn't tell anyone, Jon was once again a part of my life.

I rested my left hand across my still flat abdomen. The gems of the ring Jonathan had given me blurred through my tears. I vowed I'd quit crying—I was doing the only thing that I could do. I had to be strong and keep looking forward—for all of our sakes.

Max had Mel's car at Twin Oaks. She'd given it to him when he'd visited her in New York over Christmas. Mel had told Max that it was a bother having a car in the City, but I think that she'd hoped he would move to New York sooner than they had planned if he had a vehicle available. My needing a ride to Boston from the commune may have precipitated his move, but I think having spent the last month without seeing Mel was his primary motivator.

I had a few important mementos in my purse and the clothes on my back, everything else had been lost in my many moves over the past months. It was probably for the best. Max needed room for boxes since this was a going to be his permanent move away from the commune. Aston Martins were not known for the size of their trunks.

Max had only one thing to do before we left— he needed to set fire to Opus I.

On February eleventh, 1975, I gathered with the members of Twin Oaks and the Louisa Volunteer Fire Department as Max Miller doused the lower elements of his fantastic sculpture with gasoline and set it ablaze. It had been the most amazing piece of non-permanent public art that I had ever seen, and now it was the most magnificent bonfire I had ever witnessed as well.

On our drive away from Virginia, Max explained to me that Opus I was never meant to last. He'd said that he felt that it would have been irresponsible to leave it to deteriorate on its own. He'd been afraid someone might get injured by falling wood or that it could go up in flames during a drought and burn surrounding fields. Max thought temporal art (as he called his sculpture) was of no less importance than works that lasted for centuries. He said the awe experienced by viewers upon their first exposure to a work of art was the legacy of the piece. If that awe lived forever in just one viewer's mind, that was permanency as far as he was concerned.

Max talked (and talked...and talked) all the way to Philadelphia, where he dropped me at Clyde Dale's place. I stayed with Clyde, bunking on his couch and sleeping the days away until the weekend, when he drove me to Boston.

Always thoughtful, Clyde hadn't peppered me with questions during my stay; nor did he feel compelled to fill the silence on our drive to Massachusetts. He could tell, where Max couldn't, that I was wrestling with something big. He gave me space. He did mention he was happy to hear that I intended to go back to school in the fall. Clyde loved Penn. He was sure I'd feel the same about whichever grad school I chose. He told me about his Christmas, but didn't pry by asking about mine. When he filled me in on his little sisters back in Iowa, he said that they'd told him

Christmas hadn't been nearly as much fun without me. I knew it was an exaggeration, but it was nice to hear.

On the way to Boston Clyde told me about the plans he and Cathy were making for a summer wedding. He said they were both getting tired of their long-distance relationship and wanted to be together—it was hard living so far from the person you loved. Cathy would be joining him in Philly. It had been her decision.

I turned my head and watched the New England scenery pass as tears pooled on my lower lashes. When I looked down to blink them away, my garnet and opal ring flashed in the afternoon sun. It was my engagement ring; it was to have been my unconventional wedding ring. I thought about Clyde's words, "It's hard living so far from the person you love." I wished that I had any other option and stroked the beautiful ring Jon had now given to me twice.

Annie met us with open arms. She had fixed chicken with rice and a big salad for dinner, plus a chocolate cake with fudge frosting for dessert. Annie said she used the family recipe credited to "Aunt Elsie," then explained to Clyde that no one could ever remember an "Elsie" being a part of the Bolling clan. It was a family joke; Clyde laughed politely.

Clyde ate with gusto. I only nibbled, but it was the best meal I'd eaten in a long time. Annie understood, although she didn't say anything until after Clyde took off to explore Boston. Then, with eyes full of concern, she asked me, "What are you going to do?"

I answered her with the only sure thing that I knew, "I plan on having and keeping this baby. Other than that, I don't know." I shrugged and continued, "I still plan on going to grad school, but I don't know if I can make it work this fall. Right now… well, right now I'm just living day to day."

Annie told me not to worry. She suggested I take a shower and put my feet up, adding, "Clyde's a smart guy, but he's clueless, isn't he?" I nodded. Annie continued, "Let's just wait and talk about your situation after he takes off tomorrow. I have some ideas."

That evening the three of us ate pizza, played Yahtzee, and talked about what we liked best about Boston. Later, Clyde slept on the living room floor in my old spot. Annie and I used the new twin beds in her bedroom she'd purchased after having received my letter from Canada informing her of my pregnancy and asking her if I could be her roommate.

On Sunday afternoon, after Clyde took off, Annie and I planned the rest of my life.

We sat across from one another at her kitchen table. As I blew on my weak Lipton tea, Annie started to speak. She told me she had been pondering what I'd told her in the letter; she thought she might have a solution. She suggested that she help me raise the baby, saying she would like to be a mother, but doubted she would ever give birth.

I wanted to protest her statement, but before I could say anything, Annie hurriedly explained, "Sarie, I'm a lesbian. I've known for a long time that marriage and kids aren't my future, but if you're willing to share your child with a person that the world thinks is defective, I promise that I'll be a good mother." I hope I said, "Stop it, Annie—you're not defective!" But I think I was silent; I suppose I was stunned, but I don't know why—Annie had never shown any romantic interest in men.

As she continued to present her solution to my situation, I could tell that this was not just one evening's musings. Her plan was thorough, and, I thought, brilliant.

Annie had already made an appointment with an obstetrician who specialized in difficult pregnancies. I would see him at the beginning of the week. We would deal with the bedrest issue. She was willing to do anything necessary to keep our unborn baby safe for as long as possible.

Annie said she would like to stay in Boston if that was agreeable to me. She had already been looking into childcare, assuming I would still be interested in pursuing grad school. She laughingly assured me, "There are some good educational options in this area." I think I gave her a standard smart aleck little sister response, "Around Boston? No shit!"

She didn't want to tell Mom and Dad about the baby until after it was born. And then, she didn't want to tell them which of us was the birth mother. That was part of her plan. We were to be this child's parents equally—we would both be mommy. I told her I was fine with that, but that Mom and Dad would never believe that their responsible older daughter would ever do something so untoward as have a child out of wedlock. Actually, I was as unsure about our parents' positive response to unconventional grandparenthood as I was about my body carrying the baby to term, even though my always positive older sister took both as a given.

Annie said we would figure out the rest as we went along, just like every other couple having a baby. Her biggest concern was money, especially if I had to spend weeks on end in the hospital and didn't delay grad school. She didn't know if she could support our new family on her own. I asked her not to worry; I told her I liked her plan and I thought we could make it work.

That evening I surprised Dr. Sargent with a long distance phone call.

He seemed both relieved and delighted to hear from me; he was so talkative he didn't give me a chance to tell him how good his voice sounded in my ear. He was full of questions for me. The first was, "Where are you living—are you still *communing*?" Others followed in rapid succession.

I told him I was in Boston with Annie and answered some of his other inquiries. Then I asked him if I could talk to him about a sensitive situation. I asked him to please not be disappointed in me and explained that I was once again pregnant.

I said, "What I didn't tell you two years ago when I told you about my miscarriage was that the doctors in Boston had said it was very unlikely I would ever get pregnant again, and even less likely I would be able to carry a baby to term."

I heard Dr. Sargent's sympathetic, "Oh, Sarah…" but he let me continue.

"I didn't get pregnant on purpose, but I want to do everything I can to have this baby. It will most likely be my last chance to have a child. I want to believe since the doctors were wrong about their first prediction, they will be just as mistaken about their second." I paused, then started speaking again. "Another thing you need to know is that the father of the baby will not be part of the child's life. He's a wonderful man, but a life together—at least in the foreseeable future—is not an option for us. I'm not telling him about the pregnancy for his sake. Knowing would put him in an impossible position. He would ruin his life to be by my side; I won't let him."

I went on to explain that Annie had asked to be a second parent to my child and I had agreed. I also told him, if I was accepted, I still wanted to enter Harvard in the fall.

Unlike the beginning of our call, this time when Dr. Sargent began to speak, his words came with measured concern. He told me he understood my desire to have the baby. He reminded me that he and Margaret had wanted children, too, but after her third miscarriage it had no longer been possible for them. He told me he wasn't sure I was making the right decision not telling the father about the baby, but he would trust my judgment on the matter. Then he asked, "What can I do to help you, Sarah?"

I told the professor, thanks to him, I thought we would be all right financially, unless I had to spend months in the hospital. I didn't have insurance (not many young people did in 1975); I asked if he could extend me a loan if my medical bills began to mount up. I also asked him to not say anything about my situation to anyone. If I lost the baby, I didn't want anyone to know I had been pregnant, and, if I managed to give birth, the baby was to be as much Annie's child as it was mine. I told him of her request to keep the baby's mother a mystery.

Dr. Sargent said he had never known anyone as secretive as me, but offered to keep my confidences. He was thrilled I still wanted to get my advanced degree and said he was sure that someday I would have "Ph.D." following my name; many male graduate students were parents, he didn't see why, with Annie as my partner, circumstances should be any different for me. He also told me he planned to double my monthly stipend until I finished school so that I wouldn't need a loan. His only requests of me were that he be considered "Grandpa Sargent," and that we all come visit him in Vermillion as often as possible. Those were two incredibly easy yeses.

Dr. Sargent was my lifelong champion. I've never been able to understand his unconditional faith in me, but it gave me incredible strength. He'd been a remarkable professor, beloved by hundreds of students. When he died in 1997 at the age of ninety-two, he bequeathed the bulk of his substantial estate to endow the Jon S. Leggett Memorial Scholarship. In his obituary he requested that anyone wishing to give a memorial gift in his name, give it to Jon's scholarship. Shortly after that, USD changed the fund name to "The Sargent Leggett Memorial Scholarship for Research Travel." When the announcement was made, I thought about how happy it would have made both Jon and Dr. Sargent to know that they were being remembered together.

About ten years after the professor's death I moved to Beaufort, South Carolina. That's when I learned that the beautiful red Camellias that bloom in the heart of winter are called Professor Sargents. I thought how wonderfully appropriate it was that the flowers that cheered me on cloudy winter days in my new home had the same name as the man who saw me through the darkest winters of my heart when I was young.

—47—

Jonathan Sargent Leggett Bolling was born on June 25, 1975, about five-weeks shy of his July due date. He was a tiny baby for such a substantial name, but he grew into it. We asked our family and friends to call him "JJ." To me, his moniker stood for Jon Junior; I think Annie simply considered it a cute diminutive. She had never asked me one word about JJ's father and I had never offered her any information other than leaving him was the hardest decision of my life. If she questioned the name that I'd chosen for our son, she never said anything.

I was weak after so many months of total bedrest, making Annie JJ's primary mother during his first weeks. In truth, Annie was JJ's primary mother his entire young life. He grew up calling us "Mama A" and "Mama S." In my mind it felt like he was saying "Mama A-plus" and "Mama Satisfactory"—both good, but one exceptional. Annie had always been the more maternal of the two of us. It didn't make me feel jealous, just damn lucky.

I entered Dr. Sargent's alma mater, Harvard, in the fall of 1975, as he and I had long hoped. In 1982, I completed my dissertation and was awarded a Ph.D. in The History of Art and Architecture. My specialty was research, but I also no longer had a problem carrying on conversations concerning aesthetics with Mel Meister and Max Miller. The list of philosophers I could now quote was prodigious. As Dr. Sargent had told me, "a degree from Harvard opens many a door." And so it did —I had a successful and satisfying career.

It wasn't always easy raising a baby in Boston, but the logistics of handling a toddler became easier once Annie and I bought a three-bedroom house in Lexington in 1977. Not having to tote a diaper bag, stroller, and squirming toddler up three flights of stairs to a cramped apartment made yard maintenance and snow removal seem delightful. Shortly after we moved in, I received a house warming gift from Dr. Sargent. He shipped me Jon's plaid wingback chair and the boxes that I had stored in his attic when I'd moved away after graduation.

Before JJ was born, I'd worried about him being an only child and having so few relatives, but, as the years passed, my concerns passed, too. While JJ didn't ever have siblings, he had scads of unofficial cousins, aunts, and uncles. His Uncle Clyde and Aunt Cathy made sure that he was included with all the Dale children. When he got old enough he spent several weeks each summer with DoubleD Dale's family on the farm. Before going to Iowa, we would all visit Grandpa-Doctor Sargent in South Dakota. It hadn't been the professor's intention to be called Grandpa-Doctor, but it's what JJ called him when he was learning to talk. It stuck. He was the best Grandpa-Doctor any little boy could ask for.

As for his birth grandparents, it took them awhile to thaw. They were hurt that we'd kept JJ's birth a secret, and, truthfully, I couldn't blame them for that. Eventually they asked Annie to bring JJ to Sioux Falls for a visit—I was not included in the invitation. After the visit Annie told me of our parents' assumption, I had been irresponsible and saddled her with a baby that she didn't want. She said she'd asked them why they'd assumed that I had given birth to JJ. She said they should think of JJ as hers—I was the one who had offered to help her. She told them if they wanted to keep seeing their grandson they needed to make me feel as welcome in their home as they'd always made her feel. Annie was a determined individual; becoming a mother had made her courageous as well.

In 2004, shortly after gay marriage became legal in Massachusetts, Annie married Helena Martinez. Helena had been part of our family for years by then. I think JJ considered her another mother—if you already have two, why not three? I was always happy that

Annie had been wrong about her prediction that she would never marry or have a child. She had a brilliant and adventurous son, a wonderful spouse, and an extremely grateful sister.

Our little family of four lived our version of the fairy-tale ending, but I never stopped looking for Jon and planning our own *happily ever after*.

To follow is a copy of the letter I placed in Jonathan's greatcoat cuff on the day I left him in 1975. With Lydia de Treville's help, he did what I asked of him. He gave us forever.

> *My Jonathan,*
>
> *I'm sorry that we are not together, but I am not sorry for the decision I've made to stay in my own time. You need to be where you are. You have an exciting life to live that does not include me right now, and I have my own needs.*
>
> *Two years ago, you wrote me a letter. I know it by heart—I want to share some of your words with the hope that you will somehow recall writing them*

and they will help you understand what I have just done.

"I know that it hurts us both not being together, however, I realize this may not be an uncommon situation for us in the future…we know it is your plan to continue your education…eventually your work may call you elsewhere…I understand this…while being apart hurts, it's going to be all right in the end. We can make our separations work knowing that we are meant to be together forever…"

Jonathan, those were once your words to me. That I have chosen to follow my head instead of my heart should not come as a surprise.

I know I will find you someday in the future or past. You have proven it possible by finding me twice that we remember. How many other times in the history of the world have we pulled one another across the fractured dimension of time to embrace? Hundreds? Thousands?

Help me find you when we are both ready to be together again. Please, my love, keep a journal or day book. Let me know of your life. I hope it will be a wonderful adventure filled with the work and people who bring you happiness.

I am going to be a professional historian; I will continue to learn about research methods. If you leave your papers to an archive or hide them with George Mason's documents, I promise you, I will find them. Tell me what you are doing, where you are living, and give me clues in words or pictures as to where I might find a spot like our bench in Williamsburg so that we might meet again someday.

Jon, my last words to you are the last words you wrote to me. "Above everything, I love you. I know that we are meant for one another and that our future is guaranteed, whether we are in each other's arms or, as now, in one another's heart."

My Love Forever,
Sarah

New York Times Obituary
Sunday December 19, 2021
By Kyra T. Thurman

Dr. Sarah Bolling, Art Historian and Historical Timeline Creator, Presumed Dead at 69

Sarah Elizabeth Bolling, specialized in the history and art of Colonial America and the early years of the United States. Known for her meticulous research and computer skills, she often collaborated with writers of history and historical fiction, winning an Emmy in 2002 for her work with the documentary film maker Ken Burns. She was the mother of renowned mathematician and economist, Jonathan S. L. Bolling. She disappeared from her home five years ago; she is now presumed dead.

Dr. Bolling was reported missing December 7, 2016, by the Beaufort, South Carolina Sheriff's Department. She was declared dead in absentia on Wednesday, December 15, 2021, by South Carolina Judge Robert Tunny. She was 69 at the time of the declaration.

Dr. Bolling's specialty was creating detailed event timelines from primary source materials. In a quote from a *New York Times* interview in 2002, she stated, "I like finding factual information and leaving interpretation to others. Historical perspective changes as we change as a people. Dates and data, if recorded accurately in original documentation, remain static. I know that my timelines are incomplete—so much of what has happened was never documented, but what I find I include. That's as close to the truth as I can get."

Dr. Bolling's fame as an art historian came early in her career. Shortly after receiving her Ph.D. from Harvard in 1982, the publication of her dissertation exploring the works of Early American artist, L. de Treville caused a stir in the art world. It was through Dr. Bolling's extensive research that L. de Treville, painter of the colonial masterpiece, *The Visitor* (aka *America's Mona Lisa)*, long assumed by art historians to be a man, was, in fact, a woman: Lydia de Treville.

Ms. de Treville's other works had proven difficult to authenticate, because unlike *The Visitor,* none had been signed. Dr. Bolling discovered that while not signed, the artist's paintings bore a cursive letter "*L*," presumed to stand for *Lydia*, hidden within the body of the work. With this information more than a dozen landscapes and still lifes have been attributed to de Treville establishing her as Colonial America's most influential female artist. Interestingly, *The Visitor* and a similar portrait of Jonathan Leggett, a professor and founder of Beaufort College (1795), a precursor to the University of South Carolina Beaufort, are the only portraits ever credited to de Treville.

In 1994 Dr. Bolling surprised many of her colleagues when she left her research and teaching position at Boston College to establish a private consultancy specializing in combining history and information technology. In a 1994 *Boston Globe* article written shortly after her departure from the college she said, "I have the good fortune of being a historical researcher at a time when technology is rapidly changing how we do research. I want to be part of that change, not merely reap the rewards of other people's work. I'm not a particularly good linguist, but I find that programing language comes easily to me."

One of Dr. Bolling's first clients was the Roy Rosenzweig Center for History and New Media, part of George Mason University in Fairfax, Va. She was an early collaborator at the institute, then known as the Center for History and New Media, helping develop data bases to share colonial and early American art, craft, and folk art digitally. In 2001 she worked with the Pastime Software Company to complete PastPerfect Version 3, an application for collections archiving. In 2007 the company changed its corporate name to PastPerfect Software, Inc. According to the company's website it is now "the world's leader in collection and contact management software used by museums and archives."

In the early 2000's, Dr. Bolling collaborated with TV documentarian Ken Burns on the series, *Those Who Left*, about U.S. emigration to Canada. The documentary focused on the thousands of English loyalists who left the United States for Canada both during and after the American Revolution, and to a lesser degree, on three other periods of US emigration: the 1850 escapes of enslaved Americans following the passage of the Fugitive Slave Act; the 1896 rush precipitated by the discovery of gold in the Klondike region of the Yukon; and, the ten year period from 1965 to 1975 when an estimated 30,000 young men fled to Canada to avoid serving in the U.S. military during the war in Vietnam. In 2002, Dr. Bolling received an EMMY from the National Academy of

Television Arts & Sciences for her contributions to the documentary.

Dr. Bolling was known publicly for her distinctive style as much as for her scholarship. Often a featured presenter on educational television programs, PBS, and the BBC, she is remembered for her closely cropped hair and round tortoise shell glasses, a look she adopted while still in graduate school and retained until undergoing laser eye surgery in 2007. In public, she wore dark bespoke pantsuits and matching blouses on her five-foot frame. Once asked about her distinctive look, Dr. Bolling credited renowned fashion writer, photographer, and good friend M. L. Meister for giving her the idea. She said that she "stuck with it for a quarter of a century because it was comfortable and easy."

From 1975 until 1996, Dr. Bolling lived in Lexington, Mass. with her sister, respected LGBTQ adoption rights activist, Anne Bolling. Together they raised their son, Jonathan. For years their home was a meeting place for intellectuals and artists. New York artist Max Miller said in a 1994 interview in the *New York Times*, "Having tea and cookies at Sarah and Annie's place is as close to being part of an 18th Century philosophical salon as you can get." He also suggested that tea in this context was a euphemism, but that the cookies were real, noting that Dr. Bolling was an "outstanding baker." In an interview given this week, Mr. Miller added that he has missed his friend's "quick wit and robust profanity. Sarah always made me think of the Shakespeare line, 'And though she be but little, she is fierce.' Only her physical stature was small, in every other way she was a giant."

Dr. Bolling and her sister, Anne, were coparents of mathematician Dr. Jonathan S. L. Bolling. A graduate of MIT, he was awarded both the Fields Medal in Mathematics in 2005, at age 30, and the Nobel Memorial Prize in Economic Sciences in 2011 for his work on the economic impact of climate change on emerging markets. Dr. Jonathan Bolling, an inveterate adventurer, was presumed lost in the Caribbean Sea after his sailboat was found adrift off the coast of Belize in 2013, following tropical storm Barry. In an unfortunate twist of fate, like his mother, Dr. Bolling was legally declared presumed dead in 2015. He was 40.

Sarah Elizabeth Bolling was born on April 22, 1952, in Sioux Falls, S. Dak. Her father, William, was a roofing contractor, her mother, Catherine (Hill) Bolling, worked in the office of the Sioux

Falls Montgomery Ward department store. Dr. Bolling once said of her childhood that her parents gave her the "gift of freedom. Because I was left alone much of the time, I learned how to entertain myself at a young age. Once I learned to read, I was never bored."

In 1974, Dr. Bolling received a B.A. from the University of South Dakota in Vermillion, S. Dak. After serving an internship at the Abby Aldrich Rockefeller Folk Art Center on the campus of Colonial Williamsburg, Va., she entered Harvard University in the fall of 1975. She earned an M.A. in American History (specializing in research) followed by a Ph.D. in The History of Art and Architecture in 1982.

Upon her graduation from Harvard, Dr. Bolling was hired as an Associate Professor of Art History at the Morrissey College of Arts and Sciences at Boston College. In 1985, she moved to the Department of History, holding the Hoffcamp Family Endowed Chair in American History. In 1994 Dr. Bolling left Boston College to open a private consulting service dedicated to historical research using new technology. She remained an independent consultant and writer until 2006, when she retired at the age of 54 to Beaufort, S. C.

In South Carolina, Dr. Bolling opened her store, Fauxlonial Furnishings, specializing in Early American furniture replicas and abstract expressionist art from the mid-twentieth century. In a 2008 interview with Collin Ludlow for an article in the magazine *Art Yesterday*, when asked why she would choose such an odd combination of goods for her shop, Dr. Bolling said, "I was at the point in life where I could do precisely what I wanted, where I wanted. I wanted a small shop where I could sell two of my favorite genres. Obviously, my taste is eclectic. I chose Beaufort because I fell in love with the town the first time I saw it in 1981, while doing research for my dissertation. I could probably make more money selling exclusively online, but then I wouldn't get to look at my inventory every day. The combination of furniture that looks older than it actually is, surrounded by art that is perceived modern, makes me smile whenever I walk into the store. It's like standing in one place traveling backward and forward in time."

Dr. Bolling was preceded in death by her parents, older sister Anne Catherine Bolling, and son Jonathan S. L. Bolling. She is survived by a sister-in-law, Helena Martinez.

Her attorney in Beaufort stated that Dr. Bolling's estate had been gifted, *in toto*, to the Sargent Leggett Memorial Scholarship for Research Travel at her alma mater the University of South Dakota in accordance with instructions provided by Dr. Bolling before her disappearance in December of 2016. Dr. Clyde S. Dale, Dean of Arts and Sciences at U.S.D., told the *New York Times* during an interview this week that the scholarship established to honor two former history professors is the largest endowed history scholarship in the United States dedicated to funding student travel for the purpose of primary source research.

EPILOGUE

SCREEN PLAY PROPOSAL:
A HISTORY OF FOREVER
by Beth MacDonald

Scene — Late morning, December 9, 2016, Beaufort, SC

Tommy Gill is in his law office, coffee at his side and dark crescents beneath his eyes from spending the night reading Sarah Bolling's manuscript. He has just summarized his findings to give to Sheriff Bob Roberts and is waiting for his administrative assistant to finish typing the report.

While he waits Tommy reviews Sarah's file and peruses the information she's given his law firm regarding her final wishes. In it she's provided an account of her professional life. As Tommy reads through the file we see Sarah's life pass before us. Her career before her retirement to Beaufort, South Carolina was that of an accomplished historian and respected scholar. Another thing obvious in her recap of her life's work is the path she's discovered leading her back to Jonathan Leggett. Tommy, however, either from exhaustion or disbelief, fails to notice those details.

Scene — 1:00pm, December 9, 2016, Beaufort, SC

Tommy and Sheriff Roberts meet for lunch at an outdoor table facing Waterfront Park. Tommy plops the manuscript and a folder with his findings onto the restaurant table and says, "Bob, there's nothin' here. I don't know what Sarah was thinking—it's just her college days and a buncha crazy talk 'bout time travel." Tommy shakes his head and continues, "If any of this stuff (he puts his hand down on the pile of papers) should get out, it's gonna ruin Sarah's reputation. I think you're gonna have to investigate this just like any other missin' person's case, or, as much as I hate to say it, a suicide. She had everything pretty well planned out to settle her affairs."

Tommy and Sheriff Roberts finish their lunch. When the Sheriff picks up the folder sitting atop Sarah's memoir, the top loose pages tumble across Waterfront Park toward the wide Beaufort River. At first both men jump as though they are going to run after the pages, but then they pause, looking at one another. Sheriff Roberts says, "Just let'em go, Tom."

As they walk from the park toward Bay Street the Sheriff says, "For Sarah," while holding the remaining pages of the manuscript over a large outdoor trash can. He drops them, and we see them falling much like Jon Leggett's notes fell from the balcony on the day he and Sarah first spoke.

Scene — early morning, December 7, 2016, Beaufort, SC

Sarah places a letter and her manuscript on the old plaid chair in her office, throws on a long cape to ward off the morning chill, closes the door of Fauxlonial Furnishings, and walks through the empty streets of downtown Beaufort and its nearby neighborhood to St. Helena Cemetery.

Huge wet snowflakes fall turning the Spanish Moss hanging from the cemetery's Live Oaks into frosty bridal veils. Near the weathered bench at the foot of the de Treville graves, Sarah stops and stares at the anomalous large flakes; to her they look like sparkling confetti tossed from above to celebrate this long awaited day. A bride's unconditional smile lifts the corners of her mouth, and her dimming sixty-four-year-old eyes shine with undiminished love. As she reaches forward, her hands clasp the air, and she quietly vanishes.

Final Scene — morning 1816,
Beaufort,SC

The sun is shining. We see the two aging lovers walking hand-in-hand near the swaying grasses of the winter marshes. The Sting song "Fields of Gold" is playing in the background.

Camera pans the golden marsh grass and the azure sky of the Lowcountry. Credits roll.

The End

Beth MacDonald

Acknowledgements

Not long ago I reread Stephen King's book *On Writing*. In it he discusses writing with the door closed and with the door open. I wrote the first draft of *A History of Forever* with the door closed and triple locked. I'm not sure that I told family members, including my husband, that I was writing until I had over half of the first draft completed. When I finally cracked the door it was to Ellen Baker, a novelist whose books I've admired for years. Ellen took my very rough (and embarrassing) first draft and gave me pages of notes to digest and then incorporate into my first rewrite. One of her suggestions was that I change the name of the book to something other than *Fauxlonial Furnishings*, its original title.

I went back to work on the novel. This time, friends and family knew I writing, but other than that, my door was still closed. The only person to see my second draft was Ellen Baker. She once again gave me a sheaf of notes and a recommendation that I change the name of the book. She didn't think that *Head and Heart*, my homage to Thomas Jefferson's letter, "A

Dialogue between the Head and the Heart, 1786," would attract any more readers than *Fauxlonial Furnishings* (when I realized that it wouldn't have even attract me if I were to have seen it on a book store shelf, I knew she was right).

After my third rewrite and settling on the title, *A History of Forever*, I printed twenty copies of the manuscript and gave them out to my older sister, Mary Swanson; my husband, Mike; our son, Nicholas MacDonald, and daughter, Samantha Solberg; a long-time friend (who just happens to teach writing), Beverly Oliver; and, the extraordinary women of a multi-generational book club that I was lucky enough to have been asked to join many years ago. Besides giving me much needed encouragement, several of the book club members also edited the manuscript with care (as did my friend Bev, my sister Mary, and my husband). Without their support and encouragement, I doubt *A History of Forever* would be in your hands today.

The cover art, aka *The Visitor, by Lydia de Treville,* was drawn in oil pastels by the talented artist Jennie Yu. Jennie took my list of wishes and a few pages of manuscript and gave a face to Sarah Bolling. I couldn't have been more pleased with the result.

There is a lot that goes into making a book look good, both inside and out. This book wouldn't look nearly as good as it does had I not had help from graphic artist and long time friend, Romy Klessen. I told Romy what I saw in my mind's eye; she did her magic with the computer and "made it so."

My last and largest thank you's go to my husband, Mike MacDonald, and a place, Beaufort, South Carolina. Sitting in front of our home computer shivering in February of 2018, I bought tickets to fly from Minnesota to South Carolina, and then emailed a pleasant and professional young Beaufort realtor (now friend), Joshua Ward. When I told Mike that I was going south to look for a home in Beaufort, instead of saying, "*Honey, you're nuts*," he said, "Go for it!"

When he walked into our Airbnb room in Beaufort four days after my earlier arrival, I greeted him with, "Hi! Put down your bag—we've got a house to look at in five minutes." Mike said that he could tell by the time I'd taken three steps into what is now our little cottage on The Point that I was smitten. Mike, again, didn't balk when I made an offer on the cottage the next day even though he knew he wasn't ready to spend winters away from our then preschool age grandson. So, on January 2, 2019, Mike drove me 1,400 miles to Beaufort, then, within a week, drove home to babysit. He left me alone and gave me the time I needed to find my voice in that small South Carolina town that lives and breathes writing.

Thank you Mike, I love you, and thank you Beaufort, I love you, too.

Made in the USA
Monee, IL
01 September 2021